THE SEARCH

MAUREEN MYANT

ALMA BOOKS

1

June 1942, a sleepy day in the village, the summer sky clear, save for a charcoal funnel of smoke rising from the steelworks in the nearby town. Above the fields of growing corn the hot air shimmers, languorous and heavy with pollen. Jan feels the sun burning his neck and forearms as he crawls through the prickly stalks. He is careful to keep his head down. Although the crop is abundant this year, it has not yet grown tall enough to hide him, and he knows he could be spotted at any moment. The ground is rough, and he bites his lip to stop a cry when his knee grinds into something sharp. He rolls onto his back to rest for a moment, feeling the warm blood run down his leg. The pain nags at him, and he risks raising his head enough to examine his knee. A small piece of glass is protruding from his leg. Gritting his teeth, he pulls it out and presses hard to try to stop the flow of blood. He glances at it briefly, just enough to assure himself it isn't a deep cut, but he doesn't examine it. Blood makes him feel dizzy – it always has, since he was a small child and saw his father slice off the tip of his thumb when he was gutting a rabbit he'd caught in a trap. After a few minutes he decides to go on. He has nothing to bind the cut, and no option but to continue: they are too close behind, and could catch him at any moment.

Ahead of him there is a copse, near to Horak's farm. It will provide some cover. He crawls on, trying to keep his wounded knee off the ground. It makes for slow progress, and he thanks God he had such a good start. At last he reaches the edge of the field, with the trees only a few yards away. He risks raising his head. They are at the other end of the field, maybe a hundred and fifty metres away. He ducks down, but it's too late: they've spotted him. There's nothing for it but to run as fast as he can. He springs to his feet, wincing at the pain, and darts towards the trees, twisting round them, stumbling as his foot catches on a root. Two minutes and he'll be out of here.

Jan's chest tightens as he runs, squeezes his heart, forcing his breath out in short, painful gasps as he dashes into the yard at Horak's farm. There must be somewhere he can hide. He looks round. Blinded by the sun, Jan doesn't see the elderly mongrel slumbering near the barn. It staggers to its feet, barking, but when it recognizes him as a friend it sinks to the ground, its tail making swirls in the dust. Jan leans over to pat it, taking the chance to catch his breath. There's a pain in his side, and he pushes into it with his fist, to make it go away. The dog lies panting, its eyes begging, but Jan has nothing for it. He scratches behind its ear, whispers *sorry* and straightens up. His heart still pounding, he scans the farmyard. The barn? No, too obvious. The old cherry tree? No, the leaves aren't thick enough, and he's wearing a red shirt: they'd spot him at once. Of course – the rain barrel. Jan rushes over to it, his legs weak from all that running. Not much time. He glances around. No sign of them – there should be time to get into it.

The barrel is chest-high. Jan grasps the top and tries to haul himself up. His feet scrabble to get a grip, but the barrel is moss-covered, slippery, and he slides down, his finger catching on a rough piece of wood. He sucks at the splinter, pulling it out with his teeth, as he looks round for a stone to stand on. There's one nearby, but if he moves it, it'll be a dead giveaway. Nothing for it but to try again.

Nearly there. The muscles in his arms burn as he clambers onto the top. He kneels on the edge for an agonizing second before swinging his legs round to the inside. The barrel's almost empty because there's been no rain for weeks. He shimmies into it, landing with a light splash in a few centimetres of water. The strain has opened up the cut on his knee, and he can feel the blood trickle down his leg. He brushes it away with his fingers and wipes his hands on his shorts, wishing he had a hanky with him, something to cover it up with. Just thinking about the blood makes him giddy. He takes a deep breath to try to calm himself, but his heart hammers on.

Jan crouches, waiting. Minutes pass. There's a rustling right beside the barrel. He tenses, only relaxing when he hears the chirp of some chicks. Water, from the small puddle at the bottom, seeps into his shoes, and he shivers. But it's a small price to pay for such a good hiding place. He sniffs up the drip dangling from the end of his nose. The air in the barrel is stale. It smells like fish, like carp going off. If he doesn't get some fresh air soon, he'll puke.

Time ticks on, he risks sticking his head out. The farmyard is clear, no one in sight. Perhaps they've gone somewhere else. But then he hears a shout: "Got you!" There's an answering scream, his sister's from the sound of it. His fists clench, and he wishes he were bigger. He recognized the shout – it was Josef. He's always after Maria. He probably pinched her or stole a kiss. They act silly round each other nowadays, either fighting or giggling at nothing. Jan hates it when they do this, feels left out. He glowers: it makes him mad to think about them – stupid Josef with his spots and fuzzy upper lip, and Maria pinching her cheeks to make them look red – they're no fun any more. Jan spits into the barrel – never mind, there's always the rest of his crowd, Frantisek and Vaclav and little Karl. He pushes Maria and Josef out of his mind. Confident of a few seconds before anyone will come, he sucks in the fresh air, tastes the scent of mown grass. Luscious. He hears someone running, and ducks down, feeling a thrill at the base of his spine.

"We're coming to get you, Jan." His sister's voice, faint still. "You can't hide for ever."

"That's what you think," he whispers.

"Come out, come out, wherever you are." Josef's voice joins in, nearer.

Jan trembles. Deep in his belly there is a squirming, a fluttering of excitement. He can scarcely breathe.

The other children run into the courtyard. Jan can't believe they haven't found him. It's hard to resist sticking his head out, but he keeps as calm as he can. To distract himself he thinks of what he'll have for supper tonight. Mother said she'd make pork with *knedliche*. His stomach grumbles; surely they'll hear. A barrage of barking, and Maria squeals. She doesn't like dogs. With any luck she'll run off home, and the others will follow her – they always do.

Jan counts the seconds – nineteen, twenty. It is quiet once more; the only sound one last, lazy bark from the dog. Does this mean the others are going, or are they keeping their mouths shut to trick him into showing himself? Jan concentrates. He can hear nothing except the caw of a raven and the faint burr of a far-off motor. He relaxes. They must have gone. His eyes close, pulled down by sleepiness – it would be nice to have a nap.

A thump on the side and the barrel lurches, then starts to rock.

"Got you, Jan," shouts Maria, her round face alight as she leans over the top. The sunlight forms a halo round her head. "Come on, out you come." She tries to grab him, but he ducks out of her reach. The barrel rocks again, and he stands up.

"All right, I'm coming. Keep the damn thing still."

It's even harder getting out. His feet flail, hopelessly flapping as he strains to lift himself. Josef leans down to try to pull him out, but he doesn't have the strength, and eventually the others tip the barrel onto one side and he crawls out. His shorts are wet from the water in the barrel.

Back in the sunlight, he blinks and glares at his sister. Maria's three years older than him, much taller and fatter, nearly as big as his mother. She seems immense as she stands in front of him pointing at his shorts. "You baby. We'll have to get a nappy for you," she says.

The sun is hot on Jan's face. He kicks at a stone with the toe of his shoe. "There was water in the bottom of the barrel. I got wet when I was coming out."

"Yeah, right," says Frantisek. "Piss water by the smell of it."

"No, it isn't!"

Frantisek pushes him. He's a bit of a bully, likes to show off in front of the others. "Piddle boy, piddle boy," he chants, his voice a sneer.

Jan clenches his fists. One of these days he'll be big enough to fight Frantisek, and then he'll show him. One punch and he'll be begging for mercy. His bottom lip trembles.

"Come on, let him be," Maria says, pulling at Frantisek's arm. "He's nothing but a crybaby." The corners of her mouth turn down, making her more like their mother than ever, and she scowls at Jan.

"No, I'm not." He pushes her, but she's immovable.

"You can do better than that," she jeers.

The roof of his mouth is dry. A pulse throbs in his throat. He sees nothing through his tears of rage.

"What were you thinking of?" His mother wets the corner of her apron and wipes the blood off Maria's face.

"She started it."

"No, I didn't."

Jan says nothing. His eyebrows almost meet in the middle, he's scowling so hard. There's no point in arguing. The others are all Maria's friends when it comes down to it, and they've already told his mother he was to blame: "Like a wild animal," they said, "he went crazy, we were helping him out of the water barrel at Horak's farm, and he went for her." More trouble. He'll be lucky not to get a beating.

"Just as well your father's not home. Hitting Maria like that, and scratching her too. You should be ashamed of yourself."

"She's older than me," he mutters, glowering at Maria, who sticks out her tongue.

His mother doesn't see this; she never does. "That's enough. Go to your bed. No supper for you tonight."

He wants to ask his mother why she always takes Maria's side, but the look in her eye stops him, and he stomps off upstairs. He sits on his bed and rubs his eyes, pushing the tears away. He hates his mother, hates Maria, hates her friends. He wishes they were dead. His stomach gurgles like an ancient plumbing system. It's hours since he's eaten. It isn't right to send a child to bed without any food. It isn't fair. The tears spill over, run down his cheeks and gather in the corner of his mouth, where he licks them away. He wants to scream, but instead he kicks the door of the bedroom. His shoe dents the wood, another scuffed mark on the already shabby door. Downstairs his mother shouts: "Stop that nonsense and go to sleep."

He won't. It's still light outside, and he'll show them. They'll be sorry when they come into his room in the morning and find him gone. He opens his bedroom window and looks down. It isn't that far if he clings on to the window ledge, and lets go. He's done it before, and they didn't even come after him. It would serve them right if he disappeared for ever. Jan crawls onto the window ledge and lowers himself until he is hanging on by the tips of his fingers. When he looks down it seems much further than it did a moment ago, but it's too late to do anything other than let go. Taking a deep breath, he drops down, biting his lip to stop himself crying out as he lands heavily in the backyard. He's scraped his right knee: that's both knees hurting now, and his ankle is throbbing too. He rubs it, pressing his knuckles hard on it, bone to bone. Carefully he stands up and puts his weight on it, waiting for a moment before trying to walk. It aches, but not too much. Before he goes, he takes one last look through the window. Mother is putting bowls in front of the others. Cabbage and potato soup, from her native Poland; it smells of garlic and herbs, makes his mouth water. His little sister, Lena, looks up, spots him, opens her mouth to speak. Jan puts his finger to his mouth, and she smiles. She's a good kid.

The village is quiet at this time of night. Most people are inside, either eating or getting ready for bed. Jan slogs up the dusty road, occasionally kicking stones into the gutter, wishing he'd stayed put; he's famished. If he were at home, he could have sneaked into the kitchen when everyone was asleep, or maybe mother would have relented, called him downstairs for some food. She won't give him anything but trouble if he goes back now.

It's getting dark. The sun set fifteen minutes ago, and the moon has yet to rise. Only a few stars spatter the dusk-laden sky. Jan wonders what to do. He's not going back, but he's tired. Looking around, he sees he's near the Horaks' farm. He can sleep there. Tiptoeing past the sleeping dog, he creeps into the barn and climbs the ladder. There's enough hay there to make himself comfortable for the night. He spreads some out and lies down. The straw is full of insects that bite and make him itch, but he's too tired to let it bother him. He scratches at a couple of spots, but within minutes he's asleep.

* * *

Something's coming to get him. He's running, looking over his shoulder, but he can't see what it is. He runs as fast as he can, but it's as if his feet are encased in concrete. He can't get away. Then he stumbles, falls down. He's on the ground, crouching in fear from the thing. He looks up. It's Frantisek, grown into an ogre twenty feet tall. He stands over Jan, roaring, his pimples standing out purple in his pale face. Jan whimpers. The roaring gets louder. Jan tries to get up on his feet and run, but he can't. He's stuck in the rain barrel, the water rising. With a cry he wakes up. For a moment he can't think where he is, and his heart pounds painfully. Then it comes back to him, and he puffs out his cheeks, relieved. It's only a dream, he can go back to sleep. He closes his eyes, but the roaring is still there. It sounds like some sort of heavy traffic – lorries probably. Sometimes they pass through the village on their way to Prague, but never at night, not that he can remember. There are other sounds too: shouts, men's voices, rough and harsh. Jan sits up and strains to hear. The voices are closer, but he can't make out what is being said. Something is wrong – why doesn't he understand? He concentrates, and recognizes the word *raus*. Germans. What are they doing here late at night? Jan's heart constricts. There's been a lot of talk in the village, serious talk: men in the street, in tight groups, suspicion in their eyes, glancing round as they muttered words of warning, women pulling their children closer, the children aware that something isn't right. Jan had listened at the door while his parents spoke in low voices, but he didn't fully understand it all, something to do with an important German being killed. The Germans had been in their country now for some years, and many people didn't like it, but they just had to get on with it, his mother said. This man had been blown up, and the Germans were very angry; they blamed the Czechs. This seemed to frighten the grown-ups, though Jan didn't see why. His father has always told him there's nothing to fear if you haven't done anything wrong, and they certainly haven't.

Jan's mouth is dry. He doesn't want to be here any more. It's time to go home to his mother; he longs to feel her arms round him. Pushing the hay aside, he begins to edge his way to where he thinks the opening of the hayloft is, but he can't see anything, it's so dark. Frightened he'll fall over, he drops to his knees and crawls across the rough wooden floor, feeling his way inch by inch. It takes ages to find the ladder again. When he does, he clings to it and looks down into the black emptiness of the barn. He clenches his teeth as he turns his back to lower himself down the ladder. He counts as he goes, sure there's twelve rungs; his heart skips a beat as he counts thirteen, fourteen. How can he know for sure he'll find solid ground again? He could be entering hell. If he holds his breath, the next step will find him safe on the firm ground. It does. He leans against the ladder and thanks God.

His eyes are more used to the darkness now, and he can make out where the doorway is. The dog is barking, and he runs towards the sound. At the entrance to the barn, he stops to look out. The yard is full of menace. There is a small pool of light cast from one window of the farmhouse, but other than that, nothing. Only shadows of what? Trees? Men? Demons? With a moan, he hurtles into the courtyard, zigzags across it, dodges imaginary bullets, the clutching hands that reach from behind trees, the snares laid into the earth. Breathless, he reaches the road. He bends over to try to catch his breath, and looks down towards the main part of the village. About two hundred yards away there are a number of trucks; he can't see how many. Their headlamps are on, lighting up the scene, revealing dozens of soldiers and a few policemen. They've surrounded the main part of the village.

Without warning, a searchlight illuminates the road beside him. Jan turns round. There must be more soldiers further up towards the boundary of the village. He's trapped. He throws himself down and flattens himself against the ground. The searchlight skims over him, and he waits for a shout. Nothing. He wriggles over the grass, wincing as his scraped knees drag on the rough earth, until he reaches a tree and hides behind it to watch.

A group of policemen march into the farmyard; they have six villagers with them, all men. Jan recognizes his uncle and presses his lips over his teeth to stop himself calling out. He longs to be with someone he knows, but like an animal he senses danger. The group passes near to where Jan is crouching. He covers his eyes, as he did when he was a small child, thinking this will make him invisible. They carry on past him, up to the farm. Three of the policemen march straight into the farmhouse without knocking. In a minute or two, the farmer and his wife are dragged out. Horak is pushed over to the small group of men, but his wife is not allowed to join them, despite her pleas. Two policemen have her by the arms; her feet barely touch the ground as she is hauled off towards the main part of the village. Jan licks his lips to moisten them. He feels emptier than ever, but this is more than hunger: a hollow feeling of dread, of knowing that something terrible is happening. He wonders whether to give himself up or to run and take his chance, but he can't move. He shivers like a sheep newly shorn, though the night is warm. Another sweep of the searchlight; he'll have to hide. There's nowhere to go but up into the cherry tree he rejected earlier that day. He climbs as high as he dares, the bark rough underneath his fingers. It's an old tree, and he stops at its heart, snuggling into the crook between several branches. From here he can see into the farmyard and down to the floodlit village, where the soldiers are dragging people out of their houses into the streets. From time to time another group are marched up to the courtyard. There are one or two women among them holding tight to their husbands, but most groups consist only of men.

Jan watches as they are herded together. Occasionally someone asks what is happening, but the Germans don't reply. He feels himself drifting off to sleep in spite of his terror, and lays his face on the bark of the cherry tree. It feels warm beneath his skin. His eyes close, and he forces them open. Mustn't sleep, he might fall out of the tree.

It's been hours. In the east the sky lightens from black to indigo to deep blue. He must have dozed off, for his mouth has the thick taste of sleep. Jan scans his surroundings. Down in the village, the trucks have gone. But the farmyard is full of men. Jan scans their faces looking for his father. He cannot see him. Of course, he was on night shift at the steelworks. He'll be safe if only he doesn't come back. How can he warn him? Even as he thinks this, the rumble of a truck shakes the earth. It draws up nearby and stops. A soldier shouts an order, and two others run across and open the doors. Several men stumble out, Jan's father among them. They are all workers from the steelworks. This cannot be happening. The men are pushed into the centre of the farmyard with the others. As it grows lighter, Jan recognizes many of them: his uncle standing with his father, the farmer Horak, Arnost who lives next door, his wife, clinging to his arm, sobbing – and there on the edge, Josef and Frantisek. What are they doing there? They're only fifteen, not yet men.

Dawn. The sky is clear, promising a beautiful day. The villagers have been put into the barn with a guard of soldiers, and the door barricaded. Another truck appears, and two policemen unload some mattresses. They must be for the prisoners to sleep on. But no, the mattresses are piled up outside, standing upright against the wall. One of the soldiers – he must be their leader – calls his troops to attention and speaks to them for a minute or two. Jan wishes he knew what was being said, but he can't hear the words, and even if he could he wouldn't understand them. When the commander finishes his speech, two of the soldiers open the barn door and bring out a group of villagers. They make them stand in front of the wall, the striped mattresses a strange backdrop to the group of dazed men. Without thinking, Jan counts them.

Ten soldiers stand before the ten men. Rifles appear, and as they do, a cacophony rises from the villagers. Their pleas – "Why are you doing this?"; "Have mercy, I beg you" – are muddled with shouts from the soldiers

– *ruhig*. Shots, followed by a brief silence which is torn apart by a wail from the barn. As the bodies are dragged away, another ten men are marched out. Up in the tree, Jan watches; he wants to shut his eyes to this horror, but he can't, he has to see what is happening. He can't believe it's real, and tells himself it's a bad dream, all the while knowing that if it were a dream he'd be screaming. Here, now, in this place, he remains silent, digging his fingernails into the palms of his hands.

There's a pause, a break from killing. The soldiers in the farmyard are quiet. Mainly they stand apart from each other, smoking, eating, drinking. Most are silent, lost in thought. One soldier walks towards the cherry tree where Jan is hiding. He rests his forehead against the trunk of the tree. Jan looks down and sees the man is shaking – is he crying? A moment later he retches loudly, vomits. Jan flinches from the acrid stench. He holds his breath, petrified. When the soldier finishes, he wipes his mouth with the back of his hand. As he does so, he looks up and his eyes meet Jan's. Jan stops breathing. The moment stretches into two, three, four seconds, but still the soldier does not speak. Jan cannot look away; he thinks he will always remember this face: the wide mouth, the tiny scar the shape of a horseshoe on his forehead, the light brown fuzz of hair on the chin. His eyes are pale-blue, bloodshot and weary, with no expression. Jan waits for him to shout the others over, but instead the soldier shakes his head and walks away. Without a word he rejoins the rest of his company. Jan swallows the bile rising in his throat. He's dizzy with terror.

* * *

Two hours later. The farmyard is full of dead bodies piled together in untidy lines. Jan doesn't know how many have been shot. After he saw his father brought out, he stopped counting. His mind is frozen at that scene, as if he has a photograph in his head. Over and over he sees his father standing beside the other men. He said nothing, didn't flinch when the soldiers raised their rifles, but the impact of the bullets made his body twitch like a puppet as it folded to the ground.

The soldiers are taking another break. The one who was sick earlier is approaching the tree. When he gets there he glances behind to check if any of the others are watching. Most of them are gathered in a group, smoking, uninterested in anyone else. The soldier pees against the tree and speaks to Jan without looking up. His Czech is faltering, and it takes Jan a moment to understand what he is saying.

"Go. To the village. If they see you, they..." He mimes shooting. "In village, safe with other children. Go." He buttons his flies, and looks up. His pale-blue eyes are intense. "Go. Now."

Jan slides down the tree. He doesn't care whether he's caught or not. The soldier walks back to the rest of the company. Jan stands for a moment, uncertain what to do. Then, as he sees the barn door open and another ten villagers dragged out, he turns away and stumbles over the rough grass to the road. He staggers down to the main part of the village, the sound of gunfire deafening him, blind to where he is going.

Barely conscious, he reaches his house. It looks the same as it did when he last saw it. He had thought it would be changed. The door is ajar, and he pushes it open and creeps inside. There is no one there. His only thought is to get some food and drink. Thank God there's some stew left in the pot on the stove. Jan grabs a handful and stuffs it into his mouth. It's delicious, it always is; his mother is a great cook. Within a minute he's eaten it all. The door creaks, and he spins round. A grim-faced soldier gestures to him. Jan puts the pot aside and wipes his hands on his shorts. He looks round, but there's no escape. Walking slowly, he approaches the soldier, who pulls him outside and pushes him towards a nearby truck. He opens the door and shoves Jan inside, slamming the door shut behind him. Jan is terrified; it's dark inside the truck. Only a crack of light by the door, a thin line of brightness, stops it from being unbearable. Jan sits down by the doors and tries to peer through the tiny gap. He can see very little, a tiny patch of road with weeds growing up from a crack. He bangs on the side of the truck, but no one takes any notice. For an hour, maybe more, he waits, occasionally kicking the side of the truck, hoping someone will come and find him, but no one does.

Just as he thinks the soldier has forgotten him, the engine starts. Jan runs to the front of the truck and shouts in to the driver, "Let me go, what's happening?" There is no response. The driver changes gear, and the truck lurches forwards throwing Jan to the floor. He lies there without moving, tries to hold back the tears, which are threatening to spill over. But what's the point? There's no one here to mock him. Jan buries his head in the crook of his arm and sobs. God knows where he's going.

2

The truck judders to a stop, throwing Jan to one side. The journey has been short, but uncomfortable. It was impossible to sleep with the noise of the engine and the smell of diesel, and Jan lay on the floor, tossed from side to side as the truck rumbled over the bumpy road. He sits up, grateful that the bruising movement has ceased, and brushes the dust off his clothes. It sticks to his sweaty fingers, and he wipes his hands on his shirt, leaving filthy smears on the red cotton. He has never been so dirty in his life; his mother will be furious with him. He can hear her voice now, her Polish accent stronger, as it always is when she's annoyed – *Look at you Jan, always so dirty. How will I get that shirt clean?* – It's so clear that he looks round to see her, but of course she is not there, and it dawns on him that he might never see her again, that if the Germans killed all the men, they might also have killed the women. Tears sting at the back of his eyes, and he blinks to keep hold of them, but they spill over anyway. Before he can wipe his face, a noise at the door draws his attention and he stills, fearful and wary. Metal scrapes on metal as the bolt is drawn, and when the light and air spill in from outside, Jan knows where he is. The burnt metal smell of the furnace is unmistakeable. This is the town where his father works, worked. No – he mustn't think of his father now.

Jan uses his heels to press himself back as far as he can; he doesn't want to leave the truck to go God knows where. He squints past the soldier, who looms in the doorway, to try to make out exactly where he is. The truck has come to a standstill in what seems to be a schoolyard. He can see a school building nearby, much like the one in his village, only bigger. The soldier jerks his head to indicate that Jan should come out. Jan's knees are shaking; he knows they won't support him. He whimpers and curls in on himself as the soldier jumps up into the truck and strides towards him. The vehicle pulsates with each step. There's nowhere for Jan to go; he can't dodge the soldier's grasp. Several people stop to watch as he is dragged from the van. A little girl clasps her mother's hand tight, her mouth shocked open. After a moment or two, her mother pulls her away, but the child continues to stare, her eyes wide and wondering. The woman doesn't look at him as she hurries away. Jan longs to cry out for help, but he is too frightened; voiceless he stumbles across the yard into the school, the soldier pushing him forwards. The tarmac is sticky beneath his feet; it is a hot day, even hotter than yesterday.

The school gymnasium is full with children and women from his village guarded by a cordon of police. In the centre of the room there is a girl from his class, Karla. Her face is strained, pale. She is looking at him, but something in her eyes tells him that she is not really seeing him. Jan is pushed into the hall and told to sit down. He staggers across the threshold, his legs shaking, unable to take in what he is seeing: a haze of faces, tired and fearful. When he reaches a spot that is clear, he sinks to the straw-covered floor and puts his head in his hands. He doesn't want to look at anyone, he wishes…

A hissing whisper: "Jan, come here." He turns in the direction of the sound, sees his sisters and mother beckoning. Their faces are pallid, blurred, as if someone has tried to rub them out. He thinks he's dreaming; Jan is no longer sure what is real and what is not, and wonders what will happen if he crawls over to be beside them. Perhaps they'll disappear and he'll be alone once more. He wants to keep them there, to be able to see them, so he doesn't move. A few seconds later and his mother is beside him. She grabs his hand and pulls him to her. She has been crying; her round face is crumpled and stained with tears. "Where have you been?" she says in an undertone, looking behind to make sure none of the soldiers or police is watching.

Jan opens his mouth to speak, but no sound comes out. A picture of his father twitching on the ground flickers in his mind, and he retches. He looks down at the floor unable to speak. His mother draws him closer. Jan, who has been too old for cuddles for a year now, and who never offers his mother or his sisters a goodnight kiss, accepts this, leaning his head on her shoulder.

"Let's join the others. You can tell us later what happened." They crawl back to his sisters. Lena is asleep, her head using Maria's lap as a pillow. Maria wavers a smile at him. She is no longer angry with him. It is good to be near his family. Mother strokes his hair, and after a while he is almost lulled into a doze. When he shuts his eyes, though, the vision of his father folding onto the ground appears, and he forces himself awake.

He sits up and moves away from the others, frightened that they can see what's in his head. Mother draws him back towards her. He wants to shake off her arm, but the dull pain in her eyes stops him. Jan tries to speak, but she shushes him.

"Hush, sweetheart. It's all right. We're together now."

It's not true; papa will never be with them again. How can he tell his mother and his sisters what he witnessed? His mother rocks him in her arms, calming him with the steady motion. He looks round the room at the people there; no men whatsoever, the boys are all young, the oldest is thirteen, maybe fourteen. Everyone is huddled in family groups. Jan wonders if anyone escaped, or whether they managed to get every villager. He can't understand what is going on, why they chose to do these things to his village.

Maria catches his eye and begins to speak. Her voice is low and flat, lifeless. "We were going to bed when they came. There were three of them," she says, shuddering. "I thought they were going to kill us."

Jan gags, puts a hand to his mouth.

"What's the matter?"

He shakes his head, a tiny movement, all he has energy for. He wants to sleep, for then he can wake up from this nightmare. Maria looks at him for several seconds: he counts, seven, eight, nine… He can't bear the expression in her eyes, as if she knows exactly what he has seen, and he looks away.

She continues, "They burst into the house… they may have knocked, I'm not sure. There was a lot of noise, but they didn't wait for us to answer. Mother was half undressed. They wouldn't let her put anything else on." He glances at his mother; it's true, he hadn't noticed before, she is wearing only her undergarments, the white petticoat grubby with sweat and dirt. Jan blushes for her shame.

Maria falls silent; perhaps she too finds it hard to talk of what she's seen. Jan's eyelids droop; he's exhausted, but too agitated to sleep, too frightened of what he might see in his dreams. He tries to distract himself, gives himself a meaningless task: on what day will his birthday fall this year? His birthday is in November, five months away, but when he thinks of this, his father, whose birthday is a few days after his, comes to mind. A tear runs down his cheek. Mother shakes him, asks why he is crying. He doesn't answer and, after a few seconds, she carries on with the story that Maria couldn't finish.

"They dragged us downstairs and made us give them everything of any value. One of them held Lena while I went through our things. He had a gun in his right hand, and he kept staring at me while I brought out all our valuables." Her lower lips trembles, and her voice shakes as she goes on. "It was horrible. He was smirking, and the whole time he stroked the trigger with his finger. "I thought if I gave them what they wanted they'd go away. I gave them everything, even my wedding ring, but it was pointless." His mother pulls him closer. "When I took out the secret brick, you know, the one in the fireplace, I thought, that's it, they'll go now. All our money was there, and some jewellery that was my mother's. But they didn't. They took us outside where everyone was being gathered. The street was full of trucks and soldiers. Dozens of them. There seemed to be more of them than us." Her eyes are full of tears. "They took the men away… I… I don't know where, and put the women and children into the trucks and brought us here. God knows how long ago that was, but it was very early this morning, just after dawn." She stops speaking and pushes a fist into her stomach. "They've given us nothing to eat, only some water. I'm so hungry." She squeezes his arm. "And you, I didn't know where you were. You must be starving."

Jan shakes his head. Lena stirs, and Maria rocks her gently. It's better if she doesn't wake up. He wonders if he can speak, and opens his mouth to try, but the only sound that comes is a croak.

The day drags on. There are well over two hundred women and children in the hall, maybe as many as three hundred. All of them are tired and frightened. Every so often, some of them are allowed to go to the toilet. The smell is overpowering; a mixture of unwashed bodies, piss and shit. Jan watches as a toddler pulls at her sodden nappy until it falls to the ground. The child's mother sits nearby, looking on, but she does nothing. Her eyes are dead, as lifeless as the coal that lies in slag heaps near the mines. One of the other women picks up the nappy by the tips of her fingers and takes it over to a growing pile of dirty clothes. The child's mother turns away as the infant pulls at her dress. Jan hears someone say that the woman's husband was badly beaten by the soldiers: "He couldn't have lived after the beating he took." But no one does anything to comfort her.

Late in the afternoon, soup is brought in, a hellish grey brew. It stinks as if made from bad meat. Most people eat it holding their noses so they don't have to smell it. Jan won't touch it, even though his mother begs him to eat. He can't bear the thought of food. When night falls, they lie down on the straw and try to rest, but the air is tense with fear and crackles with the cries of babies too hungry to sleep. Jan lies awake in the darkness listening to his mother sob. He hasn't told her what he saw, but Maria whispers that they heard shots from the direction of the farm, did he know what they were. He pretends not to hear.

Another day passes. Everyone is fearful, tight with anxiety. Lena sucks her thumb so fiercely that it worries her mother. She plays finger games with Lena to distract her, and encourages Jan and Maria to join in. For a brief half hour they almost forget their predicament until one of the women tries to speak to a soldier in German. He ignores her, stands aloof, his head turned away from her. When she persists, he hits her with the butt of his rifle, and she falls down. No one moves. Five, ten minutes pass. To Jan's horror, his mother struggles to her feet and walks towards the woman, her hands in the air as a gesture of surrender. He tenses, waiting for her too to be felled. She leans over the woman and wipes the blood from her face. Jan closes his eyes. He hears his mother speak: "I would like some water." Surely now someone will hit her. But no, his mother is walking towards the door accompanied by a soldier. In a moment she returns with a bowl. Everyone in the room watches as she washes the woman's head, then tears a strip from her petticoat to make a bandage. The soldiers look on also, leaning on their rifles. She finishes what she is doing and returns to her children.

Two more hours go by. It's almost dark, nearly two days since they were taken away from their homes. They haven't had any food since lunchtime. Jan is troubled, whispers to his mother: "What do you think will happen to us?" She strokes his hair, smiles down at him. "We'll be fine as long as we're together." She doesn't mention father. Jan thinks she knows something's wrong, but he isn't going to say anything about what happened. He can't.

"Jan, where were you that night?"

He shakes his head. "I don't know, up at the farm."

"I thought you were dead." A tear runs down her face. "I thought I'd never see you again."

"I'm sorry, I was angry because I thought you were taking Maria's side. I just wanted to run away."

"Silly boy." She hugs him, and they sit silently for a moment. She takes a deep breath and asks what he has been dreading. "Was it Horak's farm? Someone said that's where they took the men. Did you see what happened to them? Did you see your father?"

Jan bows his head; she puts her finger under his chin and forces him to look at her. "Jan?"

He has to tell her. There is no possibility of lying about this. Jan opens his mouth, but before he can speak, an officer enters the room. His uniform is different, smarter than the others, and he looks stern, like their teacher does when something goes missing from the classroom, or when one of the younger children piddles on the floor. The man stands in the centre of the room, waiting. The women and the older children fall silent, don't move, but the little ones are too small to take heed, and they carry on with what they are doing: rolling up little bunches of straw and throwing them aside, chewing at the hems of their dresses and shorts, sucking their thumbs.

"Women, stand."

Uneasy glances dart from woman to woman. No one moves, and the soldier raises his voice. "Now! Stand." Slowly they get up from the floor.

"Line up here." The officer points to the door.

One woman bends to lift her baby.

"Leave it."

She ignores him and takes the child in her arms. The officer mutters in German, and two privates march over. One of them seizes the baby from her while the other one holds her. Both mother and child wail. The taller of the soldiers strikes the woman with the back of his hand, and she falls, her arms outstretched towards her disappearing child.

The officer says in a firm voice, "You will leave the children here." Chaos breaks out as he says this, and there are screams from some of the women. Jan clutches his mother's leg.

"Quiet, or we will shoot."

One of the women shouts that they can't do this, and a few more raise their voices in agreement, but they are silenced a second later by the soldier firing his gun into the ceiling. Some plaster falls down and hits a small child on the head. She is only a toddler and starts to cry, but when her mother moves towards her, one of the soldiers steps in between them and points his rifle at the child, gesturing with his head for the woman to leave. The woman looks at him in horror and goes to stand at the door. There is no doubt the soldiers mean what they say.

Mother hugs them to her, kissing them hard. Jan thinks it would be better to be shot than lose her too. He is torn now about what to tell her about papa; it seems so hard that his last words to her should be ones of sorrow and pain. But before he can decide what to do, she is gone, pulled from them by a soldier who is just a boy. Maria gathers him and Lena to her. Her body shakes with sobs, and awkwardly he pats her arm.

They fall into an agitated sleep, which does nothing to revive them. Jan wakes several times and sees that Maria too lies with her eyes open. At dawn the soldiers shout to them to get up. One child, a little boy of maybe three, howls, and this starts off many of the others. Jan tenses. After what he has seen, nothing would surprise him, and he's terrified of being shot. He grasps his sisters' hands and wills them to do nothing to draw attention to themselves. They sense his urgency, and they stand motionless beside him. The officer tells the children to line up, and they do as they're told, the older ones trying to comfort the babies and toddlers. Jan prays they won't separate the boys from the girls. He cannot bear any more pain. He has to stay with his sisters. Once they are in lines, the officer orders the doors to be opened. Jan breathes in deeply. The metallic fumes catch in his throat, but they are perfume compared to the stink inside the school. For a moment he allows himself hope: they are going to be set free, their mother will be waiting outside for them, they will be sent home. It will be terrible to have to tell her about father, but he will find the strength somehow. When he reaches the door and sees the three trucks waiting for them, he almost breaks down. Maria grabs his hand, and he squeezes it wondering how he could ever have thought her a nuisance. She smiles at him. "We'll be all right, you'll see. As long as we're together." Jan nods, but wonders whether they will be together for long.

They are bundled into the trucks, about thirty children in each. There are no seats, and they have to sit on the floor, which is filthy. Jan takes Lena on his knee so she doesn't have to sit in the muck. As they travel along the road the truck sways and bumps, and some of the children are sick. Lena pukes all over her nightdress. She starts to cry. It is her favourite, mother made it for her only a few weeks ago. It's white cotton with tiny sprigged roses on it, all of them pink. Maria tries to comfort her as she wipes the sick away with her hand.

"Never mind. It'll wash out."

Lena bites her lip. Maria hugs her tight and looks across at Jan. "I'm sorry about what happened the other day… that I teased you."

The scratches he made on her face are still livid. Jan cannot believe he lost his temper over something so stupid. He shrugs and says he's sorry too. Maria holds out her hand to him, and he takes it, twining his fingers through hers.

"I wonder where Josef and Frantisek are."

Jan doesn't answer. He wants to forget he saw them in a row of ten, their faces bleached with fear as they waited for the shots that would kill them.

* * *

He must have fallen asleep. The truck stops and, unprepared, he is thrown forwards, bumping his head on that of a boy two years or so older than him, Frantisek's younger brother, Antonin. They're all bullies in that family. He makes a threatening gesture, and Jan apologizes. There's no point in making a stand when he has to save all his energy for what's ahead. With a sneer the boy backs off. When he's sure he can't be seen, Jan sticks his tongue out. Maria giggles before she can help herself, but when she remembers what is happening she covers her mouth with her hand, her face sad once more.

Now the trucks have stopped, they can hear the sounds of a town: traffic, a dog barking, a train hooting in the distance. The doors open, and the children are told to get out. The four children at the front are reluctant to move and have to be pulled out by a rough soldier, who whacks each of them on the head. No one needs a second telling; the rest of the truck empties within seconds onto a railway platform. Jan looks around him. "Where are we, do you think?" he asks Maria.

"I don't know, Prague maybe."

Jan nods his head. "Yes it might be. Can you see a sign anywhere?" They both look around, but there is nothing to see except the train in front of them and, a few yards away, a group of women, hard-faced and unsmiling. They walk over to greet the soldiers. One of the soldiers counts the children, and a few minutes later, after some signing of papers, he and the other men leave and the women take over. They line the children up in twos and march them to the other side of the station. Although he tries hard, Jan sees no signs, and he is too scared to shout out to the few civilians they do see. Five minutes later a train steams in, and the children are shoved into one of the carriages. The seats are hard wooden benches, and there aren't enough for everyone. Jan and his sisters are squashed into a corner, against a window. It's uncomfortable, but at least they are together.

Jan drifts in and out of sleep on the journey. It goes on for hours; they pass through towns and countryside, none of it familiar. Day turns into night, and all that can be seen is an occasional light in the distance. The children are all weak with hunger for they have been given nothing to eat, not even a slice of bread. One of the little ones, a toddler, starts to cry, quickly becoming inconsolable. As she weeps, the women, who are guarding them, watch unmoved.

"What happened to the men, Jan, to father?" Maria's voice is so quiet he is not sure he has heard right. He doesn't answer, but leans against the window, feeling the smooth coolness of the glass on his face.

"Did you hear me?" Insistent.

He shrugs. "I don't know." He won't meet her eyes. Jan is sure she knows he's lying, but he doesn't want to speak about it. He can't, not yet.

"I heard shots. We all did. Are they dead?"

Jan sighs, but before he can say anything, one of the women comes over to him and slaps his face. In a strong German accent she tells him to be quiet. Although his face hurts badly from the slap, Jan is glad to have an excuse not to talk. He saw the glint of tears in Maria's eyes.

* * *

It is still dark when they reach their destination. The children are dragged out into the open air, which is sweet-smelling and fresh after the mustiness of the train. An owl hoots, making Lena jump. Jan cuddles her and whispers that everything will be fine. He can make out the dark shapes of trees against the blackness of the night. Something flies past, brushes his hair, and he gives a little cry of fear. A bat, he'd swear to it. The women order them into lines, and they are marched a short way to a large building. It's like a factory, Jan thinks when he sees it. Inside it is sparsely furnished; they are taken to a huge room with beds lined up in rows against the walls.

After a short wait, they are given some dry bread to eat. There is almost a riot as it is thrown at them in a random fashion. Jan manages to grab two loaves, enough for the three of them, and he thinks he will try to save some for later as there's no way of knowing how long it will be before they eat again. With great care, he divides each loaf into three and hands the girls two pieces each. He eats his first piece very slowly, chewing each mouthful thirty times like he used to hear his grandmother say. The bread is poor quality and stale, and turns into a glutinous mass in his mouth. The other piece is in his pocket, and he touches it, making sure it is there, his safety net for later. Although it is not nearly enough to fill his belly, the small amount of nourishment makes him feel better.

Some of the beds in the room are already occupied. Although the new arrivals make a lot of noise – the younger children are clamouring for more food, one of the babies is crying – the bodies in the beds don't move. Jan has a terrible thought that there are corpses under the grey blankets, and he stares at the nearest shape hoping it will move. For several seconds nothing, then an almost imperceptible twitch at the foot of the bed. Not corpses after all, just more children like them.

When the children have finished their poor supper, one of the women shouts at them to undress. Jan realizes he has to eat the bread or lose it, so he forces it down, though he would rather keep it for later. Once the children are naked, three of the women take them to a room with showers and tell them to wash. They have to stand in long queues for the showers can only take about ten people at a time. The water is cold, and some of the children dash in and out, taking only a couple of seconds, but Jan lingers as long as he can. The water is like needles piercing his skin, but he relishes it. It will make him clean. He grabs the small bar of soap and scrubs himself all over, digging his nails into his skin and scraping the dirt away. He's last in the shower, and a woman comes and shouts at him in German. Jan blushes at being seen naked, runs back to the dormitory out of her sight.

He waits with the others, teeth chattering uncontrollably, hoping for a towel. Like the other children, Jan stands with his hands over his genitals. None of them look at each other, thank God. It has been years since he has seen either of his sisters naked, and he doesn't want to embarrass them. There's no sign of their clothes, but Jan doesn't care. His shorts were stinking, and he doesn't want to put them on again, now he's clean. The woman shouts again and points at the beds, indicating they should get into them. There is a scramble as children from the same family try to get beds close to each other. Jan doesn't manage to stay beside Maria and Lena, but has to go over to the other side of the room. As he climbs into bed, he waves at them, tries to smile, but his mouth wobbles.

The evening is warm, and in spite of being damp from the shower, Jan soon heats up. He lies in bed trying to make out what is around him. The ceiling is high, and there is little light; he has to give up. All will be revealed in the morning. Jan is frightened to close his eyes, scared of what he will see, but he is worn out, and his eyelids droop and close. Within seconds he is sleeping.

3

Jan wakes early. He knows it's light even though he keeps his eyes closed; the inside of his eyelids is transparently pink in a way only possible when sunshine is trying to get through. For a brief, delirious instant he is happy. The sun is warm on his cheek, and he snuggles into the cocoon of bedclothes, drowsily lazy, ignoring the need to pee; he'll get up in a minute.

A niggle of unease, something's wrong. The smell. This isn't home. At home there's always something baking, filling the house with sweet aromas: vanilla, cinnamon, fruit. Here there's a tang of chemicals, cleaning fluid, bleach. Where on earth is he? He opens his eyes, sees walls that are too far away and too dark to be those of his bedroom. At home, his bed is by the wall, and the white paint is scored with pencil marks where he and his sisters have played games or written messages to each other. Here the walls are made of brick, unpainted, like the outside of a building. He looks round and sees that there are many beds in this huge room, too many to count. Fear forces his breath out quicker. He cannot think where he is... but then all at once, with no warning, the memory of what has happened punches him in his guts, and he closes his eyes. His father's body is in front of him, falling to the ground. Jan blinks rapidly to try to rid himself of the image, but each blink is like the shutter of a camera, so that every movement of his father is stilled. Jan presses his fist into his mouth and moans, bites his knuckles to stop himself from screaming out. It can't be true, it must have been a bad dream, but if it was a dream why is he not at home in his own bed? Another groan, louder this time, escapes.

Someone taps his shoulder with a touch as gentle as a feather. Jan opens his eyes, but the bright morning sunshine is dulled by his grief. By the side of his bed is a boy, probably a little older than he is. The boy holds out a sweet to him, a fruit boiling, dark red with a coating of dust and fluff, which makes it look mouldy. The unexpected kindness moves him, and he brushes his hand across his eyes, not wanting the other boy to see. The boy lays the sweet on top of the bed and gives a gap-toothed smile. He says something, but Jan doesn't catch it. When the boy says it again, more slowly, Jan realizes he's Polish. It takes him a few seconds to fully tune in to the sounds; the accent is different to his mother's. The boy must think he doesn't understand for he points to himself and says, "Janusz", enunciating the syllables.

Jan smiles. "Me too."

The boy raises an eyebrow. "What's your name?"

"Same as yours, but they call me Jan."

Janusz's smile broadens. "Enjoy the sweet; we don't get them often." He turns to make his way back to his bed.

"Where are we?" says Jan.

"Poland."

Poland. He can't believe it. His mother often promised to take the children there to see their grandparents and other relatives, but they never had enough money to visit. Before Jan can ask more, another boy sits up in bed, his hair sticking out at a crazy angle; he puts his fingers to his lips and shakes his head at them both. Janusz climbs into bed without another word.

"Where in Poland?"

"Lodz."

"Where's that?"

Janusz shrugs. "It's west of Warsaw, near Germany."

Dear God, they must be hundreds of miles from home. Why have they been brought here? What is this place? He asks Janusz, but he shrugs, saying he's not sure.

In the bed next to him is Karl, a boy from his village. Jan doesn't like him much; he's a bit of a swot, but maybe he'll have some idea of what's happening. He gets up and crosses the short space between the beds.

He shakes Karl's shoulder. "Karl, wake up, won't you."

Karl opens one eye and glowers. "Go away Jan. I want to sleep."

"Do *you* know where we are?"

Karl ignores him, pulling the sheet over his head. In spite of the warmth of the sun, Jan shivers. Why is everyone being so horrible? Surely they should stick together. Jan tries again. "Karl, where are we?"

A sigh. "Jan, I don't know, how could I? You think they told me specially?"

The door to the room opens, and Jan runs across to his bed and jumps in. He thinks it's probably best not to get caught.

A woman's voice resonates in the room, harsh sounds; she is speaking German. The bodies in the beds stir, begin to rise from their beds. Jan swings his legs out of bed, but of course he has no clothes. He stands there, beside the bed, unsure what to do. He can't see anyone he knows. None of the other children from his village have stirred. They're exhausted from their journey yesterday.

An extremely large woman, who wasn't with them yesterday – just as well, thinks Jan, there would have been no room for anyone else – comes into the room and shouts in a gruff, deep voice like a man's. Jan wonders if her face will explode; it is flushed red and shiny.

Another four women join them. They carry huge piles of clothes, so high that their faces are hidden, and dump them in the centre of the room. The fat woman points to them with a doughy finger, and Jan realizes they have to pick some clothes and get dressed. He runs across to the pile and searches for his own clothes. His shirt, a vivid red splash, is easy to find, but not his shorts. For a moment he hesitates, then chooses a pair that look to be about the right size as well as a pair of underpants and scampers back to his bedside before they can be taken from him. He dresses quickly, keeping an eye on what the others are doing. The women indicate that they should line up, and they visit the toilets before being taken into another large, austere room.

It's empty apart from several long wooden tables, each maybe twelve feet long with benches on either side. They jostle each other to get a space. Jan manages to sit at the same table as his sisters. With a pang, he realizes Lena has been crying. Her face is blotchy in the way it always is when she's been weeping. Although he's several feet away, he can see her eyes are swollen.

Maria cuddles her, but Lena doesn't respond. He stares at them, helpless.

The two people at the top of each table rise in turn and go to a hatch where they pick up some plates. One is set down in front of Jan. It has two slices of dark bread on it, and something that might be butter. He looks round for cutlery, but sees that the other children, the ones who were here before them and presumably know what to do, are wiping the bread over the butter before stuffing it into their mouths. One of them, a tall blond boy who looks older than the rest, moves his hand towards Jan's plate, but Jan sees it coming and grabs his bread. The boy retreats, a grimace sliding across his face. Careful to watch all sides and ready to protect what he and his sisters have, Jan eats the bread. It is dry and hard. He wouldn't be surprised if they'd put wood scrapings in the flour; he's heard of such things. Nonetheless, even though it's tasteless, it is food – and he's hungry, starving, so he eats every scrap. As soon as he's finished he realizes how foolish he's been; he has no idea when they'll next be fed.

When they have all finished, they are sent back up to their room to make their beds, and then to the kitchen where they have to wash the dishes they used for breakfast. All the time, the women who are supervising speak to them in German. Jan understands nothing. He follows the rest of the children keeping out of the way of the women. A couple of times he tries to find out if anyone else knows what's going on, but they're all as ignorant as him. When the other children, the ones who are not from his village, hear him speak, they shake their heads and glance at the women. Jan isn't sure, but he thinks they're warning him. A terrible thought comes to him: his mother too might be dead, shot like his father and the men of the village. It's unbearable, he has to know, and without thinking he shouts out as loud as he can, "Where are our mothers?"

One of the women turns and looks at him. She strides over to him and grips his shoulder, leaning forwards to speak. The strange-sounding words roll out in a furious stream, tumbling into incoherence. Jan makes out one word said over and over again: "*Deutsch*". He knows this means German, but he doesn't understand the rest. Her voice rises, and she shakes him in time to her words. Gradually he distinguishes the separate sounds as they are spat in his face. "*Du musst nur Deutsch sprechen.*" Still he doesn't understand. At last she stops and walks away, leaving him bewildered and frightened. He's shaking, doesn't dare look at the others in the room, but instead carries on with his cleaning duties, too terrified to speak, dusting the one spot over and over in a frenzy of rage and fear.

The morning passes in a haze of chores. He had never thought there could be so much to do: floors to be washed, potatoes to be scrubbed and peeled, clothes to be wrung out. By the end of the morning his hands are red and creased from being wet all the time, and he knows he has bruises on his back where the women keep hitting him. They beat him for so many things: a cloth not wrung out properly, a potato peeled too thickly, water slopped on the floor. He gave up counting after the twentieth slap. They hit all the children, especially the boys, at the least excuse. One boy, who is tiny, maybe only four or five years old, begins to cry, huge tears rolling down his face. Jan wishes he could comfort him – he is so small, like his own little sister, and he cannot bear to think of her crying in this way, but he is too scared to do anything, and so he stands by and watches. The women seem pleased to have got a reaction, one of them smiles showing large yellow teeth, and Jan vows that no matter how hard they hit him, he will not cry.

In the afternoon, after a lunch of salty cabbage and potato soup, they are lined up and taken to another smaller building, a house, about two kilometres away. They are forced to run, which after all they've done this morning, exhausts them. When they arrive at huge iron gates, they have a chance to rest while the women struggle to open it. For a few precious seconds they stand gasping for breath, hoping for something to drink for the day is hotter than ever, and the salty soup has left them with a pernicious thirst.

The gates are opened, and they pour through. The house looks more welcoming than the factory they have just left. It stands alone surrounded by a large garden, which is unkempt, but still bears traces of once having been cared for. There is a small orchard of apricot trees and, though they are not yet ripe, several of the children grab what they can as they pass, stuffing the fibrous fruits into their mouths. Jan manages to pocket three, and he thinks he will save them for later, give one to each of his sisters. He looks round for them, but they are at the back of the line. Lena is limping, he notices, and he hopes she'll be all right.

The women stop them in front of a large wooden door. Black paint is flaking off round the edges showing greying wood beneath. The windows are filthy, Jan spots a cobweb stretching across the top of one of them; they can't have been washed for years. Two of the women move through the line, ordering the children to one side or another. After ten minutes they are sorted to the women's satisfaction: two long lines, boys and girls. The younger children are at the front. Lena is one of the smallest. She stands near the start of the queue, wearing clothes that are too big for her. The dress she is wearing almost reaches the ground. As the girls move into the house, she lifts the dress to stop herself tripping over it, and Jan catches sight of something beneath, flapping. He peers, trying to make it out, then smiles. It's her precious nightdress. She must have managed to get hold of it and decided to keep it safe by wearing it under her day clothes. She's a smart kid for only four years old. The girls vanish into the dark interior of the house leaving the boys outside in the afternoon heat.

Hours pass. Jan is giddy with hunger. He has eaten his apricot, nibbling at the hard flesh, which catches in his teeth. Now and again, he fingers the two remaining in his pocket; Maria and Lena will never know if he eats them or not, they might even have some of their own. He'll give it another hour, he decides, and then he'll eat another one.

The scuffed door creaks open, and a tall, distinguished man beckons to them to come in. The women push them forwards into the house. It is dark inside, and blissfully cool. Jan squeezes his eyes open and shut to try to get used to the dark. Within a few seconds he can see quite well. They are in a huge hall. There is no carpet on the floor, and the wooden floorboards are scuffed and dusty. In front of them is a massive staircase, big enough for a castle. It sweeps straight up from the middle of the hall and branches off to both sides. The man marches the boys upstairs, telling them to keep away from the balustrade; several posts are missing, and they could fall through. He takes them off to the right and makes them stand in a corridor. The boys are upright and don't dare to stir. Two of the women guards are with them still, and to begin with they lash out at any movement. But eventually they get bored and start to chat to one another, only striking out very occasionally. While their backs are turned, Jan cranes his neck, but sees no sign of the girls. There is a room at the end of the corridor. Its door is open, and Jan sees several people there – a woman and some men, talking and laughing. After a few minutes the woman comes out and indicates to the boy at the front of the queue to come in. The door of the room shuts behind him. Several minutes pass. In the trees outside a bird is singing, and the smell of cut grass is in the air. It feels like home and, despite himself, Jan relaxes. The bruises on his back don't hurt so much now, and he is no longer hungry. He leans against the wall for support, but one of the women spots him, and at once he is slapped across the head. It is a hard slap, he'd swear they had it in for him since he'd shouted out the question about their mothers that morning. He narrows his eyes and stands up straight. It'll take more than a slap to get at him.

One by one the boys go into the room. Jan waits for them to return, to try to guess from their faces what to expect, but no one reappears. This is worrying. Jan senses the fear of the boys who remain; they are so frightened they don't look at each other. The line gets smaller until at last, it is his turn.

The room is spacious and bright with large windows framed by green velvet curtains. On one wall there is a picture of a man in uniform. He looks ugly, frightening. Jan recognizes him. His father used to talk to him about this man, and say how evil he was. The man's eyes seem to look right through him, and the sensation makes Jan shiver. He looks down at the ground so he can't see the portrait.

There are four people in the room. One man lifts his head as Jan enters; he has a white coat on, like a doctor. Thank God. Doctors are good people; they help you. Sometimes they hurt you, but only to make you better, like when his arm was broken and he had to get plaster on it. The doctor speaks in Czech – not very good Czech, difficult to understand, but at least it is familiar. But when he tells Jan to get undressed, Jan's fears return.

"All clothes off," he says as Jan removes only his shorts and shirt.

Reluctantly, Jan removes his underpants. They're soiled, for there was nothing to clean himself with in the toilet, and he's frightened he will be beaten for being dirty. He folds them carefully, so only the clean side can be seen, and stands in front of the adults, hands in front of his private parts. The woman has a tape measure and tells him to stand against the wall so she can take his height. She writes it down on a piece of paper along with other measurements she takes: round his waist, his chest, the size of his ears, his nose, the length of his legs, the width of his feet. The measuring goes on for what seems like hours. Then she asks him questions. At first he doesn't answer. It's so long since he has spoken that his mouth is dry and, in any case, her accent is thick, difficult to understand. She speaks more slowly, and he picks up what she is saying. The questions are easy: what colour is grass, what should you do if a boy hits you, why should you not touch an oven. Jan answers them, for a brief moment feeling proud that he knows so much, then, remembering he is with the enemy, in a much more surly way.

They make him sit in a chair and listen to his chest with a cold stethoscope, look at his teeth with a tiny mirror, examine his ears with an instrument he has never seen before. They weigh him, make him hop, jump, squat. The male doctor even holds his testicles and makes him cough. Jan does so, his face scarlet with embarrassment.

At last they finish with him. The doctor gives him back his clothes, and Jan gets back into them in record speed. He hated being naked in front of their curious eyes. Three doors lead out of the room. One goes back into the hall where they waited for so long. The one that they tell Jan to go through takes him into a room where there are several other boys. Not as many as there should be, though, not nearly as many. There were perhaps fifty boys from their village, and yet in this room there are only half a dozen. The others must have been sent through the remaining door. Jan feels cold when he tries to think what this might mean.

All the boys here are younger than him. He knows them all by sight, and knows some of their older brothers well. One of them comes over now, tries to look tough, but his voice is cracked and his eyes too bright.

"Hey, Jan," he says, "I think maybe they're going to send us home."

"You're soft in the head if you think that," says Jan, and is sorry when the boy turns quickly away. Not so quick that Jan doesn't see a tear slide down his cheek. What a stupid thing to say. The kid can only be about seven years old. He should be able to hope they're going home.

"Maybe you're right," he calls to him. "I think I heard one of them say…"

He tails off as the boy turns round. The hope is naked in his face; he is so vulnerable that Jan cannot continue. He mumbles incoherently, not meeting the boy's eyes. Before the boy can say any more, there is a diversion as one of the others draws their attention to what's going on outside.

Two trucks have drawn up and parked on the lawn. They are monstrous in the small garden. Large, painted an indeterminate blue-green colour. Jan thinks they are the ones that brought them there the night before, but he cannot be sure. A soldier runs out of the house and opens the doors to both trucks. Jan thinks they are going to spill over with more children, but no, they are empty. A moment later a large group of children are led into the courtyard. They are all from their village. The seven boys in the room press their noses against the window to watch. Jan sees Maria and draws in his breath. He can't bear this. He had thought they would be kept together. He bangs on the window, willing her to look up, but her head remains down. The slope of her shoulders tells him that she is crying. "Maria!" he shouts, "Maria, where are you going?"

She seems to have heard him. Maria turns round and looks up at the window, moves as if to try to reach him, but a woman grabs her and shoves her towards the truck. Maria stumbles and hits her shin on the edge of one of the doors. Jan strikes the window once more, but this time Maria doesn't look back, and within seconds the truck has devoured her. The remaining children are lined up in twos and pushed into the truck. Jan scours the crowd. He can't see Lena anywhere. He can only hope that she is still here in the house somewhere.

As the truck draws out of the courtyard, its tyres churning up the muddy grass, Jan wonders if he will ever see any of his family again. He digs his fingernails into the palms of his hands to stop these horrible thoughts, but they persist. When he can no longer see the truck, he leaves his place at the window and goes to a corner of the room where he lies down and curls himself into a ball in a hopeless attempt to comfort himself. Karl, the smallest of the boys, comes over to him and reaches out to touch his arm, but Jan cannot be consoled and he shrugs the child away.

Later that day they are moved to yet another building, not far from where they have been. It too is a large old house with grass surrounding it. It could almost be a family home, except for a huge fence all round which makes it feel like a prison. A nun comes to the door to let them in. Her face is like every other face they've seen in Lodz: hard, unsmiling. Jan doesn't like nuns. He knows they're supposed to be holy, but in his experience they can be as cruel as anyone he's ever met. This one reminds him of Sister Maria Josef, who was his teacher in kindergarten. She'd hit you on the knuckles if your writing wasn't neat enough. The poor logic of this always upset Jan. He used to cry to his mother about it – *how am I supposed to write better if my hand hurts?*

When they get inside and see the other nuns scurrying around, it becomes clear this must be a convent. The nuns are almost all elderly, though there are a few who are young. One of them, who is wearing a white habit, guides the children upstairs to their rooms. The boys and girls are kept apart; it's several hours, just before suppertime, before Jan discovers that his little sister has not been taken away with the others. He spots her, with a small number of other girls, and breaks free from the group of boys that have been sent to help prepare vegetables. He manages to reach her and hug her before he is grabbed from behind and sent to the boys' room without any supper. He doesn't care, he is happy just to know she's here with him.

4

A month later, they are on the move again. They are woken up very early one morning and told to get dressed. One of the younger nuns whispers to Jan, "You are going to Germany, to a children's home."

Jan shivers at the thought, Germany. Every move takes him and Lena further away from his home in Czechoslovakia, further from his mother and Maria.

"Where in Germany?"

She shrugs. "I don't know. A letter came yesterday."

Jan is used to travel by now, he knows to keep close to Lena so they won't be separated, and knows it's best to get a seat near the window so that they can get some fresh air. He saves some food from breakfast for the journey, and tells Lena to do the same. If it's anything like their other journeys it will be some time before anyone thinks to give them food.

A chance to escape; there's only two women to look after twenty-one children. They've allowed him and Janusz to go alone to the toilet, unaware that the train was about to stop. Janusz comes out of the toilet as soon as the train comes to a halt and puts his head out of the window to have a good look round. When he spots the station name he hugs Jan.

"Let's go, now! I know this place; it's not far from where my parents live. We can walk there in a few hours."

Jan pushes him away and shakes his head. "I can't. You know I can't. I have to look after Lena."

"You could... " Janusz's voice tails off. He knows Jan will not be persuaded. "Can you cover for me? Give me some time to get a head start?"

"Of course, I'll say you've got the runs." Jan remembers the sweet Janusz gave him the first day they met, and he reaches into his pocket and pulls out the bread he has saved from breakfast. It could be days before Janusz gets anything to eat again. "Here, take this."

Janusz smiles. "No, keep it. Tonight I'll be with my family. You'll need it more." He peers out of the window. A guard is about to blow his whistle. "Look, the train's about to move. I'm going to wait till it gets going, so that even if they spot me it'll be too late to do anything about it." He turns the handle of the door, his whole body tense. The train lurches forwards. Janusz opens the door. "This is it, Jan. Wish me luck." He jumps out onto the platform. Jan grabs the door and shuts it before the train can get up speed. He leans out of the window and gazes at Janusz, who is running as if the hounds of hell are after him. "Good luck," he whispers.

"What are you doing?" It is Magda, one of the women guards, frowning down at him. Jan's heart thumps.

"Getting some fresh air. I felt a little sick."

"Yes, you are pale. Where is your friend?"

"Still in the toilet. He's got the trots." Jan prays she won't notice the door is unlocked. He decides to take a chance, it's best to try to get her away from here. "I think he'll be some time, shall we go back?"

"No, you go. I'll wait in case he needs help."

Damn her! When have these women ever tried to help any of the children? Jan tries one last time, "I think it might embarrass him."

Magda shrugs. "He'll get over it. Now, run along."

Jan trails back to his compartment. His mouth is dry. When Magda finds that Janusz has escaped, he's for it. His seat by the window has gone. Lena is still where he left her, but she's sleeping now, her face flushed. There is a trace of a smile on her lips. Perhaps she's dreaming of home. He squeezes into a seat near the middle of the group and closes his eyes. Perhaps if he's asleep when Magda finds out that Janusz has gone… He's kidding himself, but he tries to sleep anyway.

A shriek of rage. Jan's stomach flips. This is it. He keeps his eyes closed and tries to breathe evenly. He hasn't a clue what he'll say.

"You! Where is the other boy?"

Jan pretends to wake with a start and puts on a bewildered face. "What?"

"Your friend, the one with the trots. He's not in the toilet." Her face is red. Behind her is the other woman, who looks even more terrifying than Magda. Her fists are clenched. Jan scratches his head. "I don't understand. He went into the toilet clutching his belly. He was really ill."

Magda narrows her eyes. "You're lying."

"No, I swear." Jan flinches from the slap she gives him. He puts his hand up to his cheek and she snatches it away.

"You'll pay for this. Get up!" She pushes him out into the corridor. Sweat breaks out on his forehead. She's in a fury; he's terrified of what she might do. Surely she won't push him off the train? It's speeding now, the countryside is a blur. He'll never survive. He staggers as she hits him on the head and on his chest. Over and over, each blow worse than the next. Jan has no breath left; he'd never thought a woman could be so brutal. He can't help himself, knows it will make things worse, but he has to, it's her fault. He vomits, horrified as it spills down the front of her dress, then thankfully he blacks out.

Voices all around him. He doesn't understand it all for it's German, but he knows enough to realize they're talking about him. He should open his eyes, but he's frightened of what he might see if he does, so he keeps them shut and pretends to sleep. There's no train sound. Have they stopped the train to try to catch Janusz? Poor Janusz, if they catch him…

They're shaking him now, it's no use, he'll have to open his eyes and face whatever is coming to him. The light is blinding, and he blinks several times to try to adjust to it.

"Get up and get dressed," he recognizes the voice as Magda's.

His eyes have got used to the light, and he sees that they're no longer in the train, but in a room. There are several adults around his bed – one is a doctor – and for a moment he feels safe, then remembers that no one can be trusted. His whole body aches when he moves, and it seems to take an age just to swing his legs out of bed. He tries to hurry for he doesn't want to antagonize them more, but his head and chest hurt so much that he gasps and lies down.

"You have a cracked rib," says the doctor. "It won't take long to heal."

"Yes," says Magda. "You got it from that other boy, he kicked you when you tried to stop him running away. Isn't that right?"

Jan gapes at her. She glares at him, defying him to contradict what has been said. He continues to stare at her, and her face flushes. Jan understands; she's ashamed. Whether it's because she lost one of the boys in her charge, or whether it's because she beat him up so badly he doesn't know and he doesn't care. He makes his decision.

"Yes," he says, "Janusz kicked me when I tried to stop him from jumping from the train."

"Do you know where he was going?" The doctor is writing in a notebook.

Jan puts his head down, tries one more lie. "I think he must be dead. The train was going fast when he jumped."

Magda smirks. She knows he's lying, but Jan stares at her, and eventually she nods. "The boy's probably right."

Jan gets up from the bed. It'll be days before he can move freely again without pain.

Jan isn't sure, but he thinks they're being prepared for something. This place is different from the convent in Lodz. It's more like a school. Apart from the handful of children from his village there are twenty or so Polish children; some came with them from Lodz, others were here already. It's absolutely forbidden to speak any language other than German. An older Polish boy, Pawel, takes him aside after he's been beaten for singing a Czech song. He looks round to check no one's listening.

"You have to speak German all the time. If you don't they'll beat you. Soon you'll be thinking in German." He lowers his voice. "Some of the little ones forget very quickly. But I will never forget." His voice is proud when he says this.

"Have you been here long?" asks Jan.

"Four or five months. Long enough. I want to go home. Don't you?"

Jan bites his lip and says nothing. His stomach twists, he doesn't want to admit he doesn't have a home any more. The Polish children's stories are very different from their own. They tell tales of being snatched from the streets of their towns and cities; some were stolen from their homes.

Pawel's story is typical; he was at home alone one Sunday, his parents had gone to church, but he wasn't feeling well, so he'd stayed behind. A few minutes before his parents were due back from mass, a truck drew up in front of their flat. Pawel thought nothing of it; they lived in a busy street. It wasn't until they hammered at the door that he realized what was happening; the dreaded Gestapo had come for him. Everyone knew they were stealing children to send to Germany where they would be brought up as Germans. There was nothing he could do: there were six soldiers, and they had guns. He was allowed to gather a few belongings together, and then he was bundled into the truck. When Pawel told Jan the story for the first time, he wept as he recalled how his parents had seen this happen, and how they ran after the truck calling his name. "I am their only child," he told Jan. "They will not survive without me. I must return home. I must remain Polish."

Jan envies Pawel's certainty that his parents are waiting for him. He would like to know why he is so sure, but there are other things on his mind too. "The day after we arrived, they took many of us away. Is that where they went then, to Germany, to another children's home?"

Pawel drops a potato into a large pan of water. "I do not think so. The others, the ones who have gone to families, were taken away in small groups, maybe one or two at a time. I think..." he lowers his voice to a whisper, "I think your friends are dead."

Jan stares at Pawel, who looks away with an indifference that infuriates him. With a roar of rage, he throws himself on the boy. "No," he screams, "no, they're not dead. I won't let them be." He pummels him with his fists. One of the women who look after them runs to see what is happening. She peels Jan off Pawel, hits him on the head. Pawel laughs until she hits him too. She shouts at them both, but neither of them answers. They stand in front of her, sullen and silent, until she gives up and leaves them alone.

Jan clenches his fists. "Why did you say that?"

"Because it's true." The boy's shoe scuffs at the ground. He still doesn't look at Jan.

Jan breathes in deeply. "How do you know?"

Pawel's hands are stuffed deep in his pockets. His eyes are full of tears. "I heard them talking," he says. "Some days after the trucks left. They said they would get what they deserved."

"But that could mean anything," cries Jan. "They could have been sent home, or to…" His voice tails off. Pawel is staring at him with an expression of pity.

"They called them little bastards. I don't think they would have done that if they were going to be nice to them, do you?"

Jan turns away from him. He looks over to the high fence surrounding the home. They're in a prison, really, he thinks. A prison for children. He wonders if what Pawel says is true about taking the children away and putting them into German families. It seems such a silly thing to do. They've broken up families – his, Pawel's, Janusz's, Josef's. All of them smashed to pieces so they can be given to some other family. It doesn't make sense.

Lena is playing over on the other side of the yard. She is throwing a ball to one of the women. The woman laughs as Lena catches the ball and calls her *Liebchen*. Jan knows this means "darling". It chills him. He wants to run across the grass and sweep her away, but he knows if he does it will lead to another beating. He tells himself he doesn't mind these endless beatings, but he can't take another today. So, instead of rescuing her, he stands watching as she twirls round the woman, laughter spilling from her mouth. She's smiling in a way he hasn't seen since they arrived, and all of a sudden he is glad that she is having a moment of happiness; that she's forgotten her mother won't be there to sing her a lullaby, or her father to lift her on his shoulders and play at giants.

It isn't often he gets a chance to speak to Lena, for the girls and boys are kept apart most of the time. Weeks pass before he manages to find a moment when she is alone; when he speaks to her, he thinks she's changed. For one thing, she speaks German. When Jan talks to her in Czech, she screws up her face and tells him to speak properly.

"Only peasants speak the way you do."

Jan gazes at her, wordless. It's not her fault; she doesn't know what she's saying. Every day the women tell them lies like this, and she's only little. It's no surprise that she takes in and believes what they say to her.

"Our parents spoke this way," he reminds her.

Lena kicks a stone away. "*Ich habe keine Eltern. Sie sind tod*."

The roof of his mouth is dry, his heartbeat quickens. Flashes of his father falling to the ground zip past him, making him giddy. His head is empty of everything save that image, falling, falling. He cannot speak. Lena is staring at him, her eyes puzzled, her mouth downturned. One of the women calls her, she runs off without a word, leaving Jan alone. He cannot see properly as his eyes fill with hot stinging tears. It's a relief when they start to fall. One of the boys from his village joins him. He has overheard Jan's conversation with Lena.

"The little ones are quick to forget."

Jan wipes away the tears and nods. The other boy continues. "When my mum and dad find out where we are, they'll come and get us."

Jan doesn't reply.

"Won't they?"

If he tells him the truth, what will happen? Jan doesn't know what to say. He wants to share his knowledge with someone, thinking that this will maybe chase away the images that disturb him so often. He can go for days undisturbed, then with no warning they intrude into his dreams and waking moments alike. So, when he opens his mouth it is with the intention of saying that there will be no rescue, but the boy's eyes are so hopeful and trusting that all Jan can do is nod; his head has a life of its own. He turns away, walks across the lawn to the house, wishing he were anywhere but here. The bell rings; a summons to the class where he will be bombarded in a foreign language, that to his horror is becoming so familiar that sometimes he finds himself thinking in German.

5

Late August, time to bring in the harvest. All over Germany, crops are being lifted and prepared for storage. Everyone knows it will be a hard winter, the fourth of this war. People work until their backs ache, their thighs throb and their heads thump. They barely talk to each other, but instead busy themselves with the endless tasks.

The Schefflers are finding it more difficult than most. It is now three years since their daughter died, killed in a road accident while cycling home from school. She'd been keen to get back to the farm to help. That was the kind of girl she was – thoughtful, eager, their little princess. Though they rarely speak of her, she's in their minds all the time; they can't stop thinking about her. She would have been fifteen in December.

As Frau Scheffler prepares the evening meal, she wipes a tear from her eye. These are strong onions, or so she tells herself. After three years, and with all that is going on, she feels guilty that she still weeps for her daughter. It is an indulgence, and she knows it, but still the tears come.

Her husband, Friedrich, comes into the kitchen. His tread is soft, and she doesn't hear him until he is standing right behind her.

"There's a letter from Wilhelm, over there, on top of the range." She speaks to divert him – she doesn't want him to see her tears. Her voice is thick, though, and he notices at once and comes to her side.

"Are you all right?" His voice wavers. "You're not thinking about Helga, are you?"

She shakes her head, not trusting herself to speak. He puts his finger under her chin, raising it up so that she is forced to look at him.

"Why do you do this to yourself? It does no good. What's done is done." He pats her cheek and goes back to the table where he cuts a slice of bread and spreads a thick layer of butter on it. They are lucky in the countryside, food is not so scarce here, and they can still eat well. He takes a bite and carries on talking, but Gisela doesn't listen. She's back in the past, where her two children are safe in bed, rather than fighting a war or buried deep in the ground in the Catholic cemetery in the nearby town.

"Well then, what do you think?"

Gisela stops chopping and stares at her husband. "What do I think about what?"

"My plan."

She has no idea what he is talking about. These days she blocks out most of what is said to her. It's easier that way. When Helga died and so many people talked nonsense to her with their pious platitudes of much better places and time being a great healer, she argued with them, but they didn't like it. She could see it made them uncomfortable when she said things like: "Is she in a better place? How do you know it's better? Are you saying she wasn't happy here with her parents?" The priest especially was embarrassed, and after a while he stopped asking her how she was, and offering to say masses for her. Instead, he'd look away when they passed each other in the street. Once, he crossed the road to avoid her, almost falling in his speed to get away from her. Stupid old fool. At least he hadn't badgered her when she stopped going to church.

Friedrich is shaking her. He often does this to get her out of her reverie. Poor Friedrich, he misses their children too, though he will never talk about it. But she can tell from the eagerness with which he grabs Wilhelm's letters and the way his eyes fill when he says Helga's name.

"Please listen to me," he says, "I read about it in the paper, about how you can adopt children."

She's listening now. What madness is this, to suggest adopting other people's children when they have their own? Her heart beats in her head, thumping a painful rhythm inside her skull.

"There are so many children who are orphans now. The government is looking for families like us to give them a home. Just think, Gisela, we could make a child happy." His eyes are bright. She hasn't seen him look like this since long before the war began. It was never in her nature to disappoint people, she had grown from a compliant child to an obliging adult, but she'd changed when Helga fell off her bike into the path of an oncoming car, and today she hardens her heart against him.

"I don't think so," she says, and goes back to her mechanical slicing of onions. Behind her, Friedrich sighs. "I thought it might help," he whispers.

For several days she won't let herself think about what Friedrich said, but gradually the idea takes hold. She reflects on what it might entail: the difficulties of raising another woman's child, perhaps it would be cheeky, or sullen, or perhaps it might be unhappy. Yes, almost certainly the child would be unhappy. Could she make someone happy again? She doesn't know. At this moment, when she can barely remember what it is to be contented and not to have a gnawing emptiness in her stomach, when smiling is an effort and laughing an impossibility, she thinks it would be easier to count the grains in a field of corn. And yet – she has to be truthful; the idea is appealing. The thought of a child running around the house, someone to look after, to love, to teach, fills her with a barely remembered emotion: hope. Perhaps it would do no harm to find out more.

She's in the kitchen when her husband comes home from the fields. He sits down heavily on the wooden chair near the range and pulls off his boots.

"Is that soup you've been making? It smells good."

She nods. "I've been thinking," she says, "about what you said." She ladles some soup into a bowl and places it on the table in front of him.

Friedrich doesn't reply. He cuts himself some bread and eats a slice before starting on the soup. He is halfway through it before he lays down his spoon. "That's better," he says. "Now, what were you saying?"

"About adopting a child, maybe we could find out more." She refills his bowl.

He shrugs. "If that's what you want."

Gisela has tested the dough for the bread. It is well risen and ready to knead. She flours the table and puts the dough down, pressing her fists into it. With slow steady movements, she flattens it, turns it over, pushing at it with all her strength. This will be the best bread she has ever made. She's not fooled by his terse response. After twenty-two years together, she knows this is as enthusiastic as he gets.

"Yes," she says, "it's what I want. Tell me about it."

Friedrich gets up from his chair and goes over to the stairs. "Are you sure about this?"

"Can't do any harm to find out, can it?"

He doesn't answer. Instead he goes upstairs. Gisela hears him walking through the rooms above. She tenses as a board creaks. He's in their daughter's room. Friedrich never goes there. It is exactly how it was when Helga left for school that day. Her books are still in the little bookcase that Friedrich made for her tenth birthday. She loved to read, lying on the rug in front of the range. The patchwork quilt that was made from scraps of material from Helga's baby clothes lies over her bed, undisturbed for three years. The footsteps cease. What is he doing? Gisela cannot stand the tension. She goes to the foot of the stairs. "Shall I make some coffee?" she calls. Friedrich grunts in reply.

She puts the old iron kettle on the range and starts to grind some coffee beans. She savours the comforting aroma. They don't have fresh coffee often enough. Usually she saves the grains and uses them three, even four times. She measures them out into the pot, careful not to spill any. There's very little left; it's hard to get hold of these days. When the water boils, she pours some over the grounds.

"Come and get this before it gets cold," she shouts upstairs.

Friedrich comes down, goes straight to his chair. His eyes are bloodshot, his eyelids puffy. Gisela hands him a cup and takes a sip from her own. For several minutes they sit in silence.

Friedrich bangs his cup down on the table, making Gisela jump. "There was never a child like our Helga."

Gisela nods. "I know."

"No one can replace her, no one."

"We wouldn't want to replace her."

"Just as long as it's understood." He makes as if to rise, but Gisela catches hold of his hand and pulls him down once more.

"This was your idea, not mine," she reminds him. "We don't need to do it." She waits for him to say something. "You said it might help."

"Help, yes. Yes I think we could do with some help round the farm. We're not getting any younger."

Gisela takes his face in her hands and gazes into his eyes. He looks away from her stare, but she persists. "I don't think that's what you meant, is it?"

He shakes his head. "No, but now that you've said yes, it's like a betrayal—"

"No," Gisela interrupts. "It's no such thing. Neither of us wants to replace Helga. But it would be good to try to help a little one, an orphan child. You must write today and say we will do this."

Friedrich rises from his chair and goes to the sink. He splashes his face with water and stands for a moment at the window gazing at the fields beyond. "I have no preference," he says, "girl or boy, it doesn't matter."

"Of course not," says Gisela, crossing her fingers behind her back in the old superstitious way that he hates so much. But she daren't tempt fate, and she is lying. More than anything, she would love a girl to teach baking and sewing and all the arts of keeping a fine house. She would not replace Helga, that was true, but in her heart, Gisela thinks she might ease the pain of the loss, just a little.

6

Jan has not seen Lena for three days. Yesterday he put his pride aside and spoke to one of the women who looks after them – he thinks of them as jailers. It hurt him to use German, and he was dismayed to find how easily the words came, without any real effort.

"*Bitte, wo ist meine Schwester*?"

"You have a sister?" The eyes that stared at him were without expression.

"Yes, her name is Lena. She's one of the little ones."

"With long blonde hair? Yes I know her." The woman turned aside and carried on with her sweeping.

Jan persisted. "Do you know where she is?"

Her eyes reminded him of hard-boiled eggs, the white a greyish black around the iris. "Here you have no sisters, no brothers. Now get on with your work." She poked him in the belly with the broom, a vicious jab. Jan bent over in pain, biting his tongue to keep from crying out.

He vows he'll find out where she is. It's early in the morning, an hour or so before they have to rise; he slips out of bed and pads across to Pawel. The wooden floorboards are cold beneath his feet; it is not yet spring, and the winter has been harsh. For the sixth day in a row, there is ice on the windows, covering the glass with a white frost. It is beautiful to look at, but lethal to touch. Yesterday, one of the little ones wanted to trace a pattern on it, but his finger stuck to the ice. When he wrenched his finger away, a little bit of skin remained on the window. Jan shiver as he recalls the cries of the child.

When he reaches Pawel's bed, Jan hesitates. It's such a shame to waken him; they have little enough sleep as it is.

"Pawel," he whispers, "wake up."

Pawel shifts onto his back, but doesn't open his eyes.

"Pawel, please... I need your help."

One eye opens, peers at him. "What is it?"

"It's my sister. I don't know where she is."

Pawel sits up in bed and looks round the room. The rest of the boys are sleeping. He puts his finger to his lips and grabs the blanket from his bed. He beckons to Jan to follow him. They cross the room, careful to avoid the wooden board that always creaks when they stand on it. In the hall there's a large window with long red curtains. The window has a deep sill; Pawel sits on it, patting the remaining space. Jan jumps up beside him, and Pawel draws the curtains so they can't be seen. They pull the blanket round themselves.

"Tell me about Lena," says Pawel. "When did you last see her?"

Jan rubs his eyes. He is tired beyond anything he has ever known. Last night he lay in his bed thinking about what to do, as he had done the night before. He isn't sure, but he thinks that he did not sleep, not for a minute. "I haven't seen her for three days now."

Pawel hits the side of his own head in a gesture of realization. "They must have sent her to a family."

Jan doesn't want to hear this. "Perhaps she's ill," he says, "sent to hospital."

"No," says Pawel. "The most likely thing is that they found a family for her."

This silences Jan. Lena, taken from him and sent to a German family. How long will it be before she forgets who she is?

"What am I going to do?" he asks. "Should I ask if I can join her?"

"I'm sorry," says Pawel. "I don't think there's anything you can do. They don't keep families together when they do this. It means nothing to them that she's your sister."

Jan thinks of the woman who told him that here they have no brothers or sisters, of her brusque tone of voice. It was as if she really hated him, hated them all. Jan knows how much the Germans hate Jews, his father had told him about it, but he hadn't realized they hated other people too. It's frightening to think of so much hatred.

The two boys sit for some seconds in the quiet of the morning. Jan breathes on the window until the frost melts and he can watch the snow drift in the wind. It's mesmerizing; he imagines himself out in it, dancing, free from care, free from memories… His eyes glaze over with longing. Pawel pulls at Jan's arm. "Come on, we should get back to bed. If they catch us…"

Back in bed, Jan lies waiting for the bell that tells them to get up. He doesn't know how he'll do it, but he's made up his mind. Soon, very soon, he will escape, and somehow he will find Lena and take her home to their village. He ignores the voice inside his head, asking him, "What home?" If there is no home he will make one for her. She is all he has now. He is ready to fall sound asleep when the clamour of the new day starts: bells and women thumping around. There's nothing for it but to rise and face the hours ahead of him.

After breakfast, when he is washing some sheets that one of the younger boys has soiled, he turns to Pawel and says, "Tomorrow, I am going to find Lena. Will you come with me?"

Pawel stares at him. "Are you mad?"

"Maybe. Will you come with me?"

"If we do this," Pawel says slowly, as if he's thinking while he speaks, "we need to do it properly. It has to be planned, and that will take time. Tomorrow's too soon." He raises his hand against Jan's protest. "Listen to me. If you don't think it through, then you'll fail. You'll be back in here… or worse. We must wait until the weather is warmer. We'll freeze in no time if we leave while there is still a chance of snow. Think about it. If she has been adopted she could be anywhere in Germany. We might have to walk hundreds of miles, sleep in the open. We can't rush at this."

Jan nods. He knows Pawel's right, and although he's desperate to act, it would be much more sensible to work out what to do: he needs to find out where Lena is, hide food to take with him, prepare well.

"Yes, you're right. We'll wait until spring. That will give us plenty of time to plan. Planning, that's the thing. What do we have to do?"

Pawel looks round to see that no one is in earshot. "The first thing is that no one, not another soul, must know of this. We must keep this to ourselves. No matter how tempting it is, say nothing. We need time to think it all through. It'll be weeks before the weather will be warm enough for us to escape, but first of all, if we're to find your sister, then we need to know where she's gone."

They are silent for some minutes as they think about this. At last Jan speaks. "The office," he says, "there must be something in there that would tell us."

Pawel pulls a face. The office is in the heart of the house; he's never seen it left unguarded.

"There must be another way. Perhaps we could ask that woman," says Pawel. "The one who likes Lena so much."

Jan nods. "Yes, she might be able to tell us something. She is very attached to Lena."

"It's worth a shot. Better that than try to get into the office."

Waltrud looks down on them. "I don't know where she is," she sniffs. "They tell us nothing."

"Please, any idea. You must have heard something."

"I'm telling you – I haven't a clue. She could be in Hamburg or Berlin or in the countryside. Anywhere. Germany's a big country."

"Yes, now they've stolen so much of other people's land." The words are out of Jan's mouth before he can stop them. He's speaking in Czech so Waltrud doesn't understand.

"You know it's forbidden to speak, other than in German." Waltrud glares at them.

"*Es tut mir leid*," says Jan. "I won't do it again. So you really don't know." He smiles up at her, trying to make it genuine. "She was very fond of you, you know."

Waltrud sniffs. “Yes, well, she’s gone now. We just have to get on with things.” She starts to move away, then stops. “I offered to take her in, but they wouldn’t agree. Said I was too young, and that I needed to be married. I would have given her a good home.”

Jan doesn’t doubt it. He doesn’t like Waltrud, for she’s mean to most of the older children, but she’s fond of the younger ones, and Lena liked her a lot.

Waltrud snorts, and with a shake of her head she moves away.

A few days later, in the garden, Jan spots the man who usually works in the office, smoking and talking with a pretty young woman who sometimes comes to help in the kitchen. He looks set to be there for some time; he is getting closer to the girl, pawing at her hair. She tilts her head back at him and smiles. Jan is torn between watching them – he’s sure they’re going to kiss – but this is too good a chance to miss. He signals to Pawel, and they sneak upstairs to the corridor which leads to the office.

“You stay here, and I’ll go to the office.”

“What if someone comes?” asks Pawel.

Jan makes a face. “Then we’re done for. I don’t know, shout or something, pretend you’re having a fit. Think of something.”

He leaves Pawel at the head of the staircase and creeps along the corridor. A floorboard squeaks, and he pauses to see if anyone comes. Nothing, he presses on. When he reaches the door of the office he leans against it and listens. The door is thick, made of oak, and it’s hard to make out any sound. He looks back at Pawel, who is watching the staircase, and mouths *I can't hear anything.* Pawel motions him on, but as he is about to try the handle there's a noise from inside. It sounds like a cough. Jan springs back from the door, his heart thumping. His mind goes blank; all his brave talk is gone, he can't think of any excuse for being here, there's nowhere to hide. Fear takes over, and he runs down the corridor, grabs Pawel and hurls them downstairs and out into the open.

"I told you," he says when he's got his breath back. "I told you there's always someone there."

Pawel shakes him off. "It was your idea, not mine."

"I know, I'm sorry."

"You chickened out. After all your brave talk. The room was empty." A furious banging from above reminds them that they should be working in the garden, clearing the snow from the path. They get on with their task. Pawel continues to berate Jan for not trying the door. "It could be our only chance."

"There was someone in there," says Jan. "I heard them. We'll have to think of something else. A diversion."

Pawel doesn't answer. He's shovelling snow like a madman, it's going everywhere instead of being piled neatly to one side. Jan stops him. If he carries on, then they will be beaten for doing a poor job. "Look I'm sorry you're angry, but there was definitely someone there."

Pawel slows down, and they carry on shovelling, making sure the snow is on one side of the path like they were told to do.

"You don't have to do this, you know. She's my sister, not yours."

"I know that. But I want to get out of here too. And if there are two of us we have a better chance." Pawel holds out his hand. "I'll stick by you, if you stick by me."

"Do you mean that?"

"Of course I do."

"Well then," Jan takes his hand and shakes it, "it's a deal. We'll think of something – I know we will."

7

It is time. The snows melt, leaving the grass to push through the warm earth. Every day there are more and more birds in the garden. Snowdrops appear, then daffodils and tulips. The warmer weather invigorates the boys; they decide they have to get into the office no matter what. They know they will have only one chance; that if the adults find out what they are planning they might as well give up now. For weeks they have watched the office to try to find a pattern to the adults' days. The office is never left empty as far as they can see. There is always someone there; when they leave, it is locked up. It seems impossible to get into it, but the boys have a plan. It is risky, but they have to take their chance. They argue over who will search the office. Both boys know that being found in the office would lead to beatings, isolation and God knows what else.

"It must be me who does it," says Jan.

Reluctantly Pawel agrees, and they set a time to carry out their plan.

Pawel hurtles down the corridor to the office, screaming as loud as he can, "Help, help. You have to come."

The door bursts open, revealing a man in army uniform. "What is all this racket?" He glowers down at Pawel from what seems like a terrifying height.

"Please, you have to come." Pawel makes his voice as urgent as possible. "The woman in the kitchen said. An accident. A terrible accident."

"What's going on?" A woman joins the soldier. She takes out a hanky and blows her nose.

Pawel tries to see into the room, sometimes there is a third person there, the man they saw in the garden with the woman, but the room looks empty as far as he can see. He pulls at their hands, starts to cry. "Please come." The couple look at each other and shrug. "I'll go," says the woman.

"No! It needs two people, she said." Pawel's screams rise, echoing down the corridor until they give in and follow him. In the rush, they forget to lock the door behind them and do not notice Jan crouching in the shadows near the top of the stairs. As soon as they pass he pelts along the passageway and into the room.

He is sick with fear as he looks round the office. His lips are dry and cracked; he moistens them with his tongue. He makes straight for the filing cabinet.

Jan pulls open the top drawer. It's full of files, all with strange lettering, thick and black. Jan draws one out, peers at it, wishing he'd paid more attention in class. He sounds it out, but he's sure it's not a name. Try the next drawer. This is it. He spots his name at once, but there is no sign of his sister's. What if they destroy someone's file when they leave? They hadn't thought of that. It would be terrible to go through all this agony and find nothing. He tries the next drawer.

It's there, third from the front. Jan pulls the file out. He grabs the papers from inside and stuffs them in his pocket before shoving the file back and closing the drawer. Time to go. As he turns, Jan hears voices in the corridor. Damn – they're returning sooner than he thought. A glance round the room shows nowhere to hide. He runs to one of the windows, the curtains are floor-length – the only option. Jan steps behind them as the door opens, thanking God that the window looks out to the side of the building where nobody goes.

"What shall we do with the boy?"

"Give him a beating. We'll round up the rest of the children, make an example of him." The man sounds pleased at this idea.

"Do you believe what he says? That he did it as a dare?"

A loud yawn. "Who knows? Does it matter. Beat him hard enough and he certainly won't do it again." He laughed at the thought. "Make me some coffee will you?"

Behind the curtain, Jan hardly dares to breathe. It's so quiet in the room he thinks they'll hear him if he moves at all. There's a tickle in his throat; he wants to cough. Christ, if he does, he might as well shoot himself. He swallows, prays, the urge subsides. The sun beats down on his head, its heat magnified by the glass. It's unbearably hot. Mustn't move. Think of cold things: ice, the showers, a swim in the river. God, he's tired, wants to sleep. Head light, dizzy. Forces his eyes open. If they find him here…

Two hours later and Jan thinks he'll have to give himself up. He's giddy with heat, fatigue and hunger, his calf muscle has gone into a spasm. If he doesn't move soon, he's going to scream. The woman left about an hour ago, telling the man not to be long. Jan thinks the man is writing. He was the last time he peeped.

A movement in the room, could the man be leaving at last? Jan holds his breath. Yes, he's going, clearing up for the day: papers rustling, drawers closing, a pen slapped down on the desk, finally the blissful sound of the door opening. Jan bites his lip to stop the cheer that's rising. Even after the door closes, he waits for five minutes, counting every second.

The seconds pass, and he decides it is safe to move. There's still a chance that it's a trap and the soldier is actually in the room, calling Jan's bluff. Jan doesn't really believe this, because there's no reason for the soldier to suspect anything, but the doubt lingers, so he won't take a chance. He moves his head to the right until it reaches the edge of the curtain and peeps round... Nothing to be seen. Carefully, he edges his whole body along, moves out into the open, bracing himself for the angry shout. Still nothing.

He's out in the middle of the room, exposed. The breeze from the open window catches the pile of paper on the desk. One of the sheets floats down onto the floor; Jan's heart misses a beat at the unexpected movement. He spins round, laughs when he sees what frightened him. But time is passing, and the soldier could return at any second. He must see what is in his sister's file. It would be too dangerous to take it, for if he is caught with it... who knows what might happen. He takes the papers out of his pocket, unfolds them and immediately feels sick. They're all in German. Well of course they are; what else did he expect? Jan peers at the strange print. He can't read the print. Damn – he can't understand a word. Pawel will be able to decipher it. He's always moaning about how easily he's picked up the language even though he hasn't been trying, has no desire to speak it. There's nothing for it. He'll have to take the papers and hope they won't be missed. He puts them back in his pocket, glancing at the filing cabinet, wondering if he should hide the empty file. What the hell, he takes it out of the drawer and stuffs it at the back, out of sight. With any luck they won't even look for it. After all, his sister has gone, so why should they want her file?

He crosses to the door, grasps the handle and pulls. It's locked. Dear God. He tries again; his hands are sweaty, maybe he just isn't gripping it properly. No – it doesn't move. He's trapped. His stomach twists, Christ, surely he's not going to be sick. Not after all he's been through. Take a deep breath, calm down. There must be a way out of here… the window.

There are two windows in the room. The open one faces the front of the house. Jan runs over to it, looks out; it's too exposed. Immediately below, there's a driveway where cars sweep up at all hours; it's also overlooked by a room where the women often sit and chat. He can't go down that way. The other window is closed; he tries to open it, struggling for several minutes before it gives way. Jan sticks his head through, breathing in the fresher air.

Although it's much less exposed here, it's still a long way down, maybe as much as twenty feet. Jan thinks back to the drop from his bedroom window, which he made all those months ago, a lifetime it seems like, and knows he'd break a leg or an arm on this drop. It's much further than anything he's tried before. If he had a rope…

Damn it. He's done for. But, wait… the drainpipe; it's about a yard away from the window… risky, but he'll have to chance it. He should be able to stretch across.

Jan squeezes through the open window and stands on the ledge. He holds on to the stone mullion, stretching out his right hand as far as he dares; it's nowhere near the drainpipe. Swallowing hard he tries again. A little nearer, but still too far, maybe six inches short. Jan takes a deep breath to calm down, stands for a moment on the ledge wondering what to do. He looks down and catches sight of the ground so far below and sways. Jesus! This isn't the time to develop a fear of heights. He is not afraid of heights. He is *not* afraid. Thinks of all the trees he's climbed, much higher than this. Takes a deep breath, looks again. This time the ground doesn't sway up to meet him. Jan notes how the ledge extends several inches beyond the edge of the window. Could it be enough to make up the gap? It's narrow, perhaps only five inches wide. No room for error. He trails his right foot along to the very end of the ledge, begins to put his weight on it. It moves. A chunk breaks off and falls to the ground. Jan feels the movement beneath his foot and grabs the mullion, stone scraping his fingernails, experiencing a horrible lurch as he thinks he too will fall. But no, he manages to steady himself, his fingers gripping crevices in the masonry. The stone crashes to the ground – impossible that no one should hear it and come to see what has happened. Jan waits to be discovered, counts once more the seconds as they merge into minutes. Five minutes pass, no one comes to see what's going on. Safe to try again. He's more wary this time, and there's less room to spare. Feels his way along until he's at the very edge with nowhere to go but empty space. Nothing for it but to try. If he fails he's dead, but he's beyond caring now. He's tired, ravenous, desperately thirsty. Jan launches himself to the right and grabs the drainpipe. He's done it. Can't believe he isn't lying dead or injured on the ground. Slides down, legs shaking so much he can't stand when he reaches the bottom. Lies on the mossy cobblestones, worn out, trying not to cry.

A few moments later, he scrambles to his feet. As he walks towards the kitchen, the siren sounds for supper. Jan runs to join the others, praying he hasn't been missed.

8

It's a bright night, the moon full and low. The stars are so thick there are patches of sky that are almost white. It's like when it begins to snow and the snow covers only parts of the ground. Jan is at one of the windows of his dormitory. He never tires of looking at the stars. When he was little, his father had taught him how to recognize some of the constellations. It was always easy to pick them out when his father was beside him to help. Now, alone, it's not so simple. Jan bows his head. It's so hard to think of his family and what has happened to them. Sometimes he thinks it's a dream, and he'll wake up safe at home one morning. He tried to explain that to Pawel once, and Pawel had looked at him in scorn.

"What rubbish. The sooner you learn that this is real, the better for you."

Jan was sad at this. He'd hoped they could share in this fantasy, hoped that someone else would pretend it wasn't real. He'd had dreams like this before, that hurt him, frightened him, but he had always woken up in the end, and he wanted to believe that this too could end with everything being better once more. Deep down, though, he knew Pawel was right, and that he had to face up to reality – and most times he could, but sometimes...

A cloud passes over the moon, pale-grey. It's the first Jan's seen for weeks; the spring weather has been surprisingly hot and dry. Now at last, it's cool, cold really, and he shivers and returns to bed. Under the blanket he huddles into a ball, his hands in his armpits trying to warm himself. He thinks of the papers under his mattress that he knows will tell him where Lena is. It's comforting to have something good to think about for a change. His eyes close, and in seconds he drops off, living a dream where he is once more at home and his parents are there to scold him.

Jan's face is wet with tears when he wakes early to the sound of birdsong in the tree outside the window. He wipes them away with the edge of the sheet. He'd die rather than let the women see he's been crying. It's not time to get up yet; everyone else is asleep. He takes out the papers from beneath the mattress and tries again to read them, but he can't. It's the writing. He's never been good at reading handwriting, and this is so strange compared to the way he was taught. Shaking his head, he puts them aside and waits for the bell that tells them it's time to get up.

It's mid-morning when the children are called to the front of the house. The officer, whose room Jan now knows so well, is there with Pawel at his side. Pawel is the colour of the porridge they are served for breakfast. The officer pushes him to his knees and addresses the little assembly of children. He speaks quickly in an accent that's difficult to follow, but they get the gist. This lowly boy, disgusting animal, played a trick, and for that he will be treated like an animal. For the next two days he will be chained up in the garden and his food will be left in a dog bowl for him to eat like the animal he is. Jan bows his head. He can't bear to look at Pawel. This is all his fault. He should tell them, take his punishment. When they are told to look on, he does so and mouths *sorry* to Pawel, who flicks his eyes to show he understands.

The two days pass, and Pawel is allowed to join them once more. Jan tries to get him alone, but the other Polish children are always with him, comforting him, passing him scraps of food they saved, for Pawel hasn't eaten for the two days he's been in chains. He refused to touch the food and water left for him in dog bowls. For this he has become a hero. They want to know why he played the trick on the officer, but he won't tell them. Jan watches all this from a distance, happy to wait for a quiet time when they can talk.

"You all right?" Pawel is beside him as they wash the evening dishes.

Jan nods. "And you?"

"Take more than that to knock the stuffing out of me."

"I'm so sorry," whispers Jan.

"Don't worry. I'm fine." Pawel scrubs at a pot. "Did you get what you wanted?"

"Yes. It's upstairs, underneath my mattress."

"Thank Christ! I wouldn't want to go through that again. What does it say?"

Jan looked at him. "I don't know," he admits. "I was hoping you'd be able to help me."

"You chancer," Pawel flicks him with some of the dirty dishwater, and they laugh, Jan harder than he has for some time. He's so relieved Pawel doesn't hate him.

Upstairs, in the half hour they have to themselves before bed, they find a corner away from the others and pore over the papers. Jan can barely control himself. He wants to know every word that Pawel is reading. Pawel is impatient with him, and tells him to find something else to do, because he's just holding him back. Jan sits on his hands so he won't flap, bites his tongue so he can't speak. At last Pawel is ready.

"This paper," he waves a creased sheet in front of him, "this is a letter of application to an adoption agency. It's from a couple in Southern Germany. Here's the address," he reads it out, "Grunfeld Farm, Seeligstadt, near Dresden. Memorize it, because we'll have to get rid of these papers before they find them on us."

"And the rest? What do they say?"

"This is a form filled in by the couple. It tells you their names, dates of birth, when they got married, the names of their children and so on. This one is a copy of a letter to the couple. It tells them that they will be sent a little girl, Helena Schussel."

"But that's not my sister!"

"They must have changed her name to make her sound German. In the letter they say that she is an orphan from the north of Germany, Hamburg. Her father was a soldier who died on the Eastern Front, and her mother when a bomb dropped on her house. Burnt to death, it says here."

Jan gapes at him. He cannot believe they would change his sister into a German.

"I don't know why you're so surprised," says Pawel. "You know that's what they've got planned for us all, or at least for the very young ones. For older ones like me..." He stops.

"What? What are they planning?"

"I don't think anyone will adopt me. Not that I want to be adopted, you understand. But I'm too old. And soon you will be too. Couples like this, they want younger children, easier to manage. No, I think they'll send us to join the army as soon as we're old enough."

Jan is finding it difficult to breathe. He thinks of the soldiers and police he saw in his village, what they did to the men. Is this what is in store for him? A brutal existence of following harsh orders. It's unbearable. He won't do it, and he knows what will happen then. Certain death.

"But I tell you what, Jan… I'm not going to wait around to find out."

"What do you mean?"

"It's time to move on. You're going aren't you? After your sister?"

Of course he is. Since he realized Lena was gone, his only thought has been to find her. He knows it will be risky; even if he does find her they will be in an alien land, friendless, with no one to tell them how to get home, if they have a home to go to. Yet he has to do this. He can't live like this, waiting for someone to come and take him to a strange home, destroying any chance of him ever seeing his family again. And the other option, he can't bear to think of that. He looks at Pawel and nods.

Pawel punches the air in triumph. "I knew it! We will go together. It'll be safer that way."

Jan is overwhelmed by the relief that sweeps over him. Pawel is older and stronger, can speak German better, if he puts his mind to it. "When?" he says.

"As soon as possible. I don't want to stay a moment longer than I have to, but not immediately, because I think we should take a little time to get ready."

"You mean for food and things like that?"

"Exactly. We'll need to save rations for our journey. And money – we'll need to try to steal some."

Jan pulls a face. It won't be easy to get money for they are given none at all. There is money in the building, but it is well guarded. "Can't we do without it?"

"No. Even if we save our rations for a week they won't last that long when we're travelling. We'll need money to buy food, and perhaps to buy a train ticket, because who knows how far away your Lena is?"

This is true and, worse, although they know they're in Germany, they don't know what part. There's a map in the room that's used as a classroom. Somehow they will have to find our where they are, and where Freidorf is, so that they have some knowledge of what lies ahead of them. As they plan what to do, Jan feels a surge of happiness, the first he has felt during waking hours since that terrible day in June, smiles as Pawel outlines some wild plans for their escape.

"I'm so happy you're coming," he says to Pawel.

"Not as happy as I am. I can't wait to get out of this place."

"Ssh, there's someone coming." They stuff the papers behind a radiator which, judging by the dust there, no one has touched for many years, and run back to their beds. When the woman comes in to shout orders at them, all she sees are two boys resting on their beds.

9

Gisela watches the child playing in a corner with a doll. The sun shines through the window – which is polished so clean the glass is invisible – and catches the golden lights in her hair. She's never seen such hair. Helga, pretty as she was, had dark hair. Truth be told, it was mouse-coloured, dull. Sometimes when the sun shone on it you could see a reddish glint, but mainly it soaked up light without reflecting it back. Gisela could look at this child's hair for hours, the way it sparkles and shifts, the soft bounce of the curls. She understands now the obsession that begot tales such as Rapunzel, and almost comprehends the Führer's infatuation with Nordic looks. She pushes the Führer out of her mind. She doesn't like to think of him for he says things that she thinks are wrong, evil even. They're not in line with what she learnt at school about everyone being equal in the eyes of God. And she doesn't like what is happening to the Jews. True, she doesn't care for them much, but they never harmed her, and she doesn't see why they should be taken away to work camps. People should be paid for their work, not treated like slaves.

"Helena," she says, her voice low so as not to frighten her. The child is nervy, highly strung. Poor little thing, to have lost both parents so young. Helena looks at her, her blue eyes open wide, but doesn't reply. "Come here, *Liebchen.*"

The child puts down the doll and approaches Gisela. She stands in front of her, hands at her side, unmoving. You'd almost think the child had been drilled in some way. It isn't natural the way she stands to attention, rigid as a soldier. Gisela puts out a hand to the girl's hair. Helena flinches away like she always does. She's like a little scared animal – a rabbit or a deer perhaps – that wants to be near people, but hasn't learnt to trust them yet. Gisela knows she must be patient with her, and she moves slowly. Helena allows Gisela to touch her hair. It's as soft as duck down. Gisela has never felt hair like it. Her own hair is thick, wiry, and feels like the bristles of a shaving brush. She sighs. She could play with this hair for hours, but she is aware of Helena's discomfort, and so she lets her return to her doll.

Later, when Helena is asleep in bed, Gisela sits in her chair by the kitchen range and sews. She is making a dress for the child. The poor soul arrived wearing a brown shapeless shift and wooden clogs that pinched her feet. Underneath the shift there was a pretty rose-patterned garment that looked like a nightdress. Gisela tried to take it from her, but Helena howled as if she was being murdered. Only after many soft words did the child allow her to take it and wash it, and then she put it on again as soon as it was dry. Gisela vowed to make her pretty dresses to replace the brown shift, but it was many weeks before she managed to get into town to buy some suitable material. There were Helga's old dresses, but Gisela couldn't cut them up to make them into smaller ones that would fit Helena. Not yet.

She's pleased with the material she found in Heidelberg, a blue cotton with white stripes, cheerful and bright. Another evening's work and it should be finished. She can't wait to see Helena's face when she gives it to her. Gisela works harder, spurred on by this thought. The light is dim, and she screws up her eyes to see better, but she's tired and, after pricking her finger for the third time, she puts the dress aside. Friedrich is reading on the other side of the fire. He looks up.

"It's pretty that. I think the child will like it."

"Do you? I hope so." Gisela pauses. She wants to talk, but Friedrich has been very quiet since the child arrived three months ago. She decides to press on. "So, what do you think of her?"

Friedrich puts aside his book. "What do you think of her?"

"I asked first."

"Yes, you did." He rubs his nose as he often does when he doesn't want to talk.

"She's pretty isn't she?"

"Mmm. Has she said anything yet?"

"Not a word. Sometimes…"

"Go on."

"Sometimes I wonder if she's dumb." The words are out before Gisela realizes what she is saying.

"No, I don't think so. She understands what we say. At least I think she does."

"Do you ever wonder about her real parents?"

Friedrich shrugs. "Can't say I do."

"I wish we knew more about her."

Friedrich nods and carries on reading. Gisela sighs. It's so hard to get him to open up. Sometimes, it's like living in a monastery it's so quiet in the house. Still, Wilhelm will be home soon, on leave for a fortnight. She shivers. They haven't told him about his new sister. Gisela hopes he'll be pleased.

The dress is finished. Gisela takes it upstairs and lays it on the chair beside Helena's bed. She will rise early tomorrow for she wants to see the child's face.

Gisela is there when Helena awakes. The child stares at her with her customary silence. Gisela nods to the chair. "Look, *mein Liebchen*. Look what I've made for you."

Helena looks round. She gets up from her bed and picks up the dress from the chair. Her mouth moves into a different shape. She is smiling. Gisela catches her breath. She could swear the child spoke. "What did you say?"

"*Für mich*?" Helena's eyes are wide, blue as the flowers that bloom each spring in the nearby woods.

Gisela nods, smiles, then laughs as the child smiles back at her. It is going to be all right.

10

The boys take several months to plan their escape. Although they are impatient to leave they know that their German is not yet good enough for them to pass as native speakers. Jan thinks he'll never manage it, but Pawel becomes more fluent by the day. By the end of July, they know they must leave soon while the weather is still warm. But they have not yet decided how they will get out.

"We can climb over the wall, late at night."

"No, we'll never get over that barbed wire." Pawel points to the tight curls of lethal wire. It would tear them apart.

"What about the gates? We could slip through after one of the women."

Pawel shakes his head. "I've watched them. There's always someone with them to open the gate. As soon as they're through, they lock it behind them."

"We could divert them."

"No way! I'm not trying that again. If we didn't get through, they'd probably kill me."

"Or try to pick the lock."

They try. Four nights in a row, with a hairpin dropped by one of their minders and bent into a shape that should be able to manipulate the levers inside the lock. One of them looks out while the other fiddles away.

They take it in turns. On the fourth night, Jan throws the hairpin aside. There are ridges on his fingers where the hairpin has dug in. "This isn't going to work. We'll have to think of something else."

The solution comes to them the next day as they work on their German in the afternoon class. The sound of an engine disturbs the class. Outside in the front yard is the truck that comes to pick up the rubbish every week. Jan is near the window and can see down to the yard. There is one man only with the truck. It is open at the back, piled high with garbage that has already been collected from other houses in the area. He leaves the truck unguarded and walks round to the side of the building where the bins are. This is it. This is the solution they have been looking for. He nudges Pawel so that he too can look.

"That's it. That's our escape route," he whispers.

The teacher looks up from her desk. "I hear talking, and I don't like it."

Pawel smiles at him, and they both put their heads down and get on with their work. One more week and they'll be free.

It is time. All week they've wondered how to get out of class and into the yard for when the truck comes. In the end, Pawel decides to make himself sick. "If I stick my fingers down my throat, I can throw up. They'll let me out to clean up, and you just have to leap up to help."

"But what if they don't let me go?"

"They will. Remember when Vaclav was sick, I was allowed out to help him."

Jan is not convinced. "It's too risky." He frowns, thinking as hard as he can. "Got it. I'll offer to go and get a bucket to clean up the floor."

Pawel shrugs. "Fine."

As the hour approaches, Jan's palms are sticky with sweat. He cannot bear to think about what they are going to do. He thinks maybe Pawel won't have to pretend to be sick, he could throw up now, he's so nervous. They have each made up a bundle with a spare set of clothes and the little food they have been able to scavenge over the past few days. Money is still a problem. They have none, not a pfennig, but it can't be helped. They've talked for hours about what to do about it, but it's all come to nothing.

The clock on the wall ticks loudly, seconds moving round to the time when the truck usually arrives. The supervisor isn't looking, she's writing a long sentence on the blackboard for them to copy. Pawel sticks his fingers down his throat and retches until he throws up. Jan looks on in horror as a shower of vomit lands on the floor beside him. He can't help it – he heaves and he too is sick. The woman who is looking after them cries out in horror, waves her arms at them, "Out, get out. Go and find something to clean yourselves with."

The boys don't need to be told twice. They exchange a triumphant glance and run from the room, across the hall and into the yard. The truck is coming up the driveway. They hide behind one of the bushes near the front door.

The truck draws to a halt almost right in front of them. The driver switches off the engine and jumps down from the cab. They watch as he makes his way round to the side of the house where the bins are. He's alone again today, just as they'd hoped. Sometimes he has a young boy with him, and they were praying he wouldn't be there. The driver returns with two of the bins and hoists them up to the open back and empties them. He trudges back to get the other bins.

Pawel nudges Jan. "Right, this is it. Time to move. You go first."

Jan runs towards the truck and throws in his parcel before he hauls himself up and over into the huge heap of rubbish. It stinks of everything bad he can think of: fish, eggs, smoke, rotten meat. For a horrible moment he thinks he might be sick again, but he thinks of breaking free from this dump, and it cheers him enough to forget the smell for a moment. Pawel's bundle hits him on the head, and he cries out. Fortunately the driver is still far enough away not to hear him. Pawel clambers in beside him and clouts him on the ear. "Shut up, you idiot. Do you want us to get caught?"

The boys push their way to the back of the truck through the piles of rotting vegetables. The stinking mess clings to them with a clammy stickiness. Jan tells himself it can't hurt, but the smell is so bad it's getting to him. Pawel pulls him down to sit beside him. "We should be fine here."

The footsteps of the driver clump nearer, and more rubbish is piled in. Jan is scared that it might all fall on top of him, suffocate him, and he takes in a deep breath. Pawel squeezes his hand. "You'll be all right. Don't worry."

"Pawel, Jan… are you there?" The call makes them jump. It is one of the younger children, sent to look for them no doubt. "Pawel, Jan, please, you have to hurry. Fräulein Weiss is getting angry."

They hardly dare breathe in case anyone hears them. Pawel's nails are digging into Jan's hand. There is the click of high heels on the flagstones in front of the house. Fräulein Weiss. They're done for.

"Boys, where are you? If you don't come back at once and clean up this filth you'll have extra duties for a month."

"Come on, driver. Start the engine," Jan mutters under his breath. "Please…" His prayers are answered. The engine turns over – and sighs to a halt. They hear the driver swear. Please God, don't let Fräulein Weiss come near! Her heels click fainter as she moves inside the house, still yelling her threats. The driver tries the starter again, and this time it works. They're off.

The truck lumbers through the streets of the village. It's so slow that Jan wants to jump out, but when he suggests this, Pawel says no.

"Sit tight and wait."

"Do you think that's the right thing to do?"

"How should I know?"

"I thought you knew everything." Jan is panicking.

"Well I don't."

Silence. Each boy fumes, mad at the other.

Jan speaks, tries to keep his voice calm. "Should we wait until it stops?"

"I should think so. We're likely to get killed otherwise."

Tears sting Jan's eyes at the sarcasm in Pawel's voice. He'd thought they'd be happy as soon as they were out of that place. Instead they are bickering like two old men.

Another ten minutes pass. The road is bumpy, and Jan risks a peep. They are in the middle of the countryside. He can't decide whether this is good or bad. On balance he thinks it is bad. A busy town would be better. It would be easier to hide there, perhaps steal some food. He wishes he hadn't thought about food. His stomach is empty after being sick. But still, the stench in this truck is enough to stop a glutton's mouth.

The truck is stopping. The boys clutch at each other in fright, but it is only to load on some more rubbish. They don't want to find themselves at some great rubbish tip, miles from nowhere.

The road is busier. They hear cars and lorries pass them. When Jan peers out he sees the houses are nearer together like they are on the outskirts of a town. They have left the countryside. "Next time it stops, I think we should make a run for it." Pawel nods in agreement. Jan is beginning to feel that he doesn't care whether or not he gets caught. Then he remembers his sister; he must escape.

The truck is slowing down. The boys crawl towards the back of the truck. They must be careful not to let the driver see, for if he looks in his mirror and they are in the wrong place, they will be spotted at once. "As soon as it stops, jump out and run as fast as you can," Pawel whispers. "Get into a crowded place and try not to draw attention to yourself. I'll be right behind you."

They are at a busy road junction. The truck comes to a halt, and Jan clambers over the rubbish and up onto the side of the truck. He pushes his way through until he thinks he is out of sight of the truck driver. He scans the street for Pawel, but can't see him anywhere. His mouth dries up. Pawel must be nearby; he said he'd be right behind him. Any minute now he'll tap him on the shoulder. Jan spins round to catch him at it, but he sees only grim German burghers bustling their way home. He notices that they avoid coming near him, and when he sees himself in a shop window, he realizes why. A large dollop of some creamy substance is smeared on his hair making it clump together in one or two oily strands. There is a smudge of red on his cheek, jam perhaps. His shorts are stained with filth. He is a disgusting sight. He tears his eyes away; there is no time to lose. Pawel must be found. The crowds are increasing. The shops and offices are shutting, and it is time for workers to make their way home. Jan cranes his neck to try to see Pawel, but still nothing. The truck has vanished, and Jan looks onto the road wondering if Pawel is still on it, or whether he has been caught.

Eight o'clock. It'll be dark soon. Jan doesn't know what to do. He's eaten some of his rations, and this makes him feel better. There is a drinking fountain in the market place with clear fresh water. He splashes some on his face and gets the dirt off. He daren't wander far from where he jumped from the truck, because he thinks that this is where Pawel will come looking for him, so he walks up and down the street constantly on the lookout for his friend. Jan feels a lump in his throat and blinks back tears. There is no point in crying. It gets you nowhere, and if he starts he won't stop. He'll cry for his father and his mother, and all the men who were shot in the village… No, he will not cry. He pinches his thigh hard to remind himself of this. Think, think, what can be done, where will he sleep, where can he pee? Oh Jesus, he needs to pee. Railway station, if there's a railway station there will be toilets there. Jan searches the skyline for clues. There in the distance, a bridge across the road. It could be the railway. He puts his bundle of clothes under his arm and starts off towards it.

As he nears it, he starts to worry. It is dark under the bridge, and he can see shadows of people lurking there. He makes up his mind to run, and he starts to jog, working up speed as he gets nearer the station. There are three men standing in his way, leering at him, and he dodges past them, feeling a cold hand grab his arm. He wrenches it away. Christ, it hurts like hell. He runs faster until he finds himself inside the station. Toilets, where are the toilets. He sees a sign and makes a dash for them, slipping in behind a man so the attendant doesn't see, for of course he has no money. He decides to use a cubicle, and once inside it he sits on the toilet relieved to be away from the shades on the outside of the station. Oh dear God, the pain. Jan sits for ten, maybe fifteen minutes as his bowels empty. He leans his head on the tiled wall of the cubicle and wishes he were dead. If he'd been caught that night, he would be better off. Jesus, his guts writhe once more and a groan slips out.

"Is everything all right in there?" A man's voice.

Jan's mind empties. Although he has understood the German, he can't think how to answer. Pawel would have known. At last he manages a quiet, *Ja, mein Herr*. The man speaks again. This time Jan doesn't understand, and he realizes that in fact he doesn't know all that much German at all. He thought he did because he could understand all that was said back at the house, but now it's clear that that was because the routine was the same every day. Up for breakfast, wash dishes, clothes, peel vegetables, lessons in the afternoon. But never any normal conversation. If the man said something about the Führer or the greatness of Germany, Jan would have a better chance of understanding, but this… this is impossible. Jan repeats what he has already said and waits. He cleans himself and flushes the toilet. When he finally opens the door, there's no one there. Jan decides to clean himself properly. The stink is beginning to get to him, so he takes off the filthy clothes and washes his body. There is no soap and no towel to dry himself, so he is still wet when he puts on his creased but clean clothes. The others he rinses, squeezing the water out as best he can. He's tempted to dump them, but knows that would be foolish. Feeling more confident, he goes back into the station. Maybe he can find a quiet corner to sleep.

11

Friedrich looks at the letter in his hand. His vision is so blurred he cannot make out the words. Dashing his hand across his eyes he wipes away the tears. It won't do to let Gisela and the girl see how upset he is. He reads it through again. Although it's over a page long, there is only one phrase he can take in: *missing in action, presumed dead*. He says the words aloud, quietly so Gisela, still in bed, will not hear him. "Presumed dead. Presumed dead." Saying it out loud doesn't make it any more real.

He's had the letter for three days now, and he knows he'll have to show it to his wife. But he can't bear to. Why should they, who were blessed with only two children, who wanted many more and lost so many before they were born, why should they lose both children? The tears course down his face, soaking his ruddy cheeks. How can he tell Gisela? He must do it today, for tomorrow Wilhelm is due home on leave, and it would be too cruel to leave it until then to tell her. Friedrich wonders about lying to her; he could say there was a telegram sent to the local post office – all leave cancelled. Yes, that's what he'll do. The twisting in his stomach lessens a little, and then returns worse than ever. He can't do that to his wife. She deserves to know the truth. He puts the letter back in his pocket. Later, he'll tell her later.

Upstairs, the little girl laughs. She's settling in now, though she's very quiet, and when she speaks, her words don't sound right. The accent's all wrong. When he mentioned this to Gisela, saying he thought her language was very poor for a child of her age, Gisela frowned and shook her head. "Poor thing, what do you expect? She's lost both her parents."

"But she says so little! Perhaps she's retarded."

"Have you seen how she helps me round the house? She's smart all right, don't you doubt it for a minute."

"But—"

"No more buts, Friedrich. She has no parents, and she's from Hamburg. That's why she sounds so different."

Helena and Gisela come downstairs. Helena is wearing one of the dresses that Gisela has spent so much time making, and she looks prettier than ever. Underneath the dress, the pink sprigs of roses peep. Nothing can persuade her to give this up, and they no longer try. She lets Gisela wash it, and that's enough. Now as they come into the kitchen he thinks that his wife looks younger than she has for years. Her eyes are more lively, and the shadows that dragged her face down have gone. Yes, it was the right decision to adopt. And now he will make her unhappy once more.

"Show Vatti what we've been doing," says Gisela.

Helena holds out a piece of paper, which has a childish drawing of a house on it. Beneath it, Gisela has printed WELCOME HOME WILHELM.

"Isn't it lovely?"

Friedrich cannot speak. His throat has closed with emotion, so he nods without looking at either of them and pushes past muttering that he has work to do. He feels his wife's eyes on him as he leaves the room, and doesn't need to look back to know that she's shaking her head, wondering at his grumpiness. Outside he breathes in the fresh autumn air; it's a sharp morning hinting of the winter to come. It isn't fair; the child might think he's angry or upset with her. He turns around and goes inside once more. She is sitting at the table, and in the early morning light she looks like Helga did at the same age, only her hair is lighter. He ruffles her curls and tells her the card is beautiful, and then, careful to avoid his wife's perceptive eye, he leaves for his day's work. As he leaves he hears Gisela say to Helena that in just one more day, Wilhelm will be with them.

As he returns home in the evening, walking towards the farmhouse with its smoking chimney and lights at two of the windows, he thinks that it looks welcoming, warm. What he would give not to have this letter in his pocket. And he feels guilt too, at not sharing it sooner. He fingers it, wishes he could tear it up and throw the pieces to the wind. His steps falter – what will he say? Should he just hand it over for her to read, or should he take her aside and sit her down, and destroy her with a few words? The child should be in bed, so he'll get it over as soon as he goes in. In his mind he rehearses what he'll say – *sit down, my darling, I have bad news.* Oh dear God, this is hell itself.

Friedrich opens the door and takes off his boots. He is chilled through, not because it's cold, although it's a clear night and there could be frost, but frozen by his sorrow. He hears a man's voice, and for a moment he thinks – good, I can put off telling her. Just for a moment, though, because it will have to be done tonight. So now he'll have to be rude to a neighbour. Gisela's laugh rings out in the house. He hasn't heard her laugh like that for years. And a child's laugh too, so she isn't in bed after all. Wishing he had a stiff drink, Friedrich pushes open the door and walks into his kitchen.

His legs give way beneath him, and he grabs the edge of the table to steady himself. He must be dreaming. Gisela rises to greet him.

"Friedrich! Isn't it wonderful? Wilhelm has some extra leave, and he managed to get home earlier than he thought."

He nods, speechless. Beside him, Gisela prattles. He's never been irritated by her chat before, but now it nags at him, stops him from thinking what has happened. He can't imagine what is going on. Then it dawns on him – the letter must be a mistake. He's never heard of such a mistake, but that doesn't mean it didn't happen. He feels his mouth stretch into a huge grin and strides towards his son, holding out his arms. Wilhelm hugs him. Friedrich hugs back, then looks at him closely. Wilhelm is pale. He looks older than his twenty years; his face is pale, his eyes huge. They look like the scorch marks on their best linen tablecloth.

"Let me look at you," he says. The scar on Wilhelm's forehead stands out – a long jagged line above his left eyebrow. He got it when he fell on some broken glass as a very young child. They thought they'd lost him then, he bled so fiercely, but he survived. And he's survived whatever it was that prompted that letter. But that doesn't matter now. All that matters is that he's here and their family is complete.

"Gisela," he says, "where's my beer? And bring one for my boy." He is so happy, so relieved, he doesn't stop to think about the deadness in Wilhelm's eyes. He doesn't notice how restrained the boy is, when talking about being in the army. Friedrich just wants to talk and to look at his son. It isn't until later, when he is on the point of sleep, that he realizes that Wilhelm has said scarcely a word. But Friedrich is a little drunk from beer and happiness, exhausted from all the worry of the past few days, so before he has time to think what it might mean, he sinks into a deep slumber.

12

Jan dreams of a feather tickling his face, making him want to sneeze. He wriggles away from it, waking just enough to see a large rat scurry onto the nearby platform. Jesus! Was that what had woken him? Wide awake now, he sits up and stretches. Every part of his body hurts. The ground is cold and hard, and he has a stiff neck. As he twists it, it makes a creaking sound, like old floorboards. His grandmother used to complain of such noises in her joints, but she was ancient. It can't be good for him, sleeping out in the open like this. Uncomfortable as he is, though, he doesn't want to move. He's exhausted and, for a brief moment, thinks with longing of his bed back at the prison house. At least it was warm. Well, no point in thinking about it, he needs to turn his mind to more practical things, like what he'll eat once his little parcel of food is finished, and how can he get hold of some money.

It's very early, and the station is not yet open. There's no one around, so he pees onto the railway line. Later he'll come back and use the washroom. Jan will explore the town a little while it is quiet. He hated its bustle yesterday, hated the way people pushed and ignored him. In the peace of dawn he can perhaps make some attempt to plan what he will do next.

* * *

The streets are almost empty. One or two cars pass by, and Jan keeps close to the walls of buildings, praying he won't be noticed. He comes to a bread shop; the smell of baking bread tantalizes, and his mouth waters. If only he had money he'd buy every loaf in the shop. The prices are on display, but they mean nothing to him. For a few moments he stands at the window and dreams. This won't help; he moves on up the street. At the end of the road there is a restaurant, and an idea comes to him. He nips round the side of the building, and sure enough there are bins there. Jan swallows hard; this will be difficult, but it has to be done. He lifts the lid of one and looks in. It's a horrible mess of rotten food, everything mixed up together. His hope of finding a nice clean loaf of bread vanishes, and he puts the lid on again. When he's really desperate he'll return here, but for the moment he still has some stale bread and an apple. Despondent, he goes back to the street and continues his walk.

Before long, he comes to a square. There's a fountain in the middle, a stone statue of a naked woman holding a pitcher from which she is pouring water into a pool. Jan smiles. He can bathe his feet there, wash and grab something to drink. More optimistic than before, he rushes across. As he leans forwards to wash his face, something catches his eye. A coin! Squinting, he peers into the shallow water, and yes – it's full of coins. Jan can't believe his luck. He takes off his shoes and steps into the water, bending down to scoop up as many of the coins as he can. They're all small coins, pfennigs and halbpfennigs, but he doesn't care. There's enough here to keep him going for some days. The main problem will be how to carry them, but that's a small problem compared to his worries of earlier.

Jan finds a seat in the square and counts out the piles of coins. As he thought, there's enough to keep him in food for several days. He cannot believe how much better he feels as a result. Part of him wants to blow a large part of it on breakfast in a café, where he can get a warm drink, but he's sensible enough to know that this would be foolish, so he wraps up most of the money in his spare shirt, careful to tie it up tightly so nothing will drop out. He's kept aside a small amount, enough to buy some fresh bread and perhaps a piece of meat. For the moment he's content to eat the remains of what he stole from the house.

"Give us a bit of that, won't you?"

It's impossible. He thought he'd never see him again. Pawel stands grinning in front of him, holding out his hand.

"You! Where have you been?"

"Here and there." Pawel sits on the bench beside him and helps himself to the apple resting on Jan's lap. "You ought to be more careful you know, counting out that money in public like that. It could have been stolen from you."

"How long have you been watching me?"

"Not long. So, where did you sleep last night?"

"In a corner of the railway station. It was horrible." Jan shudders, remembering the rat. "What about you?"

Pawel gnaws round the core of the apple before chucking it aside. "The truck started to move before I could get out. And someone had spotted me, so I thought it safest not to jump at that point. Trouble was, it was several miles before the truck stopped again, so I had a long walk back. I haven't had any sleep." He pokes Jan in the side with his elbow. "I thought I'd never see you again."

"Me too."

The boys sit in silence for a few seconds, then Pawel jumps up. "Come on, let's go see the railway station, see if it goes anywhere near where we want to be."

The railway station is filling up with people on their way to work. The boys find a map, and after a while they find the town they are looking for. It is some distance away, but when they look at the timetable, they see that there is a train going there once a day.

"I'm going to get on that train somehow," says Jan. "What are you going to do? Will you go back to Poland?"

Pawel is still looking at the timetable. He seems lost in it.

Jan nudges him. "Well, will you?"

Pawel shakes his head, slowly. "I said I'd see you get back your little sister, and that's what I'm going to do. Anyway, you'd be lost without me. Sleeping in railway stations! You'll end up sleeping on the tracks, and then where will you be?"

"Would you really come with me?"

"Of course. If I don't, you might as well give yourself up now."

The train doesn't leave for some hours yet so the boys plan how to get on the train without paying. They have enough money for one fare, but that would leave them with only one ticket and no money for food.

"The best idea is to try to slip in behind a family, preferably one with lots of children. That way we can point and say that our parents have our tickets."

"Mm, maybe. But what if they call the parents back and ask them?"

The boys think some more. "Got it," says Pawel. "We'll come running up at the last moment with bread in our arms and say to the guard that our parents sent us for it and there was a queue. There's always someone hanging out of the window so we'll point to them and say that's them."

"I don't know," says Jan. "It sounds very risky to me."

"Well, you think of something better then."

They can't think of anything better, so agree to try it. "Leave the talking to me," says Pawel.

It's time for the train. Two minutes before it leaves. They have been to the baker to buy bread. They run up to the guard, and Pawel babbles his story. The guard is impassive, argumentative. Jan knows he doesn't believe their story. It's not going to work, and they are so close. There's a woman hanging out of the window – she's looking up and down the platform. Jan waves to her, praying she'll wave back. A few seconds, then she lifts her arm in greeting.

"Look," says Jan. "There's our mother." Pawel glowers at him; he's not supposed to speak, but what else can he do?

A whistle blows. The train is about to leave. Jan starts to cry and waves once more at the woman. Once again she waves back. The guard gives in. "Go on then. In you get." He pushes them onto the train just as it moves off.

"Cry baby," mutters Pawel to Jan.

"It got us where we wanted to be, so shut up. You weren't much good out there. If it wasn't for me, we'd still be on the platform."

"Yeah, well, all right then." Pawel smiles at him. "We did it. We're on our way."

The journey is difficult. They hadn't realized there would be someone looking for tickets on the train, and they have to spend their time dodging the collector. Eventually they find the guard's van, which is full of luggage, and they crouch down behind a huge trunk. Jan worries about this because the van has no windows, and so they can't see where they're going.

"Look, it's the third place we stop. You can count to three can't you? Just stop worrying, it'll be fine."

"But what if it stops for signals? We might get off in the middle of nowhere."

"I don't think so. We'll know it's a station because we'll hear the doors opening and shutting."

Even with this reassurance Jan can't help worrying. He thinks they'll be caught at any moment, and so he is extremely thankful when at last the train starts to slow down to stop for the third time. They creep from their hiding place and walk along the corridor to the door.

"What if there's a ticket collector?"

"There won't be. They keep checking them on the train."

The train stops, and they jump down. There's no one in sight, and they walk along the platform to the small building that must be the station. Jan is worried. He had thought from the map that the station would be bigger. The town had seemed to be a sizeable one.

"This isn't right," he mutters. "There's something wrong."

Pawel doesn't answer. He is reading a notice. Jan follows his gaze and tries to read what's written there. He can't understand a word.

"Pawel, this isn't German. Where are we?"

Pawel doesn't look at him as he speaks. "We're in Poland. Not far from my home."

13

Friedrich is worried about so many things: will the harvest yield enough to keep him and his family through the winter, will the roof leak again this year, will the war ever end, what is the meaning of the letter he has in his pocket – the one that tells him his son is most probably dead, when his son sits in front of him alive and well.

It is two days now since Wilhelm returned. They have been happy days for the most part. Wilhelm is intrigued by his new little sister; he spends much of his time trying to make her say something, but she continues to be very shy and speaks very seldom. Friedrich worries about this too. She's not dumb, they've heard her talk, but although they've made allowances for her difficult past, he and Gisela fear that perhaps, after all, she's not very bright.

Gisela is making soup, chopping vegetables. Helena is trying to help her; she picks up the vegetable pieces and puts them in a bowl. Most end up on the floor, but Gisela is patient with her, takes her time and shows Helena what to do. They make a pretty picture the two of them, Gisela singing as she works. She is lost in her task. Friedrich takes out the letter and pushes it over to Wilhelm. He puts his finger to his lips and then says, "Read it."

Wilhelm's face is scarlet as he reads the letter. This is proof enough for Friedrich. He waits until Wilhelm stops reading and says, "Well?"

"I don't want to talk about it."

If his wife wasn't nearby, Friedrich would hit the boy, but he doesn't want to burden her with this knowledge. He beckons Wilhelm outside, saying to his wife that they'll take a breath of fresh air. She doesn't look up as she tells them not to be too long, the soup will be ready in under an hour.

Outside, Friedrich leads the way until he is sure they are out of earshot.

"What the hell have you done?" He has Wilhelm by the collar, nose to nose with him. His fear makes him furious.

Wilhelm pushes him aside. "I won't fight any more. I will not do what they ask me to do."

Friedrich splutters, "You have no choice. This is your country."

"What is this war about, Father?"

"I… I don't know… to get more land for us, build up the Fatherland."

"Do you think it is right to invade other countries?"

Friedrich turns aside. He never thinks about politics. He was too young for the last war and too infirm for this one, so far anyway. He's a patriot, would fight if he had to, but… "I don't know," he says finally.

Wilhelm shakes his head. "You don't think about these things, do you? Oh, I'm not blaming you," he holds up his hand as Friedrich starts to protest, "I didn't think about them either. I just went along with it all." He kicks at the wall of the house, a vicious blow that startles Friedrich.

"Is everything all right, son?"

There are tears in Wilhelm's eyes. "I thought when I went to war, that I'd be fighting other men."

A fist is squeezing Friedrich's heart. "What do you mean?"

"Do I need to spell it out to you?"

"Are the enemy sending children to war?"

Wilhelm is silent for a moment. When he starts to speak, his voice is flat, all emotion ironed out. "No, the enemy send men to fight us. I can't tell you what a relief it would be to face a soldier from another country, armed with weapons, to fight on a battlefield. Instead I've been in villages. Here in Germany, and also in some of the annexed lands. In one village not far from here, they gathered us together one morning and told us what we had to do might not be all that pleasant." He massages his temples as if he has a headache. "They said some of the older men might want to avoid it, and if they did then they could back out. And some of them did. Us younger ones laughed, made fun of them. Jesus!" Wilhelm spits on the ground and is silent. The only sound is his breath, husky with a wheeze.

"Go on," whispers Friedrich.

"They took us to the village square, brought out people for us to shoot, Jews. It went on all day. Once we'd killed them we had to load their bodies into trucks and take them away to dump them in huge pits. Some of them were children." Tears run down his face. "Many of us were shocked that first time. They gave us strong drink when we returned to barracks. Gradually one or two regained their bravado. 'They're only Jews after all, it's not as if we're killing people' – someone said that, and a few others laughed. Next time we were asked to do it, I felt sick, but no one was backing out, and you felt you'd be letting the others down if you didn't do it, so you couldn't back down. You just had to join in." Wilhelm rummages through his pockets and brings out a packet of cigarettes. He lights one up, shielding the match from the wind with his hand, and inhales deeply. "Well, last week I thought, I just can't do this any longer. There was an attack on our convoy of vehicles, and several of our battalion were killed. Body parts all over the place. I was blown clear, and was in the ditch. I crawled into the forest and hid while they were gathering up the survivors."

"It's true then, you are a deserter."

Wilhelm throws down his cigarette and grinds it into the ground with the heel of his boot. He looks older than his twenty years, lines etched into his forehead. "I prefer to think I'm a conscientious objector."

"If you're caught, you'll be shot."

"I know, but..." Wilhelm stopped, unable to continue.

The sound of their names rang through the crisp evening air. It was time for supper.

Inside the house, Gisela serves up the soup, a thick potato broth, scented with garlic and ham. She sets down the plates in front of them. Helena starts to eat, and Gisela slaps her hand away, telling her to wait. Wilhelm snaps at her, "Leave the child alone," and Gisela blinks, bewildered at the strength of his protest. It is left to Friedrich to calm them both. He doesn't want his wife to know about Wilhelm, about the killings, about the desertion. What is this war about, that they kill women and children? It's wrong, evil.

"It's all right, Helena. Mother just wants me to say grace, in thanks for Wilhelm's safe return. Put your spoon down, there's a good girl."

Helena, who was about to cry, obeys and, together with the others, waits for Friedrich to say a prayer of thanks. He sits at the table with his head bowed.

"Dearest Father, thank you..."

The others wait for him to continue, he feels their eyes upon him, but he cannot say any more. His throat has tightened so much that he thinks he will choke, and in a panic he rises and runs from the table. As he stumbles back outside, he gulps at the cool evening air, hoping it will calm him, but it makes him so giddy he has to sit down on the doorstep. Gisela joins him; she brushes some dust off the stone and gathers her skirt underneath to cushion herself before sitting down. She takes his hand and weaves the fingers of her right hand with those of his left.

"It's so wonderful to have him home, isn't it?"

14

"How can we be in Poland?" Jan's face is red, his fists clenched.

Pawel bends down and picks up a stone. He throws it onto the railway line. "We got on the wrong train."

"I don't believe you. You did this on purpose to get home. You're a bastard, a dirty rotten bastard, and I hate you." Jan walks away from him.

Pawel runs after him and grabs his shoulder. He forces Jan to look at him. "I swear, it's a mistake. You saw the timetable – you saw the platform number. Somehow we must have read it wrong."

"Some coincidence though, isn't it? Ending up near your home town? Quite frankly, it's unbelievable, so don't lie to me." Jan's heart is beating so fast he thinks it's going to fly out of his chest. He wants to punch Pawel.

"I'm never going to convince you, am I?" Pawel sounds weary. "What if I said I don't want to go home? That my father beat me and my mother was a drunk?"

Jan almost believes him for a second, but underlying the tiredness there is a hint of amusement that belies such a difficult home life. He looks Pawel in the eye. "Swear to me on the Bible that you didn't know about this."

Pawel laughs. "Sure. Bring it out, and I'll swear."

"On your mother's life."

Hesitation, proof enough. "You bastard."

"All right, I admit it. I saw there was a train coming here that left at the same time from a nearby platform. I couldn't pass it up. My family don't know what has happened to me. They'll think I'm dead. It was too good an opportunity to miss." His face is scarlet, and there are beads of perspiration on his forehead. "And they'll be able to help you. We would never have managed to get Lena back on our own."

"We managed to escape without any help. I got money for us. We hid on a train. We could have done it. I could have done it. I'll never forgive you for this. Never." Jan pushes past Pawel and runs onto the railway line.

"Are you mad? What the hell do you think you're doing?"

"I'm walking back to Germany, to find my sister. She's the only family I have for sure."

"You're a damn idiot. Germany's that way." Pawel points the other way down the track.

"No, it isn't." Jan sounds defiant, but he isn't sure. They saw no landmarks on their way here because they were hidden in the guard's van, and since they got off the train they've been walking round and round, so he's lost all sense of direction.

"Please Jan. Please come home with me. I promise you that my parents will help you."

There is a rumble and the screech of a train's hooter. They turn to see an engine bearing down on them. They jump aside only seconds before the train thunders past. Jan stands at the side of the track shaking. In that instant he feels like a tiny child, vulnerable and frightened. More than anything he wants his mother.

"I'll come home with you," he says, "but I'm not staying. As soon as I'm ready, I'll be off to find my own family."

It's dark when they reach the outskirts of Pawel's home town. It's a small town, more of a village really. Jan senses his friend's excitement as they walk down the main street, past shops and cafés.

"Our neighbour owns that shop," he says, "and that café sells the best coffee. Tomorrow we'll eat there. No. My mother will want to feed us up. I've got so thin." Pawel chatters on as they walk along the road. He's moving so fast that Jan is almost running to keep up with him. "Five minutes and we'll be there. Oh Christ, I can't wait." He is so excited that Jan catches it from him, and despite his earlier fury with Pawel, he finds himself skipping along beside him.

"This is it." Pawel stands in front of a small house. It looks deserted, thinks Jan. There's no light on, and the paintwork on the door is scuffed. There's rubbish in the small yard. It doesn't look like a well-kept house. He glances at Pawel, who is looking round in bewilderment, the excitement fading on his face. "I don't understand," he says, "this is so dirty. Not like my house at all." He bites his lip and pushes at the door. It doesn't budge, and he tries again. Nothing.

Jan pulls at his sleeve. "I think it's empty," he says. "Wouldn't there be a light on?"

"Maybe they've gone out," Pawel's voice trembles. He bangs on the door and shouts, "Mother, Mother, it's me, Pawel."

The shouts echo back on them. Pawel tries again. The door of the house next door opens, and a man looks out. "What's going on there?"

Pawel shouts over to him, “Mr Jaworski, it’s me, Pawel Zelinsky. Do you remember me?”

“Jesus Maria. So it is. Come here boy, till I see you.”

Pawel walks up the path to the house, and the man stares down at him. “You’ve grown,” he says.

“It’s been over a year. Do you know where my parents are?”

The man’s face is grave. “You’d better come in.” He beckons them both inside.

Jan feels desperately sorry for Pawel. They’d listened in disbelief as the neighbour told them how his father was arrested six months ago.

“They came for him because he wouldn’t shut up about you. He wrote letter after letter to everyone he could think of, trying to find out what had happened. He wrote to newspapers and to politicians in other countries. The newspapers didn’t print his letters of course, so he had leaflets printed and gave them out in the town centre. I don’t know whether the people in other countries got his letters, but I doubt it. Nothing gets past the Nazis.” He whispers the last words as if the walls might be listening, looks around fearfully, then wipes his brow. “Other people came to your father and told him how their children too had gone missing, snatched from the street or from their homes.”

His wife brings them food, a simple meal of bread and sausage, but oh, so tasty. They eat it while Miroslaw, the neighbour, continues with his story.

“When they came they said he was a political agitator. He was sent to a concentration camp near Kraków, in Oswiecim.” He shakes his head. “These are dreadful times.”

Pawel finishes his meal, wiping the bread round the plate to soak up the fat from the sausage. "What about my mother?"

"I don't know what happened to her. Your mother became very ill after you disappeared. She lost weight, looked miserable all the time—"

"And who could blame her, losing a child in that way? It's a terrible thing, terrible." His wife interrupts them to clear away the dirty dishes. "You must stay here with us, Pawel. And your friend, of course." She lowers her voice to a whisper. "Is he all right? He's very quiet."

"He's fine, a little tired I think."

Jan nods. "Yes, I didn't sleep last night."

The couple look at each other, suspicion flitting over their faces. Miroslaw speaks slowly to him, pronouncing each word as if to an idiot. "You're not Polish, are you?"

Jan shakes his head. "No, my mother's Polish though, from Warsaw. I'm Czech."

They smile; satisfied with this explanation. Dyta, the woman, starts to ask about Jan's mother, but Pawel is desperate to find out what has happened to his family. He interrupts her. "My mother, is she dead?"

Dyta blinks, startled by the rudeness of his tone. "No, no. Well, I don't think so. The word in town was that she left to go and stay with relatives near Krakow, to try to be nearer your father. But we don't know for sure. She was distraught when they took him away."

They chat for an hour or so. Jan stares into the fire as they talk on. He follows what they say for a few minutes: Miroslaw tells them of the German soldiers in the area, and how all of the townspeople fear them. Pawel in return talks about the children's home and the Polish children there. They ask him for names to pass to the resistance fighters, so that their parents can be told. Pawel can give only a few names, and none of them are known to the couple. They write them down anyway. Jan begins to lose the thread of what they are saying. It is hard for him to understand them; Dyta's voice is soft and Miroslaw's accent is thick. After a while he gives up and starts to dream of home. If he closes his eyes he can imagine his house. He can see his kitchen, his mother standing by the range stirring a pot of soup, Maria sitting at the table, a frown creasing her forehead as she puzzles over her maths homework, Lena in the corner drawing on the flagstones with a piece of chalk. Any minute now, father will be home. Jan sees his mother smile as she hears father come through the door.

"You are tired, little one." Dyta's quiet voice breaks into his reverie. He opens his eyes, blinks back the sudden tears. He can't trust himself to speak, nods instead.

"Come, I will show you where you can sleep." Dyta stands up and waits for the boys to follow her.

Jan remembers his manners. "Thank you for the meal. It was delicious."

Miroslaw interrupts. "Not at all. It was nothing."

Jan and Pawel know it was far from nothing. Food is rationed here, and what they have just eaten is probably the Jaworskis' meal for tomorrow. Jan holds out some coins to pay, but the couple recoil from him, upset that he would offer them money. He puts it away, feeling foolish, even more so when he remembers that his coins are German and of little use here. In silence he and Pawel follow Dyta upstairs to a tiny room where there is a mattress on the floor. It doesn't look all that clean, but they don't care. They could sleep anywhere after all they've been through.

After they've washed they lie down on the mattress and pull the blankets over them. There's a window in the sloping ceiling through which they can see the sky. The boys lie in silence, Jan wondering where his family is and whether they too lie awake in the dark, looking at the stars.

"I'm sorry about your papa," he whispers.

Pawel takes a moment to reply. When he speaks, Jan hears tears in his voice. "You'd like papa," he says. "He's good fun. He loves to play jokes on everyone. You know, when there was no answer earlier on, I kept thinking he was playing one of his jokes, that he was hiding behind the door and any minute he'd leap out and surprise us."

"He sounds great."

"He is. I really wanted you to meet him. I thought…"

"What did you think?"

"It's silly, I know. But they always wanted more children. I know that because mama often cried about it. I thought that you could be my brother, another son for them. No one could replace your own papa, but I just know you'd get on with him and mama. And they would love you."

Jan can't speak. He reaches out to find Pawel's hand. When he does, he squeezes it tight, and Pawel squeezes back. The door to their bedroom opens, and Mr and

Mrs Jaworski come in. “Good night, boys. Please God you sleep well.”

Pawel says nothing. Jan mumbles, “Thank you,” pulls the blanket over. Before sinking into sleep, he thinks of Pawel’s parents, lost like his mother and Lena, how far away she is. How will he find her now?

15

The following morning Mr and Mrs Jarowski let Jan and Pawel sleep till late. When they rise, the sun is high in the sky. Dyta seems happy to have someone to look after; she fusses round them, offering them bread and honey after breakfast, telling them they are thin and need fattening up. The boys accept the food gratefully, trying not to gobble it down. Sometimes Jan thinks he has a deep hunger that will never be satisfied, no matter how much he eats.

After their lunch of a thick potato broth, Jan offers to clear up. The Jarowskis try to stop him, but he insists, asking Pawel to help him. Mrs Jarowski busies herself in the kitchen for a while, but when she sees how well they manage – the children's home has trained them well – she leaves them to it. Jan hands another plate to Pawel to dry, looking round to check they are alone. "Pawel, we have to leave here. They're good people, but we can't keep on taking their food. And we have no ration cards. The four of us would be starving in no time."

Pawel dries the plate before he answers, "I know, but what can we do? Maybe we could get ration cards from somewhere. Perhaps mine is still in my house."

"After a year? No, even if it were, it would be out of date."

"So, what do you suggest we do?"

Jan's voice is firm. "Go back to Germany." But even as he speaks, Jan knows Pawel will never agree.

Pawel shakes his head. "I'm sorry Jan. I'll never go back there."

"I don't see why not. After all, this place is part of Germany now, an occupied country, a colony… There's more Germans here than fleas on a stray cat. You heard what they said last night, 'German soldiers on every street corner.' You might as well come with me to Germany, help me find Lena." Inwardly, Jan is crying, *please come, don't desert me*, but Pawel has his own needs.

"I'm going to find my parents, and if I can't find them, then I'll join the partisans. You'll never catch me going back to Germany."

Jan's lip trembles. "You're too young, they'll never let you."

"I'm nearly fourteen, old enough. We'll see." Pawel's face is closed, his lips tight together, he won't look Jan in the eye. Jan puts the last few plates away. There's no point in talking to him when he's like this.

An hour later they leave the Jaworskis' house. Mrs Jaworski pleads with them to stay, but they are determined to go.

"No, it's too dangerous. We have no papers, no ration books. Apart from the problem of food, if we get caught then you will be punished too. Who knows what might happen to you."

Mrs Jaworski continues to argue with them. "It's not a problem," she says, "we'll manage. We can hide you." In the background, her husband says nothing in spite of the glances she throws him. He sees the danger; they know he does. His wife continues to try to persuade them. "Please, stay one more night, build up your strength." But the boys know they mustn't get too comfortable, and they resist. At last Mrs Jaworski gives in and lets them go.

"Promise me you'll take care." She hugs them. "Where will you go, how will you eat?"

"We'll manage," says Pawel. He hesitates. "I want to try to find my parents, but if I can't, then perhaps... well, we thought we'd join the resistance."

Miroslaw takes his hand and shakes it. "There's a village, twenty kilometres west of here, Jankowice, ask for Marek Kucharski. He'll see you all right." He pauses. "In fact, you might be best to go straight to him. The resistance has a lot of information about people who've been taken away. He might be able to tell you about your parents."

"Is he a partisan?"

"I don't know for sure. It's best not to know too much, but he's a socialist and hates the occupiers, like we all do. He has no immediate family so if anyone knows how to contact the resistance, he will."

"Are you sure about this?"

Miroslaw shrugs. "As sure as I can be. I've met him several times. He's a good man. I know he'll do his best to help you. Tell him I sent you."

An hour later they are out on the road. Miroslaw has shown them the way, assured them that they are unlikely to bump into any German soldiers as the road is a quiet one, used only by local farmers coming into town for market days. It is a warm day for autumn, the late summer sun beats down on their heads as they walk in silence. Jan's thoughts are of his home; his mother, where is she now? The roadside is lined with trees, cherry trees like those at home. Their leaves are yellowing; they will fall within the month, and then winter will truly begin. Jan blinks to stop the tears that always come when he thinks of his mother, his family. Without warning the pictures of his father's death flash before him: the soldiers raising their rifles, his father's face, bleached bone-white with fear – did he imagine it, or did his father see him, hiding in the tree? Jan gasps in pain, sinks to the ground.

Pawel's face is above him, white, anxious. "What is it? Are you ill?"

Jan shakes his head; he cannot speak.

Pawel grabs his arm. "Jan, you're frightening me, what is it?"

Jan curls into himself and lies weeping while Pawel stands above him wishing he knew what to do. Jan stuffs his fist into his mouth to muffle his sobs. After a few minutes, he manages to control himself and struggles to his feet.

He brushes the tears from his face. The action leaves two dirty streaks on his face. "Let's go," he says.

Pawel stands in front of him, hands on hips. "Hang on. You can't just stop in the middle of the road like that, cry as if you're a baby, then go on as if nothing has happened. Tell me what's wrong. Maybe I can help."

"It's the trees," says Jan.

"The trees? What about the trees?"

"In June last year, when it happened... they were in blossom. I hid from the Germans in the cherry tree at the farm. And now they're bare, and I'll never see my family again." He pushes past Pawel and walks on ahead.

Pawel stares after him for a moment before running to catch up with him. He pulls Jan to a stop. "Why have you stopped believing you'll see your family again? You have to have faith, that's what you always said back in Germany when everyone cried about their families. So often you told the little ones their mothers were out there somewhere. You didn't let up." He scratches his head. "I don't understand."

Jan doesn't reply. If he speaks he thinks he will scream, so he shakes off Pawel's hand and strides on. Pawel shrugs and follows him. Once or twice Pawel tries to speak to Jan, but gives up when he doesn't reply.

A rumbling. Jan tenses. "What's that noise?"

"I don't know," Pawel is frowning.

"Quick, it's getting nearer. It could be Germans." Jan pushes Pawel to the side of the road and into the ditch, diving after him. Together they crouch in the dank mud. "I don't hear anything now," says Jan.

"Me neither, maybe we imagined—"

"No, there it is again. It sounds big, bigger than a car. It could be a lorry. If they look down they'll see us, we need to get cover."

A few yards away there is a large bush, Pawel points to it, and Jan nods in agreement. On their hands and knees they crawl through the ditch water. It is stagnant, smells vile, and Jan gags as they make their way to the hiding place. Shivering they push their way into the bush until they're sure they can't be seen. The rumbling grows into a roar. Jan parts the leaves so he can see the road. A convoy of trucks is passing. They are full of soldiers. He steps back certain they must have seen them, but the convoy continues, raising dust from the road. A minute later it is out of sight.

Jan pushes his way out of the bush and tries to wipe off some of the mud with his hands. It is useless, all he does is spread it further. "Where do you think they're going?" he says to Pawel.

Pawel is picking leaves out of his hair. "How should I know?" He sounds grumpy.

"What if?…"

"What?"

"Do you think they might be going to Jankowice? If they are it won't be safe there."

"I know that." Pawel picks up his bundle, ready to go on.

Jan has one last shot. "Why don't we go back to Germany?"

Pawel shakes his head and starts to walk. Jan stares at his friend striding down the road. He doesn't know what to do. Should he turn back, ask Miroslaw for help to get to Germany, or follow Pawel to an unknown village where they may or may not find their way to a partisan group? Jan can't make up his mind; there are too many uncertainties. How could he cross Germany on his own? Was his German good enough to pass as a native? What would he do for money? At least in the resistance there would be adults to look after him. But he has a bad feeling about that convoy of trucks. If he follows Pawel, he could be walking into a trap.

Jan kicks at the road, sending a cloud of dust into the air. What to do, what to do... He takes out one of the coins he'd found in the fountain and tosses it in the air. "Heads, I follow Pawel, tails I go back to Germany." The coin falls a metre or so away. He trudges over and looks down at it. For a moment he stands there, then he stoops to pick it up. It has been decided, he no longer needs to think what to do. What will be, will be. He gazes down the road the coin has chosen for him.

16

For some years Gisela has hated going into town. It started when Helga died: the sympathetic glances and murmurs of *time heals* drove her mad. Lately, though, she doesn't mind the necessary trips as much. For one thing she likes to buy Helena little trinkets to surprise her. The smallest things bring her pleasure: a pale-blue ribbon for her hair, a bouncy rubber ball, even a pair of white socks. Helena loves them all. Every day she is becoming livelier. Her accent is less strange now, or perhaps they are getting used to it but, either way, Gisela stops worrying about where she came from and lets herself fall in love with this beautiful child, a little more each day.

She has travelled into town by bus. Wilhelm is looking after Helena. She'd thought he might like to come with her, visit some old school friends, perhaps go to the cinema that he used to love so much, but he shakes his head when she suggests it. She's a little worried about him: he's so quiet and he hasn't left the house. Friedrich too is quiet, and she's caught them whispering about things outside in the dark, more than once. Last night she thought she heard Wilhelm swear, something about *this damned war.* Friedrich hates cursing of any kind, and she waited for him to reprimand their son. Nothing, not a word. He must be getting soft in his old age. Or maybe he just doesn't want to fight with Wilhelm when he has to go back to war in a few days' time. She's dreading that parting; it has been idyllic having him home, watching him play with his new sister.

The bus comes to a halt, and she gets off. During the journey it started to rain, and she pulls out an umbrella from her handbag. She puts it up and hurries across the road to the haberdashery shop. Last week she saw some mother-of-pearl buttons that she thought would look good on a dress she is making for Helena, please God they're still there.

The shop has a bell, which sounds loudly each time someone opens the door. It peals out its tinny ring as Gisela enters, and the four customers already waiting turn to stare at her. They were talking animatedly before she came in, she'd seen them through the glass, but now they have fallen silent. Gisela nods at them – their faces are familiar, and although she has no wish to join in their gossip, neither does she want to snub them. She folds up her umbrella and takes her place at the end of the queue, waiting for their chatter to resume. It doesn't, and this makes her uncomfortable. Perhaps they were talking about her. She looks down at her shoes: they are scuffed and worn. Is this what they were talking about? How shabby she looks? Surely not, most people are not as well turned-out as they used to be; the war has seen to that. One of the women coughs, and Gisela looks up.

"We're so very sorry," she says in a quiet voice.

Gisela stares at her. What is the woman on about? Surely they're not still talking about Helga's accident? Will she never have peace from people wanting to share their condolences? She nods at the woman, but doesn't say anything in return.

One of the others pushes her way forwards. Gisela knows this woman; she is the mother of one of Wilhelm's school friends, she can't remember his name, Helmut, Herman? It won't come to mind. She can't remember his mother's name either. The poor woman is tired-looking, and she is dabbing at her eyes. Surely she hasn't had bad news about her son? Gisela waits for her to speak. She doesn't want to ask about Herman – yes, definitely Herman, she can see him now, a chubby boy with freckles all over his face – in case something terrible has happened to him. "Such a terrible loss," says the woman.

Gisela doesn't know what to say. Who is she referring to? Is it Helga as she thought originally, or Herman? She has an overwhelming urge to get out of the shop, but they are all staring at her, waiting for her to reply. "Yes," she manages at last. "Terrible."

"So unfair," murmurs one of the other women.

"Mmm," agrees Gisela, wondering how she can get out of this. She doesn't think they're talking about Herman, his mother doesn't look distraught enough, and if they're going to talk about Helga she wants to escape. Now. She turns to go, but Herman's mother has taken hold of her arm, and she is trapped. Marguerite, that's her name. She – a fervent Nazi – was embarrassed about it: it sounded too French; for a time she'd changed it to Margit, but it had never caught on.

"We saw it in the paper," she says, nodding towards a newspaper open on the counter. "Couldn't believe it at first. We thought it must be a mistake."

"It's in the paper?" Gisela is baffled.

"Why, yes. There's always a column about those missing in action."

So they are talking about Herman. Poor soul. Gisela is about to say that Wilhelm will miss him, that he was always well liked, when the newspaper is thrust under her nose, a finger pointing to the article about missing soldiers. She doesn't like to refuse it so she takes out her glasses to read it. Her heart stops, she thinks she's going to vomit. There, four lines from the top, is her son's name. She reads it through again. There is no doubt, *missing in action*, it says, *presumed dead*.

Gisela looks up, is about to tell them that it's a mistake, her son is at home this minute, on the farm, playing with his new sister – did they know she'd adopted an orphan from Hamburg? – when something stops her: the memory of all those whispered conversations between Friedrich and Wilhelm. Their words come back to her – Wilhelm determined, *I won't do it, you can't make me, it's wrong*, Friedrich stern, *it's your duty*. She hadn't known what it was they were talking about, told herself it was none of her business. In a rush she understands: Wilhelm is a deserter. She sways, catches hold of Marguerite's coat sleeve, pulls herself together. Ignoring the solicitous comments of the women, she manages to speak.

"Can I take that?" She nods towards the newspaper.

"Of course," Marguerite pushes it towards her. She hesitates, then says in a rush, "You should be proud. Your son died a hero. For the Fatherland, serving his Führer."

Gisela takes the paper and puts it in her bag. "Excuse me," she says, "I must go." She opens the door, flinching at its cheery ring. The women stand staring at her as she leaves. "How will she cope?" she hears one of them say.

Outside the rain is pouring down in sheets. Heedless, Gisela makes her way towards the bus station. Her umbrella is in her bag, but she doesn't get it out. She walks through the gutter where the rain has gathered to form a gushing torrent. The water soaks through her old shoes, but she doesn't feel it. All she feels is the pain in the place where her heart should be.

There is a flash flood on the road back to the farm, and the journey takes four hours longer than it should. By the time she gets back it is dark, and she stumbles up the track to her home, praying she won't turn her ankle in one of the many ruts made by the tractor. The farmhouse is about a mile off the main road, and she is weary beyond words when she sees at last its lit windows. Friedrich is standing in one of them, looking out for her. He opens the door and runs out to get her.

"Where have you been? I thought you would have been back before now."

She understands his anxiety. Since Helga died, they fear the worst when one of them is later back than they should be. She pats his arm. "There was a flood. The bus had to wait until the water went down."

He has heated up some stew she made earlier in the day. Wilhelm is sitting at the table with a plateful in front of him. It smells of onions and sage, and she realizes how hungry she is – she hasn't eaten since breakfast. He looks up as she comes in and gives her what now passes as a smile from him. How could she not have noticed before now how strained and pale he is?

"Where's Helena?" she asks as she takes off her coat.

"I put her to bed an hour ago. Poor mite, she was exhausted. Wilhelm chased her all over the farm. She fell asleep before she'd said her prayers." Friedrich smiles, looks happier than he has done for years. Gisela's heart twists as she thinks of what she must do now. She opens her handbag and takes out the newspaper, spreads it out in front of the two men.

"When were you going to tell me?" she asks.

Friedrich exchanges a glance with his son. Wilhelm has stopped eating, puts his head in his hands.

"Well?" she demands, hearing her voice rise. She feels hysterical, wants to scream and shout, *how dare you destroy my last bit of happiness? How dare you desert? Do you know what they do to people like you?* Gisela takes a deep breath to calm herself. "I want an explanation."

Wilhelm looks up at her. Slowly, his voice so quiet she can barely make out his words, he begins to tell her.

It is late, past midnight. They have talked for hours, Wilhelm mostly. He weeps as he tells them of the sights he has seen, the things he has done. Friedrich has heard most of it before, but for Gisela, the things he says are difficult to accept. Especially the murder of children, this is unbelievable.

"Why would they want to kill children?"

"Not just children, babies too." Wilhelm spares them no detail.

"I don't understand." She shakes her head.

"I think they want to get rid of all Jews. And in their eyes, it doesn't matter whether the Jew is young or old. They all have to die."

Gisela feels sick. It can't be right to kill so many people. Not civilians, women, children who can't fight. Where is the sense in it? A terrible fear grips her heart. Wilhelm has deserted. She can't condemn him for this, not after what she has heard, but he is a deserter, and they are sheltering him. If he is found, they will all be punished. There is no doubt about this. Yet shelter him they must. They must find a good hiding place for him. Although the farm is a mile or so away from the main road, it is not unusual for people to pass by, for neighbours to drop in unannounced. It doesn't happen all that often, especially since Helga died. They were never a sociable couple, and people find Gisela's dull gaze and Friedrich's silence hard to take. And there will be callers – now that the announcement of Wilhelm's "death" is in the paper, that priest will take the opportunity to call by.

Gisela rises from the table. "It's late," she says, "and we have much to do tomorrow. Let's sleep on this."

Upstairs Gisela undresses in silence. Friedrich is already in bed. He lies on his back staring at the ceiling. "What are we going to do?" he says as she gets into bed beside him.

"I'm going to sleep. We can talk tomorrow." Gisela plumps up her feather bolster. She lies down, knowing it will be a long time before she will sleep peacefully again.

In the morning, she is up long before anyone else. She is at the kitchen table writing when Friedrich joins her.

"What are you doing?" he asks as he pours himself some coffee.

"Writing down all the options."

Friedrich sips his coffee and grimaces; it is a coffee substitute, bitter with chicory. "Can I see?"

Gisela pushes the paper towards him, and he reads through what she has written, silently mouthing the words. "There's not much choice, is there?"

"What are you thinking?"

"I think that perhaps the attic is the best option."

Gisela nods. "Yes, I do too. We can start work on it today. It won't be long before we start getting visitors, and we need to be ready."

"What do we need to do?"

"Move a mattress up there, build a false wall that he can hide behind in case the house is ever searched."

"Are you serious?"

"I've never been so serious in my life. Our son has deserted. I know they think he's dead, and I don't think the army will come looking for him, but if they do we're in trouble. They shoot deserters, and who knows what they'll do to us if they find out we've been sheltering him. There's no room for error." She throws the paper in the fire, watching it flare up. Friedrich is rubbing his eyes. Gisela thinks that he has never looked so old, so tired. In an instant she understands that she has to be stronger than she has ever been in her life; he's about to break down. She reaches out to stroke his face. "We'll get through this, I promise you. We have a second chance as a family, and no one is going to take that away from us."

Friedrich grabs her hand. His grip is so tight that she cries out in pain. His words are measured. "You're right, we must be strong. I don't know why this has happened to us. I can't believe what Wilhelm has been through, how he—"

A noise at the door startles them. Gisela turns round to see Marguerite standing in the doorway of the kitchen.

17

Jan is hungry and tired. He longs for his mother: her smile, her cooking, the way her eyebrows used to raise when she was warning him about being naughty. One arch of her right eyebrow, and he knew he was in trouble. Most times it was enough to stop him in his tracks, although there were times when he knew he tried her patience to the limit, when he'd annoy Maria or refuse to help with the chores. He'd give anything now to hear her asking him to bring in water or throw out the slops. He thinks of when he last saw her, dressed only in her underwear, tears streaming down her face when she turned for one last look before she was pushed through the school door to God knows where. She didn't look like his mother. His mother was always in control; this woman was lost in sorrow.

He punches the side of his head to rid himself of these memories. Over the past year he has become very good at shutting out those things which disturb him. If a bad thought comes to his mind he can get rid of it by hurting himself; hitting his head does the trick, or pinching his arm. The pain from this usually drives anything else away. What he can't do, though, is control his dreams. Mostly they are happy, dreams of the past, fragments of memories: playing with his friends or chasing Maria round the local farms, a summer picnic, stuffing his mother's food into his face. Often when he is hungry he dreams about this and wakes up with his empty stomach protesting. One dream persists. The day Lena was born, he saw her when she was just an hour old, a bawling scrap in his mother's arms. She looked red and angry, and he hadn't understood why his parents seemed so happy. But they were. His father had taken him and Maria out to the nearby town where he bought them each a puppet, a present from their new little sister. The puppets were carved from wood, and beautifully dressed as Hansel and Gretel. They'd had hours of fun playing out the old fairy tale, scaring each other with tales of the wicked old woman who lived in the woods. Lately, though, when he dreams of this, it turns into a nightmare, Maria screaming for help as the old woman grabs them with her claw-like hands, and in the background, looming ever nearer, the furnace in which she is going to roast them.

A snap of a twig hurls him back into the present. Jan tenses; he can feel the muscles in his back tighten. It's probably only an animal, but he can't be sure. He wants to turn round and look, but if it is an enemy he doesn't want them to know he's heard them. He carries on walking, trying to control his fear, making himself walk at a normal pace. The sun is low in the sky and will set in a few minutes. Not long after, it will be completely dark. Twilight is brief at this time of year. Jan can't believe he was so stupid as to fight with Pawel, his only ally. After Pawel walked away, Jan had sat down by the side of the road and watched him until he was just a dot in the distance. Then he let his feelings out. Like a tiny baby he howled. The birds sitting in a nearby tree flew off at the sound of his rage. He punched and kicked the ground, not caring that his knuckles were grazed. He cried and cried, letting out his grief and frustration until, exhausted, he'd fallen asleep. There was no way of knowing how long he slept, but when he awoke his eyes were swollen; he couldn't open them properly. He saw clearly, though, that he had been wrong to let Pawel go; he couldn't go back into Germany alone, he would have to stick with Pawel. Jan had stumbled to his feet, grabbed his things and started to run along the road after his friend, but although he ran fast and didn't stop for an hour or more, there was no sign of Pawel.

He is deep in the forest now. Pine trees, thirty metres high, stretch above him like ancient giants. Some time ago the road deteriorated into a track, Jan isn't sure he remembers exactly when, and he's worried that he might have lost his way completely. It is so dark he can scarcely see his own feet, and reluctantly he realizes he'll have to find shelter of some sort where he can sleep for the night. He strains to see ahead of him, but the sun has now set, and all he can see are vague shapes. The trees block out most of the sky, and although there's a moon, its light is intermittent.

A rustle behind him. Jan can't help himself: he whirls round, but there's nothing to be seen. He holds his breath and listens: more rustling, heavy breathing like someone panting, and the sound of something or someone running. Jesus, Maria! Where can he hide? He runs to what he hopes is a tree, aware of the noises not far behind him, his heart bursting with fear as he thinks of the soldiers he saw earlier that day. Somehow, without knowing it, he must have caught up with them, walked straight into a trap. The noise is right behind him now. The breathing is laboured, like a grunt almost. Something hard pushes into him and knocks him to the ground. Jan crouches down, protecting his head, waiting for the inevitable blows. There is a scuffling noise, then nothing. The night is once more silent round him. Slowly he sits up, tense, ready for something to hit out at him. Still nothing. He tries to remember exactly what happened: the feel of the thing as it knocked him over, the noises it made. It comes to him what it was: an animal, perhaps a boar. In Czechoslovakia the forests are full of wild boar; perhaps it is the same here. But at least it is not a German soldier. Jan's mouth has dried up with fear. He tries to moisten his mouth with saliva, breathes deeply and steadily until his heart starts to slow down once more. He is exhausted. He scrabbles around on the ground to find his bundle of clothes which he has dropped in his fright. Thank God he finds them. He fluffs them up, lies down and puts his head on the makeshift pillow. A few minutes later he is asleep.

Jan is hauled to his feet, slapped awake. He flails around trying to fight off his assailants with his hands and feet. Rough hands grab his arms and pull them behind his back where they are tied together with rough rope. He opens his mouth to protest, but before he can say anything, he is gagged. Thank God he's not been blindfolded; not that it matters, the night is so dark he can't see the end of his own nose. No one says a word as he is pushed forwards and marched through the forest. He tries to guess how many soldiers there are: he gets a sense of two, maybe three, and wonders if it's worth making a run for it. Probably not: with his hands tied, his balance will be impaired, and he's unlikely to get more than a few feet before being captured again. He stumbles on, cursing his foolishness at letting Pawel go. What had he been thinking? Now things were worse than ever. Who knew what was going to happen to him now?

The march through the forest continues in silence. If he trips he is hauled back to his feet. They are with him at all times. For an hour, maybe more, they walk deeper into the forest. Jan had thought it was dark before. Now the trees are so thick there is never even a glimpse of the moon to give any idea of what is around him.

They are slowing down. Jan can smell burning, a fire and the fragrance of roasting meat; his stomach growls at the thought of food. It is hours since he has eaten. He wonders if the men have picked up his bundle of clothes. He has a dim memory of someone carrying something. There is some bread in the bundle. Jan wishes he could have it to chew on. He feels weak with hunger. A pinpoint of light ahead, Jan tries to focus on it. It's a fire. The flicker of flames is unmistakeable. It is not far away, a hundred metres, maybe two.

Round the fire are twenty or so men. Jan tries to see their faces, to read their purpose. He has never been so scared in his life. Not since the night… No, he won't think of that, he won't. He closes his eyes to try to think of something else and falls over. This time he is left where he is. The men who captured him, he can see now that there are only two of them, go up to the fire and hold out their hands to warm them. One of the men sitting near the fire gets up and comes towards Jan, a knife glinting in his hand. Jan stops breathing. He stares at the man in terror, but the man is avoiding his look; he bends down and cuts the rope that is tying Jan's hands. Jan is light-headed with relief. He flexes his fingers to get the blood flowing, reaches up to untie his gag, but immediately someone is beside him to pull his hand down.

"Leave it," the man says.

Jan blinks in surprise. The man is Polish, his accent similar to Pawel's. He's desperate to speak to them, tries to talk through the gag.

"Shut the fuck up," says another man, who joins them. "Any sound out of you, and you're dead."

Jan shakes his head frantically, points to his mouth and joins his hands in a gesture of prayer. This disconcerts the men. They look at each other.

"Take the gag off," says one of them. "But we'll ask the questions. You keep quiet until we tell you."

Jan's hands shake as he tries to untie his gag. The man nearest him is holding a knife very close to his throat. His fingers can't get a grip on the knot, and tears of frustration run down his face. The man pushes his hands away and unties the knot himself.

"Thank you," whispers Jan.

"Quiet until you're spoken to." Someone approaches with a mug of water and hands it to Jan. He takes it and gulps it down. Nothing has ever tasted so good.

"You're not from around here." A statement, not a question.

Jan stares at them. Several of the men have gathered round him now. They're a rough-looking bunch, dirty and unshaven. The stench from their bodies is overpowering. It must be weeks since they've bathed. He's as sure as he can be that they're partisans, decides to tell the truth. He tells them the name of his village.

To his surprise they seem to recognize it. They look at each other, eyebrows raised. "How do we know you're telling the truth?"

Jan thinks quickly, and then asks, "Do any of you speak Czech?"

One of them nods. "A little."

Jan starts to speak in Czech, to tell them about what happened on that day in June last year. He only says a few sentences before the man raises his hand to stop him. "Enough," he says. He turns to his comrades. "He's Czech all right." Then he asks Jan to speak in Polish, tell them what happened.

"Can I… may I have something to eat? It's hours since I had anything."

"Jozef, get the boy some meat."

Jozef, a boy of perhaps fifteen with livid spots all over his face, brings Jan some meat and potatoes. Jan takes a few mouthfuls before starting on his story. The men listen carefully, occasionally interrupting to ask him questions – *how many men were killed? How many soldiers were there? What happened to the children?* Jan answers as best as he can. Once or twice someone interjects to add a detail. Gradually Jan realizes that they already know his story. He finishes his meal, and feeling braver now that he has some food inside him he asks them about it.

"You seem to know about my village already. How can that be?"

"What is your name, boy?"

Jan tells him.

"Jan, your village is known of throughout the world. The Nazis made an example of it after Heydrich was assassinated. Do you know who Heydrich was?"

"No, I've never heard of him."

"He was the man the Germans put in charge of the Bohemian protectorate when they invaded Czechoslovakia. You do know your country was invaded?"

Jan flushes. They are speaking to him as if he is a silly child. "Yes, of course."

"When he was assassinated, the Germans attacked your village as a reprisal and as a warning to others. They killed all the men and sent the women to camps. All of the buildings were destroyed. They wanted to make it look as though the village had never existed. No one was ever sure what happened to the children. There has been no sign of them in over a year, and it was thought that they were most probably dead. Your village and what happened to it, is known about all over the world. Many people wrote about it."

Jan can't imagine his little village being famous. It's ludicrous. Cities are famous, not villages where nothing happens. But of course, something did happen there. Something terrible. Jan's stomach tightens. "Do you know where they sent the women?" he asks.

"As I said, they were sent to camps, concentration camps. They're a sort of prison. They were sent to Ravensbruck, I think."

"So the women are still alive?" Jan can hardly dare to hope. There must be something in his voice for the man's rough voice softens.

"I hope so, Jan. But you must realize that these camps… they're not good places, and although the women were taken there alive, not all of them will survive."

"Why not?"

"Well, there's a lot of illness for one thing."

"And?"

"And for another, well you saw what the Nazis are capable of."

Jan is silent for a moment, taking it in. When he speaks his voice wobbles, though he tries to keep it steady. "You mean…"

"In these camps, terrible things happen. There's a camp not far from here in Oswiecim, where they're murdering Jews, thousands of them each day."

"But my mother isn't Jewish."

"No, but sometimes they murder other people too. Well, you know that, you saw what happened to the men of your village."

Jan shakes his head. "I don't believe my mother is dead, I'm going to find her, to rescue her, and then we'll go find my sisters."

One of the men laughs. It's not a cruel laugh, but neither is it kind. He sounds impatient. He reaches into a pocket and brings out some cigarettes. Taking a twig from the ground beside him, he sticks it into the fire until it starts to burn, then uses it to light a cigarette. He draws on it deeply before starting to speak.

"Jan, we're far from Ravensbruck here, many many miles. How do you think you'll make it across Poland into Germany, find a concentration camp and get your mother out?"

Jan flushes. When it's put like this, he realizes how silly it sounds. He's eleven years old; he has no money, no way of finding his family. It all seemed so easy when he and Pawel planned it. Now he's lost Pawel, and he's here in a Polish forest, many miles from Lena, God knows how far from his mother and Maria. He looks down at the ground, not wanting the men to see the tears in his eyes.

"Listen, little one. You can stay here with us. A boy will be useful, less suspicious to the enemy. You'll be safe with us, you'll see." The man grins, showing large yellow teeth. Jan can't help it, the teeth make him think of a wolf, but the man's smile is kind, and he has no option, not here, at this time of night when he longs to sleep. He half smiles back and nods. The man holds out a hand. "You can call me Marek."

Jan shakes his hand. Marek calls to Jozef and tells him to take Jan to a place where he can sleep. Jan gets up from the fire and follows Jozef to a nearby hut. It's makeshift, covered with branches to disguise it. Inside, it stinks like a farmyard, but it's warm, and Jozef points to a grubby mattress where Jan can sleep. He sinks down on it, thinking he'll never sleep, there's so much to think about, but the warmth stupefies him, and within minutes he is fast asleep.

18

Marguerite joins Gisela and Friedrich at the table. She sits down and puts her head to one side as she talks. Her eyes fill with tears; she is full of sorrow for their loss, repeats this several times. Her wide face crumples as she talks about her own son and her fears for him. All through this, Friedrich and Gisela sit impassive, too scared to speak. Marguerite tells them how brave they are, and brings out a cake she has made. Gisela studies her face closely, looking for signs that she has heard what they were talking about.

The floor above them creaks. Marguerite glances at the ceiling, surprised. "You have visitors?" she says.

Gisela half-smiles at Marguerite. "You haven't heard then?"

"Heard what?"

"We've adopted a little girl, an orphan from Hamburg. Her father was a war hero, died at the front." She sighs and glances at Friedrich. "Why don't you go and get Helena, bring her down to meet Marguerite."

Friedrich grunts and goes to the bottom of the stairs. He climbs up, praying that Wilhelm won't call out. His prayers are answered. Wilhelm is in his room, sitting on the edge of his bed, staring into space. Friedrich puts his finger to his mouth as he goes into the room. "Stay very quiet and don't move. We've got a visitor. I'll give you a shout when she's gone."

Wilhelm nods and gets back into bed as Friedrich goes in to get Helena. She's asleep, but doesn't make a sound when he wakes her up, just smiles at him. He smiles back. "Come on, petal. There's someone for you to meet downstairs." He lifts her out of bed and carries her downstairs.

"What a pretty child!" exclaims Marguerite. She reaches out to stroke Helena's hair, but the child shrinks from her, hides her face in Friedrich's chest.

"She's very shy," says Gisela. "She's been through a lot."

"What happened to her?" asks Marguerite.

"Shortly after her father was killed in action, her mother died when Hamburg was bombed."

"Poor thing, was she with her mother when she died?"

Gisela looks to Friedrich to answer.

"Well, we don't know for sure what happened – whether she was with her mother or…" He tails off.

Marguerite tries again to touch Helena's hair, and the child burrows deeper into Friedrich's arms. He hugs her protectively.

Marguerite tuts. "You don't want to encourage this bashfulness. She needs to mix with other children. What about kindergarten? That might help her."

Gisela's voice is firm. "No, I don't think so. She's fine at home with us for the time being."

Marguerite nods. "Ah well, you know best." She looks once more at Helena, the longing shining through her eyes. "I would have loved to have a daughter, and such a beauty as this. The Führer himself would be proud to have such a child."

"If you would excuse me, I have things to do..." Gisela pauses, takes out a hanky and wipes her eyes.

Marguerite nods, rising from her seat. "Of course, your poor Wilhelm. I should go. I'll see myself out."

"I'll be at the service for Wilhelm, let me know when—"

"There will be no service." Friedrich interrupts.

"What do you mean? You have to have a memorial service."

His eyes narrow, and a muscle twitches in his cheek. "Wilhelm is missing. Who knows, miracles can happen. Perhaps he's wandering around, a lost soul, with no memory of who he is."

"Perhaps," she says. "But still, you should have a service for him."

"There will be no service," repeats Friedrich firmly.

Marguerite raises an eyebrow and turns to leave.

Friedrich and Gisela stand at the door and watch until she disappears out of sight. Helena has stayed inside, playing with a piece of wood that Wilhelm has started to carve into a doll for her.

Gisela lets out a long sigh. "Do you think she suspects anything?"

"I don't know." Friedrich shakes his head. He looks exhausted. "I don't think so, but we must be careful. Let's go inside and talk to Wilhelm."

The day has almost gone. Little work has been done for the family have argued all day about what to do. The plan to hide Wilhelm in the attic has been abandoned. Although they are as sure as they can be that Marguerite did not hear them, they cannot take the small risk that she might be dissembling. Gisela especially doesn't trust her. She's a fanatic. Before Hitler she had been a fervent Catholic, never away from the Church. That was the type of person she was, never did things half heartedly. It was all or nothing for her. No, that plan had to go. But where else could he hide? Wilhelm wanted to leave; he knew he was putting them all at risk.

"There's nowhere for you to go," argued Gisela.

Wilhelm put his head in his hands. "It would have been better if I'd died."

"No! You mustn't say such a thing. We'll think of somewhere."

After many hours of thought they have a plan. Early on, Friedrich had suggested the barn. Both Gisela and Wilhelm had rejected it: Gisela because she couldn't bear the thought of her boy sleeping in a place with so many rats, Wilhelm because he had seen a barn surrounded, the entrance boarded up then set on fire, heard the screams of the Jewish family who were hiding inside as they were burned to death. He doesn't tell his parents about this, though – best keep these scenes to himself. But Friedrich keeps coming back to this idea for try as they might they cannot come up with anything better.

"We can build an underground room. We must, for anything else is too risky. It will have to be small, just a space big enough to sleep in. The entrance can be covered with hay to hide it. Tomorrow we will start work on it. There can be no delay."

Gisela watches Wilhelm as his father speaks. His face is pale and drawn; he has lost a lot of weight. There are fine lines on his forehead. He looks older than his twenty years. She feels sick thinking of him in a tiny cell underground, but accepts that he will have to go there. There is no alternative.

Friedrich and Wilhelm work uninterruptedly for the next two days on the underground room. Gisela keeps watch for any visitors; she worries that there will be many visitors now that people know about Wilhelm being missing in action – but there is only one, a teacher from Wilhelm's old school. His words are kind as he speaks about Wilhelm, telling stories about his mischief in school. Gisela has always liked this man, and she is tempted to confide in him. She's sure he would understand that no one can be expected to kill women and children in the way that Wilhelm was. As he gets up to go, she broaches the subject.

"*Mein Herr*, have you heard any rumours about this war?"

"What do you mean?"

"About what they are doing to the Jews."

His mouth tightens. "I'm not sure what you're asking, meine Frau."

Gisela takes a deep breath. "I've heard they're killing women, children too, even the babies."

The elderly teacher looks around as if expecting to see someone listening. He takes a hanky out of his pocket and wipes his brow. "Who told you this?"

Gisela stutters, wishing she'd kept her mouth shut. "I… I'm not sure. I think I heard someone talking in a café in the town. I just wondered if it was true."

"*Meine Frau*, it is best not to speak of these things to anyone. These are dangerous times. You never know who may be listening. I too have heard such stories, about terrible things. But I speak of them to no one, do you understand?"

"Yes," she whispers. "I'm sorry, I didn't mean to upset you."

He puts a hand on her arm. "Don't worry about me. You look after yourself and remember what I said."

After he's gone, Gisela thinks about what he said. He'd looked terrified when she asked about the Jews. As if he were hiding something. But what could he be hiding, a respectable old man like that? She puts the thoughts out of her mind and carries on with her chores, mindful always to watch the track to the farmhouse, in case any more visitors are on their way.

The room is finished. Friedrich and Wilhelm take her to see it once Helena is safely in bed. They cannot risk her seeing it or hearing anything about it in case she says anything to anyone. She is too young to be let in on the secret.

Gisela looks down at it in dismay. It is tiny. When they mentioned a room, she thought they meant just that. A small room, yes, with space to walk about in. But this is little more than a box. It is about two metres deep and long, and a metre and a half wide, lined with wood to shore up the walls. Wilhelm has already taken the mattress from his bed and thrown it down along with some blankets. On one wall there are pieces of wood sticking out as a makeshift ladder so that he can easily climb in and out. "How will you live here?" she exclaims.

Wilhelm smiles. "I'll read and sleep. At night, when it's dark I'll walk in the woods so that I get some exercise.

It will be hard, but it's infinitely better than what I was doing."

Friedrich shows Gisela the wooden cover he has made for the room. It fits very precisely onto the wood that shores up the walls, and once it is covered with muck and straw like the rest of the floor, no one would suspect there was anything unusual about the barn. She has to admit they've made an excellent job of it. There are holes in the cover to let in air, and when the oil lamp is lit it is almost cosy. She worries that he will be too cold, but he reassures her that with blankets and quilts he'll be fine.

Later that night they help him move to the hiding place. Gisela weeps as Friedrich places the cover on the room. It reminds her of how the undertaker put the lid on their daughter's coffin.

19

Three days later, they come in the middle of the night. Ten soldiers, some are only boys, but a threat nonetheless, they kick open the farmhouse door and enter. Gisela is first to hear them. She lies petrified in bed, unable even to whisper a warning to Friedrich.

But Helena too has heard them. She starts to cry, a thin wail, and this forces Gisela to act. She leaps out of bed and runs to Helena's room, scoops the child into her arms as the first soldier reaches the top of the stairs. He points his rifle at her.

"What do you think you're doing?" says Friedrich from the doorway of their bedroom. He sounds angry, furious; it's convincing, thinks Gisela. This is good; they must show no fear.

"We have information that a deserter is hiding here." The boy who speaks looks the same age as Wilhelm.

"What deserter?" asks Gisela.

"Your son, Wilhelm."

Gisela clutches Helena to her chest. She imagines how she would feel had Wilhelm really died in that ambush and her home were invaded by strangers accusing him of desertion. "What?" she whispers.

"You heard." An older soldier pushes his way to the front. "Last month you received a letter telling you your son was missing in action. A few days later he turned up alive and well. It was your duty as citizens of the Third Reich to hand him over for appropriate action. Instead, the two of you conspired to hide him. We have reliable information that you have built a false wall in the attic, and that he is hiding behind this wall."

"What nonsense! How dare you come into our home and say these things?" Friedrich is standing at his full height. The soldier shrinks back from him, but only a little. Almost immediately he regains his composure.

"I have every right to search this house. Here are the papers." He hands them to Friedrich, who barely glances at them.

"I want name, rank and serial number," he says, "from every one of you. I want the name of the officer who allowed this travesty to happen. I will complain to the Führer himself. My wife and I have lost our only son, a hero, and you dare come here and call him a deserter."

There is shuffling and muttering on the stairs. Gisela can see that Friedrich's certainty has unsettled them. She peers down the stairs to try to figure out what they are saying. One of the faces looks familiar. A school friend of Wilhelm's.

Gisela calls to him, "Karl Heinrich, is that you?"

No response.

"It is you, isn't it? What do you have to say about all this, then? You knew Wilhelm at school. You were one of his best friends. You must know he's incapable of such a thing."

The boy pushes himself to the front and whispers to the officer. "Sir, could I have a word, please?"

"Say what you have to say, so we all can hear."

He blushes bright red, looks at his feet. "It's true, sir. I did know the deserter at school, but I wasn't friends with him. I would never desert, sir."

Gisela looks on in disbelief. This boy often came to the farm. He often sat at the kitchen table sharing meals with them. One year he helped with the harvest, and they paid him well. Was this to be their thanks? The boy avoids her gaze and scuttles back to his place.

The officer turns to Gisela. "Not much help to you, was he? I suggest you keep your mouth shut from now on. You, on the other hand," he says, using his rifle to point at Friedrich, "show us how to get into the attic."

Friedrich shrugs. "This is a terrible mistake you are making. I warn you for the last time, I will not let this rest."

The officer sniggers. "I'll take that chance. Now, before I lose my patience…"

Gisela sees that Friedrich is struggling to keep his temper. Before he can say anything else, she says, "It's this way," and shows them the hatch that leads into the attic.

They gaze up at it. "Is there a ladder?"

"Downstairs, in the pantry," Gisela is quick to answer. She wants them out of her home as quickly as possible. Helena is very quiet in her arms, and she prays she will stay that way.

She's barely said the words when a voice shouts from below that they've found it and will bring it up.

The officer speaks to two of the soldiers. "Take the woman and child into that bedroom and see that they don't move. You" – he points to Friedrich – "You come with us."

* * *

The attic is bare save for a couple of old chairs. Friedrich switches on the light at the request of the officer and tries to look at it as if he were a soldier searching for a deserter. To his eyes it looks as if it hasn't been disturbed for years. As of course it hasn't. He sneaks a glance at the officer. His face is impassive as he scans the attic space.

"Well," demands Friedrich. "Do you see any deserter here?"

The man ignores him and strides across the beams to the far side. There he stands in front of the gable end wall and starts banging on it. Friedrich thinks that perhaps he expected it to give way, for he looks down at his hands as if puzzled.

"Not very likely that there's someone behind there, is it?" Friedrich can't resist sounding triumphant.

The officer turns round, his face red with fury, and points his rifle at Friedrich.

Friedrich backs away. Perhaps it wasn't a good idea to taunt him. The officer moves towards him, and Friedrich sees that the rifle is in fact a machine gun. His mouth is dry; no matter how hard he tries he can't moisten it. He can't understand why he did not notice that it was a machine gun before. Not that it would matter. He's powerless.

"We'll soon see if there's anyone behind there." The officer raises the gun and lets off a volley of fire. Downstairs Helena screams, or is it Gisela? The officer strides back across the space and stands in front of the wall. For a moment he appears to be lost in thought, then Friedrich realizes that he is listening for any sounds coming from behind the wall.

"I don't think you'll hear anything," he can't resist saying. "And perhaps you can see the daylight coming through."

The officer turns to face him. "Our information was good," he says, before lowering the machine gun. He looks ashamed, thinks Friedrich.

"Can I ask where it came from?" Friedrich feels he must ask, though he knows it can only be Marguerite. It's too detailed to have come from elsewhere. She must have heard them after all, that morning when she arrived unannounced at their door. He finds it hard to believe; she sat at their table pretending to sympathize with them, cooing over Helena.

"I can't say," says the officer.

"What will happen to this so-called informer?"

A shrug. "Most probably nothing."

Friedrich runs his hand through his hair. "Do you think it right," he asks, "that someone can smear our son's name like this?"

No reply, the soldiers are being rounded up and marched out of the house.

"I expect an apology," shouts Friedrich as they leave. "You can't do this to us; our son is a hero. He died for his country." He knows this is excessive, but feels that to react any other way might betray them.

No one answers as they leave. He and Gisela stand at their door and watch the column of soldiers until they are out of sight.

"That was close," he says. She grips his hand tightly.

* * *

Later that day there is a visit from some people they know from the town. They have come, like Marguerite, to pay their condolences. Gisela spots them coming up the track and curses beneath her breath. Friedrich shakes his head, and she knows what she must do. She gets up from her seat and goes to the door to greet them. She brings them into the kitchen where they have just finished eating lunch, a simple meal of bread and cheese.

"Please, sit down," she says. "Can I get you something to eat, to drink?"

There are five of them, including the priest from their church. He takes a seat without a word. Herr Pfeiffer, an elder of the church, is the first to speak.

"Gisela, Friedrich, we are so sorry to hear of your troubles."

"Did you hear what happened last night?"

"About the raid? Yes, we did."

"And what do you think?" asks Friedrich. "Do you think it is right that we should be subjected to this treatment, after all we've been through?"

"We're here to show our support," answers Herr Pfeiffer.

"That's not the question I asked," says Friedrich. He is belligerent, ready to argue with anyone. Gisela sees his point. She doesn't want a succession of people visiting, offering sympathy. The fewer visitors they get the better. She'd be happiest if they could become social recluses and never have to speak to anyone outside the family again, but then the more realistic part of her wins through, and she accepts that she will have to speak to these people, acknowledge their condolences. "Friedrich," she says, smoothing her skirt, "it's not

Herr Pfeiffer's fault we were raided. And the soldiers too, they were only acting on orders."

At once, she recognizes her mistake. Friedrich flushes an angry red and opens his mouth to reply. Frightened of what he might say, she rushes in. "Please gentlemen, what will you have to drink? Friedrich, will you get some wine?" She pleads with her eyes for him not to say any more. He nods to show he's understood and vanishes to the store room where they keep a small supply of wine and beer.

Gisela's hand shakes as she pours the wine. One of the men notices and speaks quietly to her, telling her to leave it to him to do. She pretends not to hear him and carries on with the task, taking care not to spill a drop. The raid by the soldiers is not mentioned again. Instead the men talk of Wilhelm, call him a hero, praise him with lavish words until Gisela can't stand it any longer. She wants to tell them the truth, that he deserted, and she's proud of him for refusing to kill any more women and children. She knows, though, that this would be suicide. Behind their friendly faces lies God knows what. She doesn't know whether any of them are members of the Nazi party, but there have been enough mentions of the Fatherland to make her think that there is sympathy with Hitler's aims.

At last they rise to go. They have not stayed long, perhaps only thirty or forty minutes, but it seems like hours. As they are about to go, Helena wakes up from her afternoon nap and starts to cry. The noise startles the men, and Gisela sees immediately that they are suspicious. Perhaps they believed the raid was justified after all.

"Who is that?" asks the priest.

"Haven't you heard?" says Friedrich, his voice softening with pride. "We've adopted a little girl. Two months ago. Gisela, you should go and see to her."

Gisela takes the chance to leave the room and runs upstairs to Helena. She lifts her out of bed and soothes her before starting to go downstairs with her. At the bottom of the stairs she hears the priest ask if they will be bringing her to Mass.

Friedrich mumbles a reply, which she doesn't pick up. She prays he's put the priest off. The thought of going to Mass, facing the treacherous Marguerite, makes her feel sick. She takes a deep breath and goes into the room.

"What a beautiful child," says one of the men. He comes nearer as if to greet her, and immediately Helena clings to Gisela.

"She's very timid, isn't she?"

"Not really. After all, she's been through a lot, losing both her parents, then moving to a new family," says Friedrich.

The men lose interest at the lack of response from Helena and make their farewells.

This time Gisela doesn't watch them leave. She sits at the table, head in her hands, and sobs. Friedrich pats her on the back, murmurs soothing words, but it doesn't help. She can't stand this endless pretence. This game they are playing. Not until Helena runs over and strokes her face does she manage to pull herself together. Gisela wipes her eyes with her apron and smiles at the child. "Come on, there's work to be done," she says to no one in particular.

* * *

The soldiers' visit has affected Helena badly. She rarely smiles, and she is as quiet as she was when she came to them two months back. She follows Gisela everywhere, watches her every move. One day in town she starts to scream when she sees a soldier. She makes so much noise that Gisela abandons her shopping to take her home at once. People are staring, and Gisela doesn't want attention of any kind. It's too late, though, the faces are turned towards them, and she sees the knowing looks exchanged between the town gossips. She lifts Helena into her arms and hurries towards the bus station. Gradually Helena's sobs die down.

But there are footsteps behind her. She hears her name called. Someone is running to catch up with her. A man. Gisela daren't look round. She runs as fast as she can, there's a bus in a few minutes' time, she has to get out of this place. She turns a corner, and the station is in sight; she relaxes. She can see the bus and the queue of passengers waiting to get on. Whoever is following her won't want to make a scene with so many people around.

"Gisela, please, wait."

She recognizes the voice, Wilhelm's old teacher, Herr Knoller. He's not so bad, it won't do any harm to speak to him, so she slows down to allow him to catch up with her.

"Thank you." He is out of breath, an old man. Immediately she feels guilty for running away.

She waits for him to speak, but it takes him a moment to catch his breath.

"I heard about the raid," he says, "and I wanted to let you know that if there's anything I can do… anything." He looks into her eyes, and she gasps; the look is so direct. He is reading her mind, he knows all about Wilhelm, everything. She lowers her eyes and says nothing.

"You know what I'm saying, don't you?"

She cannot take the risk. Gisela takes a deep breath, forces a thin smile. "I have no idea what you mean, but thank you for your offer of help. It was very distressing to have Wilhelm's name sullied in that way. If perhaps you would like to write to the authorities…" She breaks off, unable to continue.

He smiles, a kind warm smile, a smile that can be trusted. "You are very careful," he says, "that is good. You need to be careful. But you also need to know your friends, and remember this, I am a friend. You know where I am if you need me."

Gisela can only nod. She is clutching Helena so tight that the child starts to cry once more. She bends to soothe her and, when she looks up, Herr Knoller is gone. She looks round, but he is nowhere to be seen, and for a wild moment she wonders if she imagined the whole scene. She feels comforted, though. His presence was a good one. Feeling better than she has since the soldiers came, she gets on the bus. All the way home, she thinks about the old man's words. Can he be trusted, could they ask him for help in hiding Wilhelm? The more she thinks about it, though, the more she thinks she has imagined that he knows everything. He was only offering to help, like lots of people, probably meant he'd say a prayer for them or some such pious nonsense. She has read far more into one look than was actually there. By the time she reaches the track where she leaves the bus, she has decided to say nothing to Friedrich. This is their problem, theirs and no one else's. No one is to be trusted. They must deal with it themselves.

A month since the soldiers' raid and Helena continues to fret. She has lost her smile and remains as silent as she was when she first arrived three months ago. The silence is unnerving. Gisela thinks that it would be good for her to see Wilhelm, but she is frightened to suggest this to Friedrich. He too has been very quiet these past few weeks.

They are very careful with their visits to the barn, taking care to go there only after dark, and to check carefully before they do so that there is no one in the vicinity. Friedrich insists that only he should go at first, but Gisela will not allow this. She needs to see her son, to check that he is well, even though it breaks her heart to see the space where he is confined.

The days are getting shorter. At night the temperature falls to freezing, and Gisela frets about Wilhelm. She wants to bring him back into the house, but Friedrich will not have it.

"You saw what they did, shooting into the wall like that. They're ruthless. Next time they could bring dogs, and where would we be then? Dead, the lot of us."

She knows he's right, but begs nonetheless. "What are the chances of them coming back? They've been once. They found nothing. To come again would be harassment."

"Have they punished that woman for her lies?"

"No," she concedes. It is true. Marguerite is free, Gisela saw her in town, the day before yesterday. She crossed the road to avoid her.

"Don't you think if they were sure she was lying, she'd be locked up?"

"I don't know, Friedrich. She's a party member. Perhaps she has influential friends."

"Perhaps, or maybe they're just biding their time waiting for us to slip up, to relax, and they'll be back. With more men, for a more thorough search."

Reluctantly she agrees with him, and Wilhelm stays where he is. She'd hoped they might revert to their original plan of the false wall in the attic, but Friedrich's argument is persuasive. She talks to Wilhelm about it.

"I want to bring you inside, but Papa thinks it's too risky."

"He's right, Mutti. I think they'll be back."

He's so pale her heart aches for him. His cheekbones are pushing through his skin for he isn't eating enough. Although she tries to feed him well, as often as not he barely touches what she gives him. It breaks her heart.

"I don't think so. They searched so well the last time, what possible excuse could they have?"

"They don't have to have an excuse. We think that Marguerite, you know, Herman Durr's mother, has told them she heard you discussing where to hide me. She'll keep on pressing for another search. I don't know whether they'll listen to her, but I suspect they will. We have to be prepared for the worst."

* * *

A few days later, and the worst is here. This time they haven't bothered to wait for the cover of night. They have come prepared to search the whole farm. When Gisela sees them marching up the track she feels as though they have sent the entire German army, there are so many of them. Her heart is hammering as she goes out to greet them. Friedrich is in the fields, mending a fence. There is no one to warn Wilhelm, to tell him to stay quiet and still.

The officer stands in front of her. He is so close she can smell the sweat from him, a stale smell like cabbage. She recoils from him. Once again he has papers. He thrusts them into her hand, but she lets them drop to the ground.

"You're wasting your time," she says.

His voice is loud, grates on her. "We'll see. Where are your outbuildings? This time we'll do a thorough search. This time we'll find him."

20

Jan is welcomed into the band of partisans. He's not sure he's happy with this, but there seems little he can do about it. With the disappearance of Pawel, a lot of his hope went too, and he is resigned to living rough in the forest and doing whatever is asked of him. For some time he hopes that Pawel will somehow find him, but as the days turn to weeks his hope fades.

His tasks are simple to begin with. Easy jobs that anyone could do: picking up supplies from a village, taking messages to other partisans. He and another boy, Zygmund, who is just a little older than he is, are often sent together to do this. The idea is that even if they are seen, they are unlikely to be suspected as resistance fighters because of their age. Gradually they are trusted with more difficult tasks – laying traps, digging holes; Jan doesn't like to think about this for the holes are deep, and he thinks they might be for graves. He hates the Nazis, but it scares him to think of bodies tumbling into these holes. Soon he learns to block out these thoughts in the same way that he never thinks of that day in June last year.

He's becoming stronger. The winter is harsh, and he's always hungry even though there is usually enough to eat. The men are well supplied by people willing to help with food even if they are not prepared themselves to endure the hardships of the forest. But even though he's hungry he can feel muscles developing through all the hard work, digging these holes. And he can run fast too. He found this out one day when he was picking up supplies and was spotted by a German army patrol. They chased him for a mile or more, but he easily outran them and was careful to run in the opposite direction from where the partisans were. This act earned him extra rations that night.

"You're a bright boy, Jan," said Marek.

Jan thinks every day about this. He thinks that if he earns their respect, maybe the partisans will help him find his family. When he confides in Zygmund, though, he laughs at him.

"Don't you understand? They are only interested in destroying the Nazis. Helping you is the last thing on their mind. And don't go thinking they rely on you. You're expendable. All of us are. Even Marek."

"I don't believe that. They'd be lost without Marek."

"Maybe so, but it's the greater good that counts."

"The greater good?"

"I've just told you, defeating the enemy. Besides that, everything else is unimportant. If a few of us were to die, so what? There will be others left to fight, others who will run their errands."

Jan looks at his friend. "You sound bitter. You've never told me how you came to be here."

Zygmund shrugs as if he doesn't care, but his eyes are burning with anger. "I am Jewish. The choice was between here and a concentration camp. My family arranged for me to be hidden on a nearby farm, but the woman became nervous, and eventually I felt I had no choice but to go. She didn't try to stop me. It was lucky for me that a few days later I met Marek and he helped me. I was starving by then, pretty desperate." He smiles at Jan. "I'm not bitter, just..." he falls silent.

Jan takes a chance; this is the longest conversation they've had. Usually Zygmund does what he has to do in near silence. "What happened to the rest of your family?"

He's gone too far. Zygmund gets up as though the question was never asked. "We have work to do, let's get a move on." The conversation is over. Jan doesn't really understand what has happened, but he recognizes a sadness in his friend that is at least as great as his own. He follows him into the forest where they start to gather firewood. Jan chatters on, tries to get him to speak again, but he remains silent. A few days later one of the men tells him that they found out some months ago that Zygmund's whole family was murdered. Gassed and cremated in a concentration camp. Jan never asks him about his family again.

One day, not long after this, Marek takes Jan to one side. He offers him a cigarette, which Jan takes, feeling very grown up. "What age are you, Jan?"

Jan draws on the cigarette, and immediately the smoke catches in his throat. He splutters, can't stop coughing. What a baby he is. After what seems like an age he gets himself under control. "What month is it?" he asks. Not so long ago he would have felt stupid asking such a question, but there is nothing to differentiate the days, and he has lost track of the weeks.

"It is December, December the eighteenth. A week to Christmas."

Christmas. The word sets off so many memories that Jan is almost overwhelmed, but he only says, "Then I am almost twelve. My birthday is two days after Christmas day."

"Nearly twelve, eh? You are a good size for twelve, Jan. Tell me, do you like what we do here?"

Jan is flattered by this conversation with Marek. He's noticed how the other men respect him, how they fight to sit beside him at meals, laugh at his jokes, keep the best seat for him. It's flattering that Marek is treating him like a grown up. He thinks carefully before he speaks. "I think what we do, we do because it's for the greater good."

Marek throws back his head and laughs; his white teeth glint in the firelight. "You've been listening to the comrades, Jan. The greater good! Marvellous."

Jan doesn't know whether to laugh or cry. He knows he's being laughed at, and it hurts, but he doesn't want to show it. He gives Marek a wavering smile. Marek smiles back.

"Jan, you're a good worker. You do what you have to do, and you never complain. I don't know if you realize it, but recently we've had a few losses."

Jan nods. Over the past few weeks there have been times when the men come back from raids or ambushes depressed and angry. He knows of at least six men who have died.

"I'd like you to do more direct work for us. Not killing, you're too young for that. But I have a very important job for you."

A flutter in his stomach; no, it's more than a flutter, an ache. Jan's scared, but he doesn't want to show it.

He waits for Marek to say more, but Marek is getting up, stretching his arms and yawning.

"I'm off to bed now. Take your time and think about it. There's no pressure, but it would be a great help to us."

Jan stares after him, lost. What can it be that they want him to do?

Marek ignores Jan for the next week. He is always with the older men, laughing and joking, plotting. Jan longs to be one of them, wishes Marek would speak to him like that, but he never does. One of the older men, Wlacek, has been delegated to give the boys their tasks. The usual sort of things: cleaning up, peeling vegetables, nothing that seems to Jan to be important. Nothing that would gain him an approving word from Marek. One day, as Jan is gathering firewood, he flings down his load and stamps his foot. Zygmund looks round, his eyebrows raised. "What's up with you?"

"I'm better than this!"

"And?"

"I'm not going to do it any more."

Zygmund stands very still, his eyes are enormous in his pale face. "Has Marek asked you to do something else?"

"Yes, what of it?"

"Nothing. But I think you should know: he asked me first, and I said no."

Jan shrugs. "So?"

"So, think carefully about what you're getting into."

Jan doesn't want to admit he doesn't know what he is being asked to do, so he starts to pick up the firewood that lies scattered all around him and says nothing.

Zygmund helps him, and they start the walk back to the camp. When they reach it, Zygmund holds out his hand to Jan. "No hard feelings?"

"Of course not."

"Have you told Marek yet that you'll do it?"

Do what? wonders Jan, but he is nonchalant as he says, "No, I'll catch him later."

Zygmund grasps his hand tight. "Good luck," he whispers.

Later that evening, Marek comes to him. "I've been watching you for the past week. You seem unhappy. No, that's too strong. Dissatisfied. I get the feeling you're ready to move on. Am I right?"

Jan nods.

"So, you'll help us?"

"Yes," Jan's voice is barely audible.

"Good man! Tomorrow evening. I want you ready and fresh. Make sure you get a good sleep tonight."

Jan is swelling with pride at being called a man, but it's not enough to divert him; he has to know. Swallowing hard, he says, "Marek, what is it that you want me to do?"

Marek shakes his head. "Tomorrow, Jan. Tomorrow, all will be clear."

Jan can't sleep. Try as he might, it is impossible to relax. There are too many things to think about. It's clear that he wasn't the first choice for this special task; they asked Zygmund, and only came to Jan when Zygmund refused. But he is a year older than Jan. Still, it's not as flattering as it might have been. He is their second choice. And he has not yet been told what it is he has to do. It's not killing, though. At least it's not killing. He knows someone has to do it, but it's a man's job, not for a boy. And despite what Marek said earlier, he's not a man. Not yet. Jan's thoughts continue to whirl for hours until at last he falls into a deep sleep. For the first time in months, he dreams of his father. At dawn, he wakes with tears running down his face.

The forest is darker than anything he's known since the night the partisan group found him. Jan can barely make out the figures of the other men as they make their way to the ambush point. Marek has told him that there is a group of soldiers expected along that road late that night. They are on their way to a village where two of them have sweethearts, or think they have. The girls are actually members of the partisan group and have told their "boyfriends" that there will be a party with plenty of girls for any soldier they might care to bring with them. The soldiers have told the girls there will be ten of them.

The plan is to ambush them. The partisans will hide in trees, and on Marek's signal will shoot. Jan worries about this; what if someone hears? But Marek is clear that it is far enough away from the army camp for gunfire not to be heard. If their bodies are found, however, the girls will be blamed, so it has to look as if there has been a mass desertion. This is not as unlikely as it sounds as the regiment is due to be sent to the Eastern Front in a few days' time, and according to Marek's information there is widespread unhappiness about this; one of the soldiers has already told his "girlfriend" that he'll kill himself rather than go to the east, where the Russians are massacring the Germans.

Marek ordered the group to dig a mass grave. Most of the day has been spent digging it, a narrow trench six or seven feet deep, and maybe thirty feet long. Jan was one of those who dug it, and he's terrified he'll fall into it in the dark, though as Marek pointed out this is unlikely, because of the huge mounds of earth surrounding it.

When they reach the ambush spot, Marek tells Jan what he has to do. He gives him some matches and a feather. Jan looks at them, bewildered.

"It will be clear in a minute what they're for. You'll be up a tree with the rest of us. I want you to watch carefully to see where the soldiers fall. As soon as the gunfire stops you must find each soldier. We have to be sure they're dead, so I want you to hold the feather under their noses. Count to one hundred. If there's any movement in that time, call one of us, and we'll finish them off." Marek wipes the sweat off his forehead. "Do you understand?"

Jan nods. His heart is hammering in his chest; he's not sure whether it's apprehension or excitement. Marek shoves him towards a tree, and he shimmies up it. There are already two men up there. They're ready to shoot; he can make out the outline of the rifles, and prays they won't shoot him by mistake. He tries to make himself comfortable, but the bark is scratching his skin, and he has cramp in his right calf. He flexes his foot to try to ease the cramp. Above him, one of the men whispers that he should try to keep still. It's not easy to stay in the same position when he's so uncomfortable.

The night is full of sounds: the wind in the branches, scuffling below them, the grunting of a boar as it looks for food. Nothing that could be soldiers on their way to a good night out, though. Jan closes his eyes wishing he'd slept better last night. He'd love to go to sleep now, but forces his eyes open. It would be dreadful to let Marek down. But it's so boring…

A song, men's voices. Jan grips his branch. This is it. His tiredness flees; he's wide awake, listening for Marek's signal. Above him, one of the men shifts slightly, must be to get a better line of sight. The moon's up now, but it's still hard to see anything clearly. The singing's getting louder. Any moment now. Yes, there it is, three hoots like an owl.

The sound of the gunfire is deafening. Jan almost falls out of the tree; he has to grab on to his branch to stop himself falling. A bullet whistles past his ear; he's sure it's grazed him, but when he touches his ear it seems fine.

One of the soldiers almost escapes. He was last in line, a little behind the rest, and when the shooting started he was quick off the mark, but Wlacek pursues him through the trees and gets him.

Jan climbs down from the tree. The ambush was so sudden and so bewildering he's not sure where all the bodies are. He strikes a match and looks around. The match is dropped as he stumbles over something. He strikes another and gasps at what he sees. He is standing in a mess of blood. There is a soldier with a hideous wound in his head. His brains are all over what was his face. No point in wasting time holding a feather under his nose. He's dead for sure. Jan calls out to Marek, and he and one of the other men come over and lift the body to take it to the pit. Jan continues with his search. Ten metres away there is another body. He lights a match and holds the feather under the man's nose. Nothing. Once more he calls to Marek.

Jan isn't sure how many soldiers there were. Marek expected at least ten, and he's only found five bodies. His eyes are tired from straining to see. Wlacek cries out; he's found another. Marek creeps up behind Jan. "You're doing well, but there's still four to be found. Try over there," he points to the east.

Ten bodies. They seem to have found them all. Jan stands back and watches the men shovelling earth into the mass grave. He's dizzy, feeling sick, walks a little way away from the rest, stumbles over another body. Jan bends over the body with the feather and starts to count. He's used to this by now, one, two, three. A movement. Jan holds his breath and waits. The man opens his eyes.

"*Bitte*," his eyes close again.

Did he imagine it? Jan's so tired he thinks he must be dreaming. He opens his mouth to shout to Marek.

A tight grip on his wrist. "Please, let me go. I have a wife, children." There are tears running down the man's face. "I don't want to die, please."

Jan can't move. He is back at Horak's farm, watching ten men at a time being lined up to die. He looks down at the man; his face has been replaced by that of his father. "Father," he says. "Tati, is that you?"

The grip is tightening. Jan winces from the pain. When he looks again, his father has gone, the German soldier is there instead, eyes open wide in fear; there is a shot. A hole appears in the centre of his forehead. Jan looks round to see Marek standing there.

"You should have shouted for us at once," says Marek. "They're the enemy. Do you think they'd show any mercy to you?"

Jan gets to his feet. His head is lowered; he doesn't want anyone to see his tears. "I'm sorry," he mutters, "I wasn't thinking." He pushes past Marek and hurries off. When he is sure he is out of sight, he leans against a tree and vomits, wishing he'd never agreed to go with the group that night.

The men are jubilant. It's been a while since they managed to kill so many in one strike. There were eleven in all, even better than they'd thought. The mood is good, and when they get back to the camp there is more rejoicing. One of the men gives Jan a drink. He gulps it down, thinking that it's water, wondering why it's in such a small glass. As it hits his throat he gasps. It must be vodka. He clutches his throat, and the men laugh, not unkindly. One of them says, "Take your time, little one. This is firewater, and a child like you should drink it slowly. Try again." He hands Jan another small glass. Jan looks at it wishing he could throw it away. But he realizes it's a compliment to be given a drink by the men, and so he sips at it. This time it's not so bad. He takes another sip. His head feels light, it must be because he slept so little last night. But it's not sleepiness, it's more than that, it feels good. It takes away the bad feelings he has about tonight. Marek's right, he would have killed him if it had been the other way round. If only he hadn't seen his father's face, though. He takes another sip. It wasn't his father; he has to hold on to that. His glass is filled up, and he gulps down some more vodka. It's getting easier to think about all the things he normally hides from himself: the killing of his father, the loss of his mother and sisters. He tries this out, and no, it doesn't hurt as much as it usually does. This vodka is good stuff. Jan empties his glass and holds it out for some more, but one of the older men spots him and immediately tells him off.

Jan is feeling bold. Isn't he now a man after all? And this old guy, what does he know? He ignores him and waves the glass at Maciej, who has the bottle and is offering it round. Maciej fills it up without a glance, and Jan lifts it to his lips, letting out a cry as Wlacek knocks it out of his hand.

"Did you not hear me, boy? This is not a drink for youngsters. Get yourself off to bed!"

"Leave me alone," says Jan, but it comes out all wrong. Something isn't working right. His words are slurred. He looks up at the man who is smiling down at him.

"You'll be sorry in the morning," says Wlacek. "You'll have a head like a bear."

"Better than a head like an ugly old pig," says Jan and giggles.

Wlacek cuffs him. "I won't tell you again, bed."

Jan tries to hit him back, but when he stands up he finds his legs are not holding him properly, and when he takes a swipe at Wlacek, not only does he miss him by several feet, he falls in a heap at his feet. He tries to get up, but can't. The last thing he remembers before falling unconscious is the sound of everyone laughing at him. Bastards.

* * *

Jan opens his eyes to bright sunlight and closes them again at once. The light hurts not only his eyes, but his head too. It feels as though someone has put it in a vice and is squeezing it. He groans. Even that hurts.

"Drink this," Marek hands him a cup.

"What is it?"

"Water. No more vodka for you, little one. We had to clean you up last night before you went to bed. There was vomit everywhere."

Jan sips the cool water. Somewhere in his mind is a memory of everything spinning, like being on a swing and a roundabout at the same time. His stomach lurches just to think of it. He gulps down the water and holds out the cup for more.

"So, little one," says Marek, "you're a man now. You've seen things that only men should see."

"You forget what I saw in my village," says Jan.

"So I do, so I do. And what you saw in your village – does that make you want to kill the men who did that to your father?"

Jan doesn't reply. The memory of his father falling has come to him with full force. Last night he thought he could think of it without pain. Now he realizes that he was wrong to believe that the pain had gone; it will never go. He pushes the memory aside, but it is replaced at once by a vision from the night before: the face of the man as he spoke of his children, the look of terror as he was shot. Jan closes his eyes to try to get rid of the memory, but it won't go away.

"Jan?"

"I… I don't know." Jan looks up at Marek as he says this and catches a glimpse of something fleeting in his eyes. Disappointment perhaps, or sadness. Maybe even relief. It is gone before he can decide what it is.

Marek smiles at him, ruffles his hair. "Maybe one day, little one, maybe one day." He strolls off to join the other men.

Jan lies down again, his head still aching. He's feeling sick. But whether it is from last night's drink, or from what he saw, he isn't sure. He clutches the blanket close to him, wishing it were his mother.

21

The officer takes off his gloves and lays them on the kitchen table. Gisela stares at them; she has never seen such fine leather in her whole life.

"So," he says. "Let me tell you about what has been happening in this little corner of our Fatherland."

Gisela looks up at this. There's something about his tone that worries her. "What do you want with us?" she asks.

"All I want is for you to listen," he is standing with his back to the range and has lifted the bottom of his jacket so as to warm his rear. "But perhaps you know already?"

"Know what? I don't take much notice of what goes on around me these days," says Gisela. "I have recently lost my son, but then you already know that."

"Your son, yes. Well, we can talk about that later. I want to tell you about one of your neighbours, the Bielenbergs. They own a farm not far from here."

Gisela knows the family. They are good folk, the woman is a little older than she is, and she was kind when Helga died. Came round, but didn't say the usual stuff which angered Gisela so much, just held her hand as Gisela wept. Her heart grows cold. "What about them?"

"Perhaps you should take a walk up past their farm. I'd do it one day soon, before the smell gets too bad.

Then you'll see what happens to traitors who hide Jews."

"Jews?" says Gisela. "But they're not Jewish."

"Maybe so, maybe so, but they had a whole family of vermin living in one of their barns. Up in the hayloft, behind the hay. They squealed like the pigs they are when we went in with hayforks."

Gisela's hand is at her mouth. She doesn't trust herself to speak.

"So, now you see what happens to traitors. The Bielenbergs are hanging from a tree, for the ravens to feast on."

Gisela can't help it; there are children in the family, she has to know what has happened. "All of them?" she whispers.

The officer studies the ceiling. "All of them. And the Jews too, all dead. Impaled on hayforks. It makes you think doesn't it? Hardly worth taking the risk, is it?"

Gisela wants to be sick. The Bielenbergs had four children; surely they didn't kill them. But after what Wilhelm has told her of what ordinary soldiers are ordered to do, she could believe anything. And the SS are worse. She pulls herself together; she has to be strong, call their bluff. "I don't know what you mean," she says.

"Well, it's obvious isn't it? You have a farm with outbuildings. Perhaps you too, have Jews living there. Or," he says, narrowing his eyes, "maybe your son is hiding there."

She may vomit, her tongue sticks to the roof of her mouth. The officer is watching her closely; she stares back at him, unblinking, unglues her tongue. "Yes, we do have outbuildings. No, our son is not hiding there.

The only thing you'll find in our barn is hay." She stands as tall as she can. "Our son is dead. He died a hero, fighting for the Fatherland. I don't understand why you are bothering us, and I will complain about it, I guarantee it."

He went on as though she hadn't spoken. "And so, I thought, I'd give you a chance. You tell us where your son is hiding, and we'll spare you and the child. We can't spare your son. An example has to be made of him. To deter the others, you know how it is," he rubs his eyes as if weary of it all. "Just tell us where he is."

Friedrich steps forwards. "Wilhelm is lying in a grave somewhere, unmarked, in pieces, blown to bits by a shell exploding. Go on, search the barn, search the house, search all you like. You won't find him here or anywhere else. He's dead, dead." He sits down at the table and starts to weep.

For the first time, doubt sweeps over the officer's face. He moves away from the fire towards the table and picks up his gloves. "Come with me."

They stand outside the barn. The band of soldiers has searched all the other outbuildings. "This is your last chance," says the officer. "Just point us in the right direction and you'll be spared."

"Our son is dead," repeats Friedrich once more. He sounds so weary, so sad that Gisela herself starts to wonder if something has happened that she doesn't know of. They are standing near the trap door that is well hidden by the hay spread thickly over the floor of the barn.

"Very well." The officer beckons to his men. Their rifles have bayonets attached, and one by one they stab at the pile of hay at the back of the barn. Nothing. The frustration on the officer's face would almost be amusing if the danger weren't so clear. He allows the farce to go on for five, maybe ten minutes, his face becoming more flushed by the minute. At last he gives the order to stop.

Although Gisela is feeling a sense of relief she is very much on her guard. Righteous indignation is the correct approach to take, she decides. "Last time you harassed us I said we would write to the authorities. We didn't because we are in mourning. This is too much. This time we will complain. And to Hitler himself if necessary."

The officer's face surely cannot get any redder. He shouts to his men to line up and marches them out without another word.

Gisela and Friedrich walk back to the farmhouse together. Gisela's heart is pounding with fear. She knows how close they have come to discovery and feels it is only a matter of time before they come again. For some reason, the Nazis are deeply suspicious of them. She thinks it must be because of Marguerite, but wonders why the woman seems so determined to frame them. As she nears the farmhouse she hears Helena crying; she must have woken from her nap. Gisela runs to the house and upstairs to the bedroom. Helena is sitting up in the bed, crying with great heaving sobs that seem fit to burst her chest. Gisela gathers her into her arms. "*Liebchen, Liebchen, Mutti ist hier.*"

Helena twists and turns in her arms as if demented. Rage rises up in Gisela; she wants to tear the soldiers apart for she knows that the stress of all this is affecting Helena. "Ssh, ssh," she tries, but the child will not be quietened. She carries her downstairs, cuddling her closely. In the kitchen Friedrich is sitting at the table writing in his beautiful copperplate.

"What are you doing?"

"I'm writing a letter to complain about how we have been treated."

"Do you think that's wise?" Gisela is beginning to regret her words to the officer, thinking that perhaps it's best after all to lie low for a while.

"It was your idea," he doesn't look up from his task. He is concentrating on making the letter sound as good as possible.

"Well, yes, I know. It's just—"

He interrupts her. "We have the upper hand, now, for a brief moment. But if we don't complain they'll start to wonder why, and then they'll be back. More soldiers, a more thorough search. We can't live like this."

Helena has stopped sobbing. Gisela lets her down on the floor, and she runs to the corner where her one doll is kept. She grabs it and hugs it to her. Gisela watches for a moment before turning once more to Friedrich.

"You're right. It would look suspicious if we didn't write. Let me see what you've written."

He hands the paper to her, and she scans it, murmuring the words to herself: patriotic Germans, loss of our only son, outrage at this invasion of our privacy at a time of mourning. "You should add 'unjustified' before invasion. It makes it stronger."

Friedrich takes it from her and looks at it again. "I'll write it all out now, and we can add more as we think about it."

That evening they take extra care when they visit Wilhelm. Instead of using a torch as they normally do, they walk to the barn in the darkness. It is nerve-racking, for Gisela expects Nazis to leap out at her from behind every tree; she jumps at every rustle of the leaves When they reach the barn, they sweep aside the hay and give the coded three knocks followed by five seconds of silence, then another two knocks to let Wilhelm know it's safe to come out. The trapdoor is pushed up, and Wilhelm comes out. He staggers a little as he does so.

"What was going on? This afternoon… they were back weren't they?"

"Ssh, not here. Let's get back to the house."

They make their way back in silence. The shutters are already shut so no one can look in on them, and the lights are on. Wilhelm blinks as he comes into the light. With a pang Gisela notices his pallor; his skin is grey and sickly. Poor Wilhelm who always looked so brown and strong – he is fading away.

"Tell me what happened," he says.

When they've finished telling him and shown him the letter they're going to send, he sits very still for a few moments. Then he gets to his feet. "I have to go," he says. "There's nothing else for it. If they find me here, they'll kill you too, and I won't have that."

Friedrich bars the door. "You're going nowhere. If you leave, the worry will kill your mother and most likely me too. We will go back to our original plan and build a false wall in the attic. They've shot into it so they know there was nothing to it. They won't do it again."

"They'll be back, you know they will."

Friedrich shakes his head. "I don't think so, not this time. The officer looked very upset when he left, and when the authorities get our letter..."

It takes two hours to convince him. Only when Gisela says that if he leaves, she will come after him, search for him in every city in Germany, does he at last agree.

Friedrich thumps him on the back. "Just as well too, son. For if she goes, who'll look after me?"

Wilhelm smiles dutifully at this weak joke, but the smile doesn't reach his eyes, and Gisela thinks back to the past with sorrow, to a time when his laugh filled the kitchen.

They send off the letter the next day to the Kommandant of Wilhelm's company. They don't expect to hear anything back, the best they hope for is that no one will search the farm again, but one bright morning two weeks later, a letter comes for them.

Gisela hands it to her husband. "You open it, I can't bear to."

Friedrich takes it from her and opens it. It is a single sheet of crisp white paper, with an official crest at the top. He starts to read it aloud.

"Dear Herr and Frau Scheffler, thank you for your letter. I have investigated your son's case in some detail. While I am sorry to have to tell you that we are in no doubt that he died following an attack on our company, I am pleased to let you know that steps are being taken to punish the person whose malicious gossip caused you so much distress. Please be assured of our sympathy in your time of loss, and that you will no longer be harassed. Heil Hitler." He squints at the paper. "I can't read the signature."

Gisela grabs it from him and reads it to herself. She cannot believe what is written there. Her eyes are shining as she takes it in. "It's too good to be true," she says to Friedrich, who is sitting stunned at the table.

He looks up at her. "I hope we have heard the last of this. It worries me that they're admitting it came from gossip. That means what we suspected is true, that Marguerite did hear us that day. I don't see her letting this go."

Gisela is determined to look on the bright side. "She'll be punished. She won't bother us again."

"I hope you're right," says Friedrich. He jumps up from the table. "Dammit, you are right. It's time to celebrate. I'm going to tell Wilhelm."

The hope that they won't be searched again lightens Gisela's heart, but she is not foolish. She knows they have to be careful, and Wilhelm stays for the most part in his tiny space behind the false wall in the attic. For one thing, Helena mustn't know that he's still at home for she might say something to betray them. Luckily she's so young that she almost seems to have forgotten that she ever saw him, and she rarely mentions him. When she does, both Friedrich and Gisela are careful not to react. They hope that by doing so she'll forget all about him. And it seems to work. As the stress leaves Gisela, and she is more relaxed, so too does Helena blossom. She starts to speak more, and her accent sounds less strange. Gisela knows she should seek out other children for her to play with, but she seems happy enough with just their company. Time enough for other children when she is of an age to go to school. Gisela can't bear to think of her going to school. Not only does she dread the indoctrination it will bring, she doesn't want to be separated from this lovely child who has brought back some joy into their lives.

It is almost springtime, a year since Helena came to them, and Gisela decides she would like to buy her a present. This means going into town, something she has avoided for many weeks now. When people called to see them in the aftermath of Wilhelm's "death" she was so quiet and sad-looking that they gave up trying to talk to her, and soon they were left in peace. Friedrich arranged to have their food supplies delivered. It's been hard, for they've had to feed four people on food meant for just two adults and a child, but Gisela is good at making meals go further by adding potatoes and vegetables from the farm to eke out the little meat they have.

There's a difference in the town. It's not just that the buildings are shabbier; the people look more tired, less confident. The news from the war is not good. The Allies seem to be gaining strength, and the Eastern Front in particular is no place to be. Every day there is a huge list of casualties. Gisela doesn't read the newspapers, though; she leaves that to Friedrich, barely listens as he tells her what is happening. She feels detached from this war; detached from the country she loved so much. It seems to her that everyone has turned mad.

The shops have little in them, and she wonders whether she will manage to buy the child anything at all. The haberdashers where she used to love to shop, is closed. She stands with her nose against the window, trying to see what has happened to it. Is it shut for good, she wonders, or just for the day? The little that is in the window looks tired and out of date, and she thinks it may have closed down. As she stands there, wondering where else she can try, she feels that someone is staring at her. It is not pleasant, and even as she turns round, she knows who she will see standing there.

But it takes her a second to fully recognize Marguerite. The plumpness has left her cheeks: they are now sunken and pale. Her mousy hair has turned grey, but it is her eyes that strike Gisela with force. They burn with hate.

"You," breathes Marguerite. "You dare to show yourself here in this town." Her breath is foul, smells of death, and Gisela recoils. She manages to control herself, however, and stands her ground.

"What are you talking about?"

"I don't know how you did it. I don't know how you managed to keep him hidden from the SS, but I wish they'd found him."

"I assume you're talking about my son, the same son who was blown to bits, who died for his—"

"Spare me the histrionics, *meine Frau*," Marguerite spat the last two words at her. "I know you were hiding him, I know because I heard you and your husband plotting. I heard it all. Your faces when you saw me! How I laughed as I walked home that night!"

Gisela turns to walk away, there's no point to this encounter. Marguerite follows her, shrieking at the top of her voice. Thankfully most of it is incoherent. She hurries across the road, praying that Marguerite won't follow her. It's maybe too soon to hope, but the noise seems to be lessening. She takes a risk and glances back. The parish priest is holding Marguerite, seems to be gently chiding her. She's so busy watching she doesn't look where she's going and bumps into someone coming the other way.

"Excuse me," she says, without looking up. It is rare that Gisela ever looks at anyone outside her family in the eye these days.

"Gisela." The voice is that of Herr Knoller, Wilhelm's old teacher. "How are you?"

She licks her lips, wishing her mouth didn't dry up with fear every time someone speaks to her. "I'm all right," she says, thinking as the words come out that she sounds like a sullen school girl.

"Are you really?" His voice is so kind that she wishes she could go to sleep to its tones. He sounds as though he really cares. She daren't look up at him in case he sees the tears in her eyes.

She says, "Yes, I'm fine. Really."

"Your friend isn't so good, though." He nods at the scene across the road. Marguerite is still shouting, though in a feeble, hopeless way. She punches the air around her, like a madwoman.

Gisela nods. "Yes."

He puts a finger under her chin and raises it so that she has to look him in the eye. "She's a dangerous woman, that one. Like a bear whose cub is threatened."

"What do you mean?"

"She's been doing everything to try to stop her son being sent to the Eastern Front. Informing on her neighbours, telling lies. She told the mayor of the town that her next-door neighbour hadn't put up a flag for the Führer's birthday. Turned out she'd taken it down, hidden it in a cupboard in her house. They found it when they searched the house the other day."

Gisela is struck by this. So it's not only her family that Marguerite is targeting. "Why did they search her house?"

"She went too far in claiming that Wilhelm is a deserter. Your letter set the authorities thinking. They started to think that she was up to something, had something to hide."

"You know about that?"

"Yes, the whole town is talking about it."

Gisela blushes to think that the whole town knows her business. He hurries to reassure her.

"Please, don't worry about it. It isn't gossip. It's… Well, everyone knows that you lost one child already, and there's a lot of sympathy for you. When people heard your farm was searched, not just once but twice, well…"

"Well what?" asks Gisela. She can't imagine that anyone would have objected, not officially at any rate. These days it's best to keep your head down. He seems to know what she's thinking for he gives a sad smile as he answers her.

"Nothing, really. Everyone's too… Well, you know how it is. But there was a great deal of sympathy for you, please believe me."

Gisela says nothing. There's nothing to say. After all, if it had been another family who'd suffered like theirs, would she have spoken out? She knows the answer only too well, thinks of the Jewish families in the town, driven out years ago, disappearing to God knows where. Did she speak out then? Did anyone?

"Gisela, I know what you're going through, and I can only repeat, if I can ever be of any help, you only have to ask."

Yet again she has the impression that he knows about Wilhelm. She nods and thanks him before adding, "Why is Marguerite doing this?"

"She wanted to keep her son safe. She thought that if she gave the SS good information, that they would release her son from the army or at least ensure he had a desk job away from danger. Instead she's ensured that he'll be sent to the Eastern Front. He goes next week."

Despite everything, despite all the terror that Marguerite has caused her family, Gisela feels a sharp pang of pity for the woman. The Eastern Front. It's everyone's worst fear these days. The casualties are high; the conditions terrible. Gisela can't condone what Marguerite did, but she can begin to understand it. "I see," she says.

"You're a remarkable woman, Gisela." Herr Knoller smiles at her, before raising his hat and taking his leave of her. She watches as he walks down the street, hoping she'll never have to ask for his help. He seems genuine, but who can be trusted these days? She shrugs and continues to walk down the street in search of that elusive present for Helena.

They decide that this day will be a special one for Helena. Gisela has made a cake. She couldn't find anything that would pass as a present, but Wilhelm has whittled a piece of wood into a puppet for her. Gisela made dresses for it out of scraps of material, including Helena's old nightdress which is now too small for her. Friedrich performs a little play for the child. Helena watches entranced as the puppet dances around her. "More, more," she cries as the puppet twists and turns in a frenzy. Gisela and Friedrich join in with her laughter, and for a brief moment their cares are forgotten. Gisela wishes Wilhelm could join them, but takes comfort in the fact that he can hear the child's laughter and hopes that it will bring a smile to his face.

Wilhelm smiles little these days. He is only too aware of the danger he has put his parents in. For a week or two after the letter came from his Kommandant, he let himself believe they were safe. But as the time goes on he is falling further into despair. He reads the paper every day, but it is nothing but propaganda, and he wonders if he will ever be free of what he has done. The war has gone on for ever, since before he was an adult, and it feels like this is all he has ever known. Sometimes he thinks he should try to escape to the other side and throw himself on their mercy. It surely can't be worse than what would happen if he were discovered here.

Today it is worse than ever. He hears the laughter from down below and feels abandoned. The laughter is an offence to him. He doesn't begrudge them their happiness, how could he when he has been the cause of so much worry to them, but laughter seems inappropriate when death is lingering so long in the land. He puts his hands over his ears to try to block out the sound, but it is there in his head, mocking him.

22

Two days after the attack on the soldiers, Jan and Zygmund are sent to a village to pick up supplies. They've never been sent so far away before, it will take them most of the day; Marek tells them it is twenty kilometres, maybe more. He walks with them to the edge of the forest and gives them directions. Jan wonders if they will ever find their way back as the directions are complex. But Marek makes them repeat them many times before allowing them to go. At last he is satisfied that they know what to do.

"Take care," he warns. "Stay by the edge of the road, so you can hide if you hear anyone coming. There aren't any troops stationed anywhere on the road, so you should be all right, but be on the lookout anyway. When you get to the village, go to the baker's. He'll tell you what to do after that."

The two boys set off down the road. The sun is shining, and for a time it feels almost as if things are normal. They walk briskly, chatting as they go along about school and how they miss it. Jan thinks he must have changed a lot. Two years ago, he hated school, despised his teacher and lived only for the afternoon when they were free to leave the classroom and roam the village. Now he would give anything to sit at a desk knowing that he could go home to his parents and their nagging about learning to read and write so he can better himself.

"Were you clever at school?" he asks Zygmund.

"So so. Not the top of the class, but nearly there. I wanted to be a doctor."

"And now?"

"Now, I want only for this war to end. After that I'll think about what to do. If I'm young enough I'll go back to school, and we'll see what happens then."

Jan falls silent. He can't imagine the war ever being over. Yet surely one day it must be. At night the talk is of Allied victories, and Marek has said that it won't be long now before the Russians get here. Marek is always upbeat, trying to motivate the men, but Jan isn't sure if he believes everything he says; sometimes there's an air of desperation surrounding him, the look of a man being hunted.

They continue to walk along the road, kicking up dust as they go. It's good to be out in the sun for once. It heats them through. Even in summer the forest can sometimes be chilly. And dark. Out here in the open, Jan remembers how light it can be. Although he is now used to the forest and its gloominess, he misses sunlight, the open expanse of sky. It's a joke among the men that he follows the patches of sun around their part of the forest as much as he can. But one of the problems with so much sunlight is that they get thirsty. Marek has given them each a bottle of water, but it soon becomes apparent that it will not last for the twenty kilometres they have to walk.

Zygmund takes a tiny sip of his water and sighs. "I want to gulp all of this down. All of it. In one go."

Jan looks at his bottle. Less than half a litre left, and they've only been walking for an hour. Even at their quickest pace, that's only about six kilometres. And they haven't been walking particularly fast. "We'll have to find a stream. There must be one somewhere."

Zygmund shakes his head. "No, I don't think we should wander from the road. It's complicated enough as it is. We'll just have to ration ourselves."

"I wish we'd thought of it sooner," says Jan, holding up his bottle to the light. No matter how much he stares it doesn't get any fuller.

They continue to walk along the road, listening for any sound of traffic. There's nothing, only the sound of a blackbird singing as it builds its nest. The cheerful song makes Jan feel better, but then, underneath the song, drowning it out, there is something else, a rumble. "What is it?" asks Jan.

"I don't know," says Zygmund. "But we'd better get off the road." He drags Jan to the side of the road where they drop down into the ditch. For several seconds they crouch there listening as the rumble gets louder. It's much louder than a truck, then a screech of a horn alerts them to what it is. "A train," they say simultaneously.

"Might as well get back on the road. There's nothing anyone can do if they see us from a train."

Jan frowns. "They might report us."

"On what grounds? Two boys out walking on a summer's day; what's suspicious about that? No, the only problem is if someone stops us and starts questioning us about where we're from, where we're going, that sort of thing. Your accent would be a giveaway."

"Yes, of course, you're right. Let's get on with it." Jan springs out of the ditch and back onto the track.

A few minutes later they realize why the train sounded so loud. The railway line is very near the road. Jan frowns as he looks at it. "Marek didn't mention a railway line."

"No," agrees Zygmund. "I wonder why not."

"Do you think we've lost our way?"

"I don't think so," says Zygmund. He thinks for a second. "No, we couldn't have. We had to turn left at the first fork in the road, then right at the next one, and that's what we did. No, it'll just be that he forgot or didn't think to mention it."

"Mmm. Yes, you're right. And most probably it will lead to the village, so we can follow it."

Zygmund shakes his head. "I don't think so. We should follow Marek's instructions exactly. Otherwise we could get completely lost."

It's nearly midday now, and the boys are hungry. All they have with them apart from the water is some bread. Jan wants to stop and eat it, but Zygmund insists they carry on. "We should try to get at least halfway, maybe more, before we eat anything. We won't get anything else to eat until we reach the village."

Jan scowls, he knows his friend is right, but, nonetheless, he's starving. He kicks the dust on the road, raising it into a cloud, which catches in his throat and sets off a coughing fit. Damn, now he'll have to use some of his precious water. He gets out the water and takes a sip. He swirls it round his mouth, feeling the dryness disappear, even if only for a moment. Reluctantly he screws the lid back on. Zygmund is watching him. "I know it's hard, Jan," he says. "But we have to be sensible."

Jan nods, he doesn't want to waste energy speaking.

They carry on in silence. Jan stares at the ground as they walk. His feet are sore, his head aches from the sun. The forest's coolness would be most welcome now. He thinks of the tall pine trees with longing. How they stretch up into the sky, the sharp scent of the needles rising from the ground. You never feel thirsty in the forest. Out here in the open it's so dry and dusty, and a wind has sprung up making the dust swirl round. Jan has rarely felt so hot and miserable. He's so sorry for himself he doesn't notice that Zygmund has slowed down, is pulling at his shirt to slow him down too.

"What is it?" he snaps, when he finally realizes.

"Up there, there's a train, stopped."

"So what?"

"We need to be careful, going past."

"I don't see why. Nobody's going to get out and come after us." Jan quickens his step. He really is in a bad mood. Zygmund has to run to catch up with him.

"Look, Marek put me in charge. You'll do as I say."

"Will I? You wouldn't even help him when he asked you. I don't know why he put you in charge."

Zygmund holds out a hand to Jan. "I don't want to fight with you, Jan. I'm bigger than you, it's hot, we're hungry and tired. There's a thousand reasons we shouldn't fight, not least because we're on the same side."

Jan turns away. He knows Zygmund is right, but he doesn't want to admit it. He waits to see what Zygmund will do now.

"Jan?"

"What?"

"Are we friends?"

Jan goes to kick at the dust, then remembers just in time what happened when he last did it. He raises his foot so that it skims over the ground. Despite his ill temper he can't help smiling at himself. When Zygmund sees the smile, he takes it as a positive response and gives Jan a friendly thump on the back.

Jan shrugs it off. "What are we going to do now?"

Zygmund is about to answer when they pick up a noise coming from the direction of the train. "Ssh, do you hear that?"

They listen, trying to make it out. It sounds like someone crying. No, it's louder than that. Sounds like many people crying. Someone calls out for help and is joined by what seems like a hundred other voices.

"Is that crying, do you think?" says Jan.

"I don't know. It's horrible – I don't like it."

"Neither do I," Zygmund is frowning. "Should we go and see what it is?"

The two boys stay where they are, locked in indecision, then Zygmund starts to walk towards the train. He beckons to Jan to follow him. Together they approach the last of the wagons. As they get nearer, they can smell something foul, a dirty, animal smell, worse than the smells they are used to in the forest. Jan tugs at Zygmund's arm.

"I know what these wagons are. I've seen them at home. They're used to transport animals when they're going to slaughter."

Zygmund sighs and shakes his head. "Oh Jan, it isn't animals that are in these wagons. When did you ever hear an animal shout help, or ask for water."

"Then what is it? What's making that noise?" whispers Jan.

"It's a transport."

"I know that!" Jan is indignant.

"No, I don't mean it's a form of transport, I mean it's a transport of Jews to the concentration camps."

"Oh," Jan is silenced. "What will happen to them?"

Zygmund doesn't answer, and Jan remembers what he has been told about Zygmund's family, how they all died in a concentration camp. He feels stupid for having asked such an ignorant question, for not having guessed as quickly as Zygmund what was going on. "I'm sorry," he whispers.

"It's all right," says Zygmund. They are now only a few yards away from the wagon, which is at the back of the train. There are so many in front, they can't see the engine. There is less crying now, more of an underlying moan, an extended groan, which makes Jan want to run away as fast as he can so he won't have to listen to it. But he can't run away. The road is right beside the railway track, and he has to pass this, has to get to the village to carry out his task. His steps falter and Zygmund has to pull him on.

"Don't make this harder than it is," begs Zygmund.

They are right beside the wagons now. They are made of bare, dirty wood. Some of the wood is broken, and when Jan glances over he is shocked to see faces peering through. Faces of old people. No, not all of them are old; there are children too, and young men and women. The smell is unbearable: unwashed bodies, faeces, urine. It's all there. There's another smell too, something rotten, terrifying. It makes Jan want to vomit. He knows only too well what it is: dead bodies. He has smelt this before, rats caught in traps on local farms in his village, sheep dying when they are trying to lamb.

"Water, please. Can you give us water?" The voice is weak, scarcely audible. A woman's voice. It could be his mother, his sister. Jan doesn't hesitate, goes over to the wagon and pushes his water bottle through the largest hole he can see. A hundred hands seem to appear from nowhere and grab the air around it, but the woman has it.

"Thank you, child," she says, "but what are you doing here?"

Jan doesn't know what to say, then thinks why not tell her the truth. Maybe the knowledge that there are people out there fighting the Nazis will give her hope, so he tells her.

"I wish you luck," she says when he finishes speaking. "What's your name?"

"Jan."

"Jan. A Polish name, but you're not Polish, are you?"

"No," says Jan. "I'm from Czechoslovakia."

"And why are you not still in Czechoslovakia? Are there no partisans there?"

Jan is silent for a moment, then says, "My village was destroyed by the Nazis, my father killed, my mother and sisters have disappeared."

"I'm sorry," she says. She disappears from view.

Another voice calls out for water. Jan feels desperate that he has no more to give. Then he remembers his bread and digs it out. Once again the hundred hands appear, snatching it away. "I'm sorry," he says, "I have no more. I'm sorry."

Zygmund has done the same with his bread and water. Now they have none, and more than half of their journey still to make. But at least they have some hope of finding some more. Zygmund joins him, pulls him away from where they are standing.

"We'd best go. There's nothing more we can do here, and if the Nazis spot us, we've had it. Come on, you've done all you can."

"But it's nothing," rages Jan. "Nothing. How can we leave them like this?"

"Jan, there is no more we can do."

"We could try to unlock the doors—"

"You have the keys then, do you?"

Jan hits his head against one of the wagons. He bursts the skin on his forehead and feels the warm blood spill down his face.

"What do you think you're doing?" Zygmund drags him back from the railway's edge. He marches him along the road; they're still beside the train for there's no other way past. Jan tries to block out the voices, the cries and pleas as he passes. He counts twenty wagons; it's nearly the end. As they reach the front of the train, the engine starts up once more. The sound of steam chuffing out of the engine almost drowns out the moans of the people in the wagons. Almost, but not quite. Jan had thought he would never again hear such desperation from human beings, had thought he had heard it all that morning in his village, and now, here it was, back, drilling into his mind, sending him mad. He must be going mad for he can hear someone shouting his name. Is it the woman he spoke with? No, it is not her voice. It is the voice of a younger person. Who amongst these poor souls could know his name?

"Jan, Jan! It's me, Pawel!"

Jan comes to. "Pawel? Pawel? Where are you?" He looks frantically along the wagons, searching for a clue. Nothing. Then he spots a small brown hand poking through a hole in one of the wagons near the middle of the train. He runs towards it, conscious that the train could begin to move any minute. Zygmund is right behind him, trying to pull him back.

"Let me go, he's a friend. I must speak to him." He wrenches himself away from Zygmund, and in a second is by the wagon.

"Pawel, what happened to you?" Jan is trying to get the door to open. He scrabbles at it with his fingers, but nothing moves. He looks round for something to attack the door with, but there's nothing but stones. He picks one up and bashes the door with it, but it doesn't move.

"Jan, leave it. There's no point. Even if I did escape they'd only shoot me. And if they see you..."

"Where have you been?" Jan is breathless with excitement and fear.

"In the forest with partisans."

"Me too!" The train is moving now, and Jan has to run to stay beside his friend. Behind him, Zygmund is shouting something. He turns to him. "What is it?"

"Tell your friend to lie about his age, you know, when he gets to the camp. He has to say he's at least fifteen."

"Did you hear that?"

"Yes," says Pawel. "Why?"

"Never mind that. Did you find your parents?"

There's a deep sadness in Pawel's voice. "No. Look, Jan, you must get away from here, before they spot you."

The train is going faster, and Jan stumbles back from the line, crying out his goodbyes to Pawel, before falling onto the ground. He lies there for a second, stunned, before he gets up. He is brushing down his trousers when he hears a bang and a warning cry from Zygmund. He looks up at the train to see a soldier standing at the window of one of the wagons, rifle raised and pointed straight at him. For a heart-stopping moment he thinks the soldier is going to shoot him, but the train is going too fast, and the soldier must realize he has no chance of hitting him. He lowers the rifle, and Jan lets out his breath.

"Jesus, Maria! That was a close thing." He turns to speak to Zygmund. Zygmund is lying on the ground, arms splayed out across the road. This is no time to play the fool. Irritated, Jan kicks him on the ankle. "Come on you, get up."

Zygmund doesn't move, and Jan's heart starts to beat faster. He leans over him and shakes him. "Zygmund, get up. We have to go." His hand feels warm and wet. He looks down at it; it's covered in blood. Jan yelps and wipes it on his shirt, on the grass by the side of the road, on the road itself, to try to get rid of it. All the time, he's shouting at Zygmund to get up. But Zygmund doesn't move, and the blood which has turned his dirty white shirt dark-red spills over onto the road.

Night has fallen. Jan doesn't remember it getting dark, but the sun has gone long ago to be replaced by a peppering of stars and a hangnail moon. He sits where he has for many hours, terrified to move. For a long time after it happened he thought that Zygmund was merely wounded. He kept talking to him, chattering on about Pawel, what they'd done together, what great friends they'd been, told him the story of their escape, though he'd told it to him many times before. All the time he held Zygmund's hand, telling himself it was still warm. But it was warm only from the sun. Now that the sun has gone, it is cold. Cold as the stones on which he is lying. He can no longer pretend. Zygmund has gone for good.

The night is a terrifying place to be. The hoot of an owl is sinister, the face of a friend becomes that of an enemy, the breeze in one's hair becomes the touch of one who wishes you harm. Jan thinks of what he must do now. He has missed the meeting in the village. Marek would have expected them back before now. He wonders if anyone will bother to look for them or whether they will be forgotten within a day or two, replaced by other, fitter, stronger boys. No point in such thoughts, he moves away from Zygmund and lies down at the side of the road, hoping he'll fall asleep.

In the morning it begins to rain. Huge drops fall on the road. The rain mingles with the dust to produce a musty smell, which reminds Jan of summer thunderstorms in his village. Within a few minutes the rain is hammering down. A blessing. Jan stands under it with his mouth open, tasting the sweetness of rain as it falls. He feels too as if it is washing away any blame for what happened yesterday. A baptism almost. Zygmund's body lies where it fell. There is nothing he can do about it. Zygmund was bigger than him; he can't carry it any distance, and he has no tools to dig a grave. He will have to return to the forest and tell Marek what has happened. A long way, and with no food and only the rain to nourish him, he doesn't know if he can do it. He has to, though. But before he does, he must say goodbye to Zygmund. Jan kneels down on the ground beside his friend's body. He closes Zygmund's eyes and mouth, and whispers sorry to him, then stands up. As he does so, he notices something glinting on the road beside the body and bends down to pick it up. It is a ring, a plain gold band. Jan examines it; most likely it is a wedding ring, probably belonged to his mother. For a moment he considers leaving it with Zygmund, but that would be a waste; anyone finding the body would steal it. Jan weighs it in his hand: it's heavy for such a small ring, and is probably worth quite a bit. He puts it in his trouser pocket, making sure it's safe at the bottom. It'll come in useful. He scans his surroundings trying to remember the way they came. Easy enough, the railway was on their left as they walked along. Jan turns round, so that it's on his right and sets off to find help.

The heavy rain leaves puddles everywhere. Jan washes himself in one, and then drinks from the next one he finds. As he does so, he wonders whether it will make him ill. He feels sick already, but that is probably because of what happened to Zygmund, or hunger. Hunger, his stomach tightens at the thought of food. He is very weak, and his legs tremble as he walks along in the thunderous rain. The road looks very different from yesterday; the dust has turned to mud and makes his journey more difficult. Every step is an effort. It is useless, he needs to sleep, but if he lies down in this rain, he could drown. Jan forces himself to carry on, trying not to think of food, trying to keep the vision of Zygmund lying on the ground with his blood spread out like a cloak all around him, trying to remember the way back. His mind is so busy with this that at first he doesn't realize he's passing an orchard. The apples and pears hanging from the trees don't register with him. Without thinking, he kicks an apple out of his way, the mud splashing over his shoes and trousers. He looks down at the smashed fruit in the road, then up at the branches above him. He ignores the pears; they are the size of bullets. The apples, although small and green, far from ripe, look promising. He reaches up and starts to pull them from their branches; he has to twist hard to free them from the tree. Some he shoves in his pocket for later, the largest one he starts to eat, wincing at its sourness, grimacing at its hardness. When he looks at it, there is blood on the flesh, his gums have started to bleed. But he perseveres, it will give him some nourishment.

A fork in the road, a choice to be made. Jan looks down both tracks, trying to remember which way he came yesterday, hoping he'll recognize some landmark. But the countryside is unremarkable, fields stretching out as far as he can see. He closes his eyes and pictures himself and Zygmund leaving Marek. Marek making them repeat the instructions – these would need to be reversed. "Turn left at the first fork, then right at the second, go straight along the road until you get to a crossroads, then turn right, the village is about five kilometres down that road," he mutters. "We never reached the crossroads so this must be the second fork, so I go left here." He peers down the track wishing he knew for sure it was the way. Nothing for it but to try. He thinks he has about two kilometres to go before he reaches the first fork, then it's not far from there. His grits his teeth at the thought of facing the men without the provisions he was supposed to pick up. A few sour apples will be no substitute.

He's almost there, about five hundred metres to go. Jan slows his pace. Now he's back, he's frightened of what Marek will say, of what the others will do. Some of the men are very short-tempered and, without food, dangerous. Perhaps he was wrong to come back, he should have gone on, completed the mission. He slows his pace, not just because of his fears; it's slippery underfoot. The rain has made the forest treacherous. Tree roots, always a nuisance, lie waiting to trip him up, for his feet to lose their grip.

He reaches the outskirts of the camp and stands behind the broad trunk of a pine tree to watch what is going on. The men are restless, huddled together in groups. There is whispering, looking round to see if others are listening. Something's wrong; he feels it in the pit of his stomach. A twig crackles behind him, and he twirls round, Jozef is there, his spots more livid than ever. Jan nods to him, and he joins him.

"What's going on?"

Jozef picks up a twig and throws it as far as he can. It lands twenty or so feet away. "Your guess is as good as mine. I tried to hear, but they cuffed me round the ear."

"It doesn't look good. Did you pick anything up at all?"

A grimace. "I'm not sure. There was something about moving."

"Moving?" Jan doesn't like the sound of this. He's become used to this half existence in the forest. "Why would we move?"

"I don't know. Where's Zygmund? Did you get the supplies?"

Jan can't answer him. He stares ahead, trying to see Marek. He'll have to tell him before anyone else.

"Jan?"

Jan starts to move towards the main part of the camp; Jozef follows, muttering about Zygmund. He's picked up that something's wrong.

A cry rings through the forest, then a shout and the sound of scuffling. Jan's heart pounds – what is happening? Have the Germans found them? He turns to Jozef and mouths "What's going on?" Jozef paler than Jan has seen him, shrugs. They creep towards the disturbance and, as they get nearer, Jan sees that two of the comrades are fighting. Marek rushes over to pull them apart.

"What's going on here?"

The taller one, Piotr, who only recently joined them, says, "He called my sister a whore."

It comes to Jan, then, that Piotr's sister is the girl who was going with a German soldier. But she was doing it for the greater good, he's heard the men say this many a time and, because of her, eleven German soldiers were killed the other night, but he won't think about that. That can go to the place where all his bad thoughts go.

Marek interrupts before either man can say anything. "We've no time for this now. We have to move, all of us."

Jan pushes himself forwards. "Why?"

"Who said that?" Marek looks round, he frowns when he sees Jan. "Where have you been? I expected you back sooner."

Jan splurts out, "Zygmund's dead, shot."

Marek shakes his head, closes his eyes. Jan waits for him to say something, but he is silent. "It wasn't my fault," he cries.

"You will tell me about it later. But now we must move, because the Germans have taken in Piotr's sister for questioning."

Piotr gasps, "What?"

Marek turns to him, his voice is soft as he speaks to him, as if he were trying to calm a frightened child. "I'm sorry, Piotr. Word came from your village early this morning. Apparently there should have been another soldier with the group we captured that night, but he was ill and couldn't make it. When the rest didn't return, he told his captain where they'd been going. I suppose they then put two and two together." He ducks as Piotr tries to punch him. Two of the other men step in and pull Piotr back.

"I told you," yells Piotr. "I told you it was too risky. But you wouldn't listen, and now they've got my sister." His face is scarlet with rage, and his eyes brim over with tears.

Jan whispers to one of the men, "What will happen to his sister?"

Piotr overhears and starts to cry. "You want to know what will happen to her? Go down to my village in a couple of days' time and you'll see. Her body will be hanging from a gallows. And they'll torture her first. Why do you think we're moving? They'll break her down until she tells them exactly what she knows about us, then they'll hang her or, if she's lucky, shoot her."

"Piotr," says Marek, "it's a risk we all take, you know that, and your sister knew… knows that too. She chose to do what she did, no one forced her."

Piotr throws Marek a look of pure hatred. "Try telling my mother that. Kasia was all she had left."

Marek sighs and shakes his head. "I'm sorry, Piotr, I don't know what else to say." He turns to the rest of the men gathered round and starts giving orders.

"Gather together anything of importance. Make sure nothing is left that can identify us, for they'll use that against our families. Guns, knives, ammunition, we need all of that. Wear two sets of clothes, if you have that many" – he grins as he says this, for many of the men have no change of clothes – "and bring as much food as you can carry. Everything else will have to be left. We have little time, so get a move on. We'll meet back here in half an hour."

The next thirty minutes are a blur of activity. Everyone rushing round collecting their belongings, getting ready to go. Everyone except Piotr; he sits staring into the dead ashes of the fire, tears streaming down his face.

After the time is up, Marek addresses the group of men. Jan counts them; he's never seen them all together in one place before. There are twenty-four of them. "We have to split up. Those of you who have a safe house to go to, I suggest you go there. If you can take a comrade with you, then do so." He pauses. "How many of you have somewhere to go?"

There's a murmuring among the group, then a show of hands. Jan counts fifteen. Marek holds up a hand for silence. "Please don't tell anyone where you are going. That way, if anyone is captured, they can't be tortured into telling the Nazis where you have gone. The rest of you spilt into threes. You're on your own for the next few days. The usual methods of communication apply. Look out for signs after a week has passed. With any luck they'll have given up the search by that time." He raises his clenched fist in the air. "Comrades, I salute you. Good luck to you all!"

Jan tugs at Marek's shirt. "What about me?" he whispers.

"You can come with me."

They are walking back to where Zygmund died. Marek wants to bury the boy; it's wrong to leave him unburied. He and Jan carry spades as well as a little food. The others have dispersed to God knows where. The journey is tense. And slow. Marek insists on stopping many times to listen for the enemy. As they walk, Marek asks Jan about what happened. Again he tells him it is not his fault that Zygmund is dead, but Jan's guilt lies heavy on him. If only they had not stopped by the train, they should have kept on walking, ignored it, or if only he had not run alongside the train to talk to Pawel. It's all his fault.

"Do you really think that?" asks Marek.

"Yes... No, I don't know," says Jan. "But I should have realized that there would be soldiers guarding the train, and that they would have guns. I don't know what I was thinking."

"But you could say that of Zygmund too. He should have realized about the guards too."

Jan wipes his eyes. He doesn't want Marek to see the tears, but it's too late.

"Don't cry, little one. You're not to blame. You didn't shoot Zygmund. He'll have suffered very little," says Marek. "He must have died immediately."

Jan wants to believe this more than anything. He can't bear to think that Zygmund was dying and he did nothing to help.

They reach the spot. Zygmund's body lies where it fell. They're about twenty metres from it. Marek stops Jan from running forwards. "They could be watching out for us. The guard will have reported it, and they may suspect that someone will come to claim the body. I think we should dig a grave for him, and when it is dark we can carry his body back and bury him properly."

They retreat into a nearby wood, and in the middle of it, where they can't be seen from the road, they dig a grave. Jan is used to the work for he has done it many times before. He had never thought he'd be doing it for a friend, though. When they finish, Marek sits down with his back against a tree and rolls two cigarettes. He lights them and hands one to Jan. "This is dangerous work," he says. "I think maybe I was wrong to allow boys to join us."

Jan says nothing. He draws on his cigarette and tries not to cough as the smoke reaches his lungs.

"He was only twelve when he joined us, some said it was too young, but I said he had nowhere else to go, and we should take him in."

"But you were right. He did have nowhere else to go. I think you did the right thing."

"Do you?" says Marek. "Do you think I should have made you stay? After all, it stopped you looking for your sister."

"I still want to find her," says Jan. His voice is shaky.

"You haven't answered my question."

"I don't know. I was lost, and you took me in. It was only right that I should work for you. I had to earn my keep."

"But the things I asked you to do. Dangerous things, and now Zygmund is dead..."

With a jolt, Jan realizes that far from blaming him for Zygmund's death, Marek blames himself. He doesn't know what to say. Marek has always seemed to be so much in control. It's worrying to see this other side of him.

Darkness falls. They wait for an hour for the moon to rise, but it's waning and gives little light. Marek throws a stone onto the road to see whether there's any reaction. He tries again, to make sure, and when it remains quiet he whispers to Jan to follow him, and they creep along the road to where Zygmund's body lies.

"You take the legs, and I'll take the upper half of his body," says Marek. Together they lift him; Jan is surprised how light he is, but then everyone is thin these days. Perhaps he could have managed to carry him on his own after all. By the time they reach the place where they are going to bury him, though, he is panting, exhausted.

"We'll rest for a moment and then bury him," says Marek. He lights a cigarette, but doesn't offer one to Jan. Jan wishes he would, for although they make him light-headed, the cigarettes take the edge off his hunger. Marek smokes in silence. The red tip of the cigarette glows red in the darkness. Jan watches, waiting for it to die.

"Right, let's get on with it," Marek stubs it out on the ground beside him and jumps up. "We need to be careful. If we put the body at the edge, we can roll it over, and it will fall down."

Jan's arms shake with tiredness as he lifts Zygmund for the last time. When Marek says the word, he lays him down and steps back to allow Marek to roll the body over. It lands with a thump at the bottom of the pit they've dug. Without a word, Marek hands him a spade, and Jan starts shovelling earth on top of Zygmund. He swallows to keep back the nausea that's threatened him all day. Jan tries to think of pleasant things as he carries on with his task, but he can't do it, and tears fill his eyes. At last they are finished.

"Let's go," says Marek.

"Aren't you going to say a prayer or put a cross on the grave?" asks Jan.

"He was Jewish. I don't think a cross is appropriate, do you?"

Jan feels the blush stealing up on him and is thankful for the dark. "But, a prayer…"

"I don't know any Jewish prayers." Marek is curt. He strides off into the night, back the way they have come.

Jan doesn't know what to do. It seems so barren to leave Zygmund in this way, his death unremarked, with nothing to mark his grave. He looks round, but sees only stones. Quickly he gathers up a dozen or so and lays them on the soil in the shape of a Z. "Goodbye, Zygmund," he murmurs, before running to catch up with Marek.

23

A brown envelope, their name and address typed; it has to be an official letter. Gisela looks at it, places it on the kitchen table in front of Friedrich and waits. He continues to eat his breakfast. She wipes her hands on her apron. "Aren't you going to open it?"

"It's addressed to you too," he says, before picking up his cup and gulping down the rest of his coffee.

Gisela's mouth is dry. "Who do you think it's from?"

He gets up and starts clearing the table. "How should I know?"

They're terrified, both of them. Official letters are rarely good news. Neither wants to open it, but they both know they have to. Gisela breaks first. She grabs it from the table and tears open the envelope, bringing out a one-page letter. Her eyes flicker over it, scanning the contents. Without a word, she gives it to Friedrich, then sits down at the table and puts her head in her hands.

"We'll write back and say no," says Friedrich.

"How can we? Have you read what it says? It's all about the war effort, pulling together. If we say no, they'll have us down as traitors. And it could raise suspicions again."

"How can we have members of the Hitler Youth to stay? How? Will you answer me?" Friedrich thumps his fist on the table. The noise startles Helena, and she starts to cry.

Gisela picks her up. She's such a nervous child; it'll be a wonder if she ever recovers from all she's been through. She strokes her hair; that usually calms her.

"What are we going to do?"

Gisela cuddles Helena. "Why don't we write back, say we don't need anyone, that there's little harvest to bring in this year?" That much is true. They were able to plant little last year, and what there is they could easily harvest by themselves.

"We could try, I suppose. But it says here that the young people are from the cities, and that they're being bombed. It's to keep them safe as much as anything." Friedrich is looking old, thinks Gisela in surprise. He's only forty-two, but looks many years older. She wonders if she too has aged in this way. For years she has avoided mirrors. Helga's death put ten years on her. She hands Helena over to Friedrich and gets up from the table.

"Where are you going?"

"There are some things I have to do in town."

"What things? Can't they wait? We need to sort out this problem."

Gisela leans across the table and takes one of his hands. "I hope that's what I'm going to do."

Standing in front of Herr Knoller's house, Gisela wonders if she's doing the right thing. What if she's wrong in thinking he knows about Wilhelm? What if she's misjudged his kind words? What if he's really a Nazi? Her hand, which is hovering near the knocker, drops to her side. Perhaps she should leave it; they can try writing to the authorities as she suggested, tell them they don't need any Hitler Youth to help with the harvest. No, it won't do. This is their only real hope. Before she can change her mind she takes the knocker in her hand and raps sharply on the door. It resounds along the street. She looks round to see if anyone is watching. No one. She listens to hear if he's coming to the door. Herr Knoller lives alone. His wife died many years ago, in childbirth if Gisela remembers rightly. The child, who was a boy if her memory is correct, also died. She holds her breath as she waits for him to answer the door. A minute passes, more than enough time for him to answer. He must be out. Gisela stands in front of the door wanting to kick it down in frustration. She'll leave a note, just a few words to say she called. Nothing else, nothing incriminating. She rummages in her handbag for some paper and a pencil, jumps back in shock from the door when Herr Knoller shouts from behind it, "Who is it? What do you want?" His voice sounds shaky, perhaps he's ill.

"It's me… Gisela. Wilhelm's mother," she adds.

The door opens a crack, and Herr Knoller peers round. He's pale and thin. Much thinner than when she last saw him, a couple of months ago. His eyes look huge in his face. "What do you want?" he says.

This is not the response she'd hoped for. In her mind she'd envisioned him welcoming her in, offering her coffee, perhaps some cake. She can't reply she's so disappointed, but then manages to stutter out, "I… I'm sorry to disturb you. This is a bad time, please forgive me," and turns to go.

"Gisela, wait." He opens the door and beckons her in. when she doesn't move, he reaches out and grabs her arm. "Come in, quickly."

She's inside. It's a large house, perhaps six or seven rooms, and the hall is dark and dingy. It lacks a woman's touch, she thinks. The walls are painted a dark, mustard yellow that reflects on his face, making him look bilious. The wooden floor is partially covered with a long rug, elaborately patterned. It looks eastern, Turkish perhaps, but it's hard to tell for sure because there's so much dust around. She sneezes.

"Bless you," he says.

"*Gott sei dank*," she says, giving the traditional response.

He moves through to the sitting room. The blinds are down, making the room dreary. It could be a beautiful room, the ceiling is high, and there's a wonderful stove with blue ceramic tiles in the corner. It's not lit today, though. "Sit down," he gestures to a chair. Gisela sits down and waits.

"It's good to see you, Gisela. Are you well?"

This has been a mistake. She's come to him thinking he's an ally when all he did was say some kind words to her. She's imagined the whole thing. He knows nothing about Wilhelm's desertion. She'll make her excuses and go.

"I'm well, thank you."

"And your husband?"

"Yes." Her hands are sweating. She has to get out of here. She rises to go.

His voice is soft, almost a whisper. "I know about Wilhelm."

She sinks back into her seat, heart pounding. Her mouth is dry; she can't speak. She waits for him to say something else.

"I saw him, when he was on his way home. I was out walking near your farm. I thought nothing of it. Just that he was on leave. Then I heard he was missing, presumed dead, and I realized."

"Did anyone else see him?"

"I didn't see anyone, so I doubt it. Anyway, if they had, if they had anything to go on other than what Marguerite said, your place would have been searched over and over until they found him.

Appalled, Gisela stares at him. Although she guessed that he knew something, she's horrified to have it confirmed. "What will you do?" Her voice is tense with fear.

He picks up on the fear, sits down with a sigh. "What do you take me for? I want to help you, Gisela. I'll only do what you want me to do. This regime is… How can I put it? It's abhorrent to me. I'm not going to harm you, or Wilhelm, if that's what you think."

"Thank you," she whispers. Her hands won't stay still; she pleats the material of her skirt between her fingers. "I hope you don't mind me saying, Herr Knoller, but you don't look well."

He grimaces. "Hunger is a terrible thing."

There is rationing, but most people manage. "Hunger? But don't you have enough to eat?"

A pause. "I share my rations."

"But why? For you, there is no need—" She breaks off as she realizes. "Oh."

He nods. "Yes, I too am hiding someone."

Her eyes widen. "Who?"

"My wife was half Jewish. Her father was Jewish, no one around here knew about it because they were not a religious family and they came from Berlin. Anyway she died long before all this nonsense started. The daughter of one of her cousins contacted me in desperation four years ago. She left her daughters with me, saying she'd be back for them. She has not returned, and I fear she never will."

"My God. But the danger."

"You can talk of danger, you're hiding your son at great cost to yourself."

"He's my son. I have no choice."

"And I too have no choice. You know what is happening to Jews. How could I not shelter these children?"

Gisela is silent. She had no idea such things went on. He was taking a huge risk in telling her.

"Why did Wilhelm desert?"

The question takes her by surprise. "He was being asked to kill women and children. He couldn't do it."

Herr Knoller nods. "I thought so; I hoped so. I mean," he rushed to explain, "Wilhelm was always a gentle, kind boy at school. I couldn't imagine him doing the sorts of things I'd heard about."

"And yet he did." The words are out before she can stop them.

"He must be feeling terrible." His voice is sympathetic. "And you too." He rises from his chair. "Can I get you something to drink?"

Gisela blinks back her tears. "No, thank you. You must be wondering why I've come."

"I assume you need help."

"Yes," Gisela takes a breath. "This morning we received a letter. From the government. They want us to take two young people from Berlin, members of the

Hitler Youth. It's supposed to help us with the harvest, but also to get them out of the city, away from the bombing."

"I see."

"Do you?" asks Gisela, for she is still not sure that the old school teacher has fully grasped what is going on. He seems to have aged a great deal, and there is no sign of these children he is supposed to be hiding.

"You're frightened they will find your son and betray him. You want me to hide Wilhelm here."

Relief sweeps through her. "Yes. Could you?"

He nods. "Of course, but I can't feed him. My rations are barely enough for three, I could not share them out any further."

"Of course not. We will bring him food."

Herr Knoller gets up from his chair. "We must think about this carefully for people will talk if they see you coming here regularly."

Gisela blushes; she has not thought about this, but of course people will gossip. "I'll send Friedrich," she says, thinking even as the words form in her mouth how impossible it will be. He'll need to work on the farm, even if they do have help from the Hitler Youth he'll need to supervise them.

"No, I have a better idea. Later today I will put an advert in the local newspaper for a part-time housekeeper. You will apply for it, and no one will think anything other than that you need some extra money."

It is agreed. Gisela leaves the house lighter of heart.

"You did what?" explodes Friedrich. His face is purple with rage.

"I asked Wilhelm's old teacher for help."

"Why him? Can he be trusted?"

"Yes, I think so," Gisela tells him about the Jewish girls and about the plan of her becoming a housekeeper.

Friedrich mops his brow. "I don't know, it seems very risky."

"No riskier than keeping him here for the Hitler Youth to sniff out." Gisela is abrupt; she thought he'd be more enthusiastic than this.

Friedrich goes to the door. "I'll need to think about this," he says. "I'm just not sure if the old man can be trusted."

The next day Friedrich agrees to the plan. Together they tell Wilhelm. He says nothing.

"Tell us what you think," begs Gisela.

"I think I would be better to give myself up," says Wilhelm.

Cold fear clutches at Gisela's heart. He is so depressed that she fears he will walk out of the house at any moment. "Don't say that," she says, "the war could be over any day now."

Wilhelm gives a snort which might be a laugh. "You've been saying that for months. The war's been going on for almost five years now. I don't see it ending soon."

Friedrich interrupts him. "The Eastern Front's falling apart. Russians could be here within a few weeks. Everyone says so."

"And you think they'll forgive me? You think they'll just pass over what I've been doing?"

"They'll only want the bigwigs. They won't care about ordinary soldiers like you."

"I don't know," says Wilhelm.

He's extraordinarily thin, thinks Gisela. Not for the first time does she wonder whether he eats everything he's given. The knuckles on his hands stand out, and his face is gaunt. "Wilhelm," she says as gently as she can, "we're in a pickle. If you stay here, the Hitler Youth may find you. We can't refuse to have them, and Herr Knoller, well, he's a good man. He'll look after you."

"I don't have much choice, do I?"

"No," says Friedrich.

The letter confirming the arrival of the two Hitler Youth comes two weeks later. It is late August. They have missed most of the harvest, so will be of little help. The day before they are due to arrive, Wilhelm and Friedrich leave the house late at night to go to Herr Knoller's house. Gisela hugs him fiercely. "I'll see you soon, for now that I'm the housekeeper, I'll be there at least twice a week. Don't be any bother to him."

Wilhelm nods. He pick up the bag that's been packed for him, with food and clothes, and turns to his father. "Let's go."

They have chosen to walk over the fields to the town. Petrol is scarce, and in any case you never know when cars will be searched. It's almost fifteen kilometres, but it has to be done. Gisela fears for Wilhelm's strength for he has had little exercise for months. Friedrich will have no problem other than thinking up an excuse if he's seen on the way back. It will be light when he's returning, and it is likely he will be spotted. They fret about this, but there's nothing that can be done about it other than pray he's not seen.

It's fully dark by ten o'clock, and they set off. Gisela watches them as they stride across the upper field, Wilhelm a head taller than his father. "I should be worrying about him settling down," she says to herself, "rather than this constant anxiety about whether he'll be caught. Whether we'll all be caught." She watches until they're out of sight, and then closes the door and goes upstairs to bed.

The field is boggy after the recent rain. Friedrich wishes he'd had his boots mended, he's been putting it off for weeks; water seeps through the worn sole, chilling his feet even though the night is warm.

"You'd be better off without me," says Wilhelm out of nowhere.

"Don't say that," says Friedrich. He's never been a demonstrative man. When the children were little, he rarely hugged them, often watching in envy as Gisela swung them round and played easily with them. Strangely he's more at ease with Helena than he ever was with either of his own children. Feeling brave, he reaches across and hugs Wilhelm awkwardly. "It would kill your mother to lose you."

"She would get over it." He pauses. "And now you have Helena..."

"You're not jealous are you?"

Wilhelm's face is not visible in the dark. "No," he says, "not jealous. Not in that way." He shifts his bundle to his other shoulder. "I suppose I envy her innocence. I can't believe I was once like that."

It's hard to know what to say. Friedrich knows only too well that Wilhelm's guilt is immeasurable. He's seen the tears on his son's face after another sleepless night. Heard the cries of anguish when he does sleep, watched the weight drop off him like melting snow in spring. He's tried many times to comfort him, to tell him he was only carrying out orders, but Wilhelm cannot be consoled. He wishes his son still had his faith, could believe in absolution, for if ever anyone was truly sorry for his sins, it is Wilhelm. But his faith had died when he killed innocent civilians, when he stood with a rifle in front of people who had done nothing other than be in the wrong place at the wrong time or who had the misfortune to be Jewish in an inhospitable land. Yet Friedrich feels he has to try.

"You mustn't blame—"

"Who?" Wilhelm sounds angry. "Who mustn't I blame? Surely you're not going to trot out that shit about me not being to blame. I pulled the trigger, I stood in front of men, women and children who didn't deserve to die, and I killed them."

"I know, I know," Friedrich's voice breaks. "But you were carrying out orders."

Wilhelm's voice is softer. "Don't you think I tell myself that every minute of every day? You'd think it might make things easier, but it doesn't. All I can think is why didn't I disobey, why didn't I kill myself rather than shoot innocent people."

"Because we all want to survive in the end," says Friedrich. "We all want to live, and we'll do what it takes to keep on going."

Wilhelm doesn't say anything for a moment then, so softly that Friedrich isn't sure he's heard properly, he says, "Do we? Do we want to live?"

* * *

It takes longer than they planned to reach Herr Knoller's house. The ground is uneven and wet, and makes their journey hard. It is cloudy too, and difficult to see in the dark. After almost three hours they find themselves on the outskirts of the town. This is the most dangerous part of the journey for if they are spotted they will be asked for identity cards. Fortunately Herr Knoller lives near the edge, and they get to his house easily. He answers the door and drags them inside before they have time to knock. He has been looking out for them.

"Herr Knoller," Friedrich's manner is stiff and formal.

"Please, call me Hans. You too, Wilhelm."

They sit down in the kitchen while Hans makes them coffee. Its aroma reminds Friedrich of happier times.

As they drink the coffee along with some homemade schnapps, which Friedrich has brought as a gift, Hans tells them of where Wilhelm will hide.

"I have a cellar. It's not deep, you'll have to stoop." He nods at Wilhelm. "And I doubt anyone knows it's there. The entrance is in a cupboard through a trapdoor, and I keep the trapdoor hidden by piling up rubbish on top of it. From outside the house no one would know it was there. You know you'll be sharing it?"

"Yes," says Wilhelm.

He's abrupt, rude-sounding, thinks Friedrich, and rushes in to fill the silence. "We're so grateful to you, aren't we Wilhelm?"

A grunt. Friedrich could shake him, but Hans only laughs.

"Leave him be," he says, "he's tired and cross. I've put another mattress down there, and hung up a curtain to give the girls some privacy. When you've finished your drink, I'll show you."

Hans takes them out into the hall. There's a wide staircase sweeping up to the floor above and under the stairs, a cupboard. Hans pulls the door open. As he said, it's full of rubbish, cardboard boxes, old newspapers, bundles of clothes and shoes. He pulls them out and reveals the trapdoor. When he lifts it up, he presses a switch just inside, and a dim light rises from the cellar. There's a fixed ladder which Hans starts to climb down, followed by Friedrich and Wilhelm. There's only half a dozen steps to the bottom, and none of them can stand upright. Hans beckons them on. "It's better through here," and they move into the main part of the cellar. It's a room about four metres square with a concrete floor and, just as Hans had said, a curtain hanging down to separate part of the room. In the part of the room that was to be Wilhelm's was a mattress with some blankets and a pillow. Nothing else.

From the other side of the curtain, a young girl's face appears, pale and sleepy.

"Go back to sleep, Hannah," says Hans. "It's your new friend, like I told you."

The girl smiles at them and vanishes behind the curtain. She's very young, thinks Friedrich with a pang, about the age Helga was when she died. "What age is she?" he asks.

"Ten, and her sister's eleven. They're very quiet. Too quiet, I fear."

"What do they do all day?"

"I teach them," says Hans. "Maybe you can teach them too."

Wilhelm says nothing, dumps his bundle on the floor and lies down on the mattress. It's a signal to his father to go. Friedrich touches him on the shoulder, but he shrugs him off. "I'll be seeing you," he says.

The road home is long and weary. Friedrich wonders if he'll ever see his son smile again. When he reaches his home, he opens the door gently so as not to disturb his wife and creeps upstairs. He undresses quickly and gets into bed beside her, relishing the warmth coming from her body. She shifts slightly to make room for him, and he spoons into her. It's so comfortable he thinks he could lie like this for ever.

24

Jan struggles to keep up with Marek whose long legs set a brisk pace. They've been walking for two days, mostly in silence. Marek doesn't want to speak, and Jan is scared to. Since they buried Zygmund, their mood has been low; Marek blames himself for Zygmund's death, but Jan thinks it's his fault. If only they'd never stopped by that train. They are also hungry. For the most part, food has been scarce, though they managed to get a good meal last night in the house of a comrade. The food was given willingly enough, and a bed for the night too, but Jan felt that the woman was pleased to see them go. Her smile when they said they were leaving was much broader than that when she had to welcome them into her small cottage. Who could blame her, though; she had three small children to protect. Jan didn't think arguments about the greater good would have much impact on her. She drew her children close to her while she watched her husband talk to Marek. From the look on her face it was clear she feared him joining the partisans; it was one thing to help them, but to leave your family is something else. Jan knows that Marek, like many of the partisans, has no close family. Zygmund had told him he had a fancy for a Jewish girl, but she had disappeared into a ghetto in Lodz. Soon after that he had joined the partisans, and all his energy went into becoming a leader.

The countryside is different here. More open, fewer trees. This worries Jan, there's nowhere to hide. But they have seen little activity on the two days they've been walking. An old man with a cart and horse earlier today, that was all. They'd hitched a lift with him for a few kilometres, relishing the chance to rest their legs. Just before he let them off Marek had spoken to him softly for several minutes. They seemed to be bargaining. Jan heard a sum of money being mentioned, but he was too tired to try to hear what was said. If it were important, Marek would tell him.

It is several hours since they left the cart, several hours since they last ate. Jan's stomach is gurgling like water swirling down a plughole. Sometimes it's worse getting a good meal, for it reminds you of what you're missing. He hurries behind Marek whose stride has lengthened; he seems to have endless energy.

"Where are we? Do you know?" Jan is worried that they've lost the way. They must be many kilometres away from the rest of the group.

"I know where we are, don't you worry," Marek smiles at him. He reaches into his jacket and pulls out some bread, breaking off a piece to give to Jan. Jan tries to eat it slowly, but he's so hungry it disappears in a few seconds.

"That was foolish, Jan," says Marek. "You don't know when you'll next have something to eat."

"I know, I'm sorry." Jan digs his nails into the palm of his hand.

"Never mind. Here, have some more," Marek hands him the rest of the loaf. This time Jan takes a small piece and chews it slowly before putting away the rest.

"Good boy, you're learning."

* * *

The sun set half an hour ago yet there's no sign of them stopping anywhere. Jan's so tired he could cry, but he forces himself to keep moving; he doesn't want to be a burden to Marek. There are few houses around; it is a desolate part of the country. Field after field, some of them with tired-looking crops. The farmhouses are shabby. Every time they get near one they have to be very quiet in case a dog hears them and starts barking. Finally, as the moon rises, Marek stops and looks around. A hundred metres to the east, there is a farm building. He points it out to Jan. "We'll sleep there. I had hoped we'd manage more tonight for we're not far from where I want to go, but I can see you're exhausted."

"No, I'm not," says Jan, feeling his eyelids droop as he says this.

"Yes, you are," Marek gives him a friendly push towards the barn. It stinks inside, but Jan doesn't care. He finds some hay and lies down on it. Not even his empty stomach can stop him falling asleep.

Jan wakes to bright sunshine. Marek is nowhere to be seen. In that instant he goes to pieces: Marek has disappeared, leaving him God knows where. The soldiers must have captured him; they've killed him, and any minute now they'll storm the barn and bludgeon Jan to death. He hears footsteps and sits petrified, waiting to be found. A cheery whistle, he recognizes it as Marek's. Thank God, he's safe. Jan jumps up to welcome him.

"Were you worried?"

"No," says Jan.

Marek opens his hands to show Jan two eggs. "You can eat it raw," he says, giving one to Jan, "or you can keep it until later when maybe, just maybe, we'll find someone to cook it for you."

Jan looks at it, he's so hungry he wants to eat it immediately, but the thought of a cooked egg is enticing. He hands it back. "I'll keep it for later. What are we going to do now?"

"We're going to meet someone, an old friend of mine who I hope will be able to help us."

"Where, when?..." The questions bubble out of Jan, but Marek won't tell him any more.

"We have to go now, before people start moving around," he says, pushing Jan towards the open air. "Hurry up."

"This is Anatole," Marek introduces the tall young man in front of him. Jan shakes his outstretched hand. "I'm Jan," he says.

"Anatole once lived in the town near where your sister is."

It's hard to take it all in, to understand what is happening. Marek's words stream out, too fast for Jan to comprehend: the border, Germany only a few kilometres away, his sister within reach, only two more days' walk. Anatole brings out a map, explains it to Jan. "You are here, see. And here," he points to a spot a few centimetres away, "is the town where I used to live." Jan looks at the piece of paper, wishing he'd paid more attention in geography lessons in school. He looks round at Marek. "I don't understand."

Marek sits down and takes out a cigarette. "You have to go and find your sister. This is your chance."

"But why now?"

"You're too young to do this work, and you want to find... what is her name?"

"Lena," says Jan. In a rush he says, "Will you come with me?"

"I wish I could, but I'm needed here. Anatole will take you across the border. He's used to going across, and he'll get you there safely. Or as safe as you can be these days. But after that you're on your own."

Jan has a thousand questions; they tumble out of his mouth. Marek laughs at his haste. "Slow down, little one. Save your breath. Come on, let's cook those eggs."

They go through to Anatole's kitchen where he produces a bowl, some more eggs and some ham. He takes Marek's two eggs, cracks them into the bowl along with some others and adds salt and pepper before whisking them. Meanwhile, Marek is melting butter in a frying pan. He takes the bowl from Anatole and lets the eggs slide into the pan while Anatole tears up the ham and adds it to the omelette. A minute later it's ready, and the three of them sit down at the table to eat. Anatole produces some bread, apologizing that it isn't fresh, but Jan doesn't care. He's eating his omelette – it's just as he likes it, soft and runny inside – thinking that not even his mother could produce something so perfect.

Once they've eaten, Marek tells Jan to clear up the dishes. Jan does so slowly. He feels that something is coming to an end, that very soon, Marek will tell him to go, and he'll be alone. Tears prick his eyes as he wipes the dishes and puts them away. He's terrified of being on his own, thinks about asking to stay with the partisans, but in his heart he knows this is too good an opportunity to miss. When will he get a similar chance? It could be years before he's so near her again, and by then he'll have changed beyond recognition, and maybe she won't recognize him. His hearts stands still at this thought; he has no choice. In two days' time he could be with Lena once more. He goes back through to the other room to tell Marek of his decision.

The plans are made. Jan discovers that the man who gave them the lift has agreed to lend him his cart and horse. "It's costing a lot of money," says Marek, "but we'll manage."

Jan remembers the coins he stole from the fountain. "I have money," he says.

Marek raises an eyebrow. "Do you?"

Jan runs to his bundle and takes out the money. He spreads it out in front of Marek. "Take it," he says.

Marek lifts up one of the coins, examines it and smiles. "We can't use this in Poland. No, Jan, you keep it. You'll need it when you're on your own in Germany."

Jan's disappointed. He wants to help Marek, feels shame that he is costing him money. Then he remembers. He feels in his pocket; it's still there, down at the bottom. He pulls out Zygmund's ring and gives it to Marek.

"What's this?"

"It was beside Zygmund's body. It must have fallen out of his pocket when he fell."

Marek hands it back to him. "Keep it… to remember Zygmund."

"No, you have it. You can sell it, use it to buy supplies."

"What would Zygmund want you to do?" asks Marek.

Jan considers the question. He wants Marek to have the ring, doesn't want the partisans to go short because Marek has paid for his transport to Germany, so he has to be persuasive. Got it. "I think Zygmund would want you to have it." He pauses and smiles. "For the greater good."

Marek laughs and takes it from him. "All right. If you're sure."

The plan is simple. Marek will go back to the old man's village and pick up the cart and horse. He has told the man he wants it to carry furniture from one house to another, for a friend who is moving. The man wasn't keen, but the money offered was good, and he agreed, but on condition that Marek gave him his ration book as security as he was worried he would never see his property again. Anatole will drive the cart and horse across the border with Jan hidden under vegetables. He is used to crossing the border, but he does not usually have transport.

Jan can hardly concentrate as they talk about the plan and everything that has to be done. He has such mixed feelings about it all. It's been hard living with the partisans, some of the men were rough, but he's fond of Marek, looks up to him like an older brother, and he knows he'll miss him greatly. He's scared too of what's ahead. Anatole has agreed to drive him some distance into Germany, but they will only have the cart for two days, and so he cannot go all the way. He brings out another map; It is very detailed, more so than the one Jan has already seen, and he spends some time teaching Jan how to read it.

"This here," he points to a green patch. "This is open countryside, and where you see this symbol" – he shows Jan what looks like a rough drawing of a tree – "this shows that there's woods. You can take cover there."

Jan studies the map. It's all very hard to follow, some lines are paths, other thicker ones are roads, those that have lines through them are railways, a cross is a church, if it has a circle underneath it means there is a steeple. He'll never remember it all.

"Do you remember the name of the farm?" asks Marek.

For a frightening moment Jan's mind goes blank. He's forgotten. This is terrible; he'll never find Lena if he doesn't know the name of the farm. Marek must have noticed the puzzled look on his face, for he speaks to him softly. "It's all right, it will come to you."

And it does. "Grunfeld," he stutters. "That's what it's called."

Anatole examines the map, he stabs his finger on a spot near the middle of the page. "Got it!"

Jan looks over his shoulder at the map, and there it is, Grunfeld farm. He takes a deep breath. In a few days' time he could be with his sister once more.

* * *

The day arrives. Early in the morning Marek sets off to get the cart, and Jan gathers together his small bundle of belongings. He has very little: the clothes he is wearing, a spare pair of pants, trousers and a shirt. Anatole has given him a jumper. It's too big, and it's been made from scratchy wool, but it will keep him warm at night. There is also the money, enough to keep buy some basic provisions for him and Anatole when they reach Germany, and there will be some left over for when he finds Lena.

He and Anatole sit in the autumn sunshine and wait for Marek. Jan is sleepy and closes his eyes. He allows himself to dream of the days ahead. First of all a day's drive in the cart and horse; followed by a day's walk to the farm. He tries to picture Lena's face when she spots him, how happy she'll be to see her big brother, she'll jump into his arms, and he'll hug her tight, but, no matter what, he cannot remember her face. In horror he opens his eyes – what is he going to do?

Anatole senses his agitation. "Is something wrong?"

"I can't see her face. Lena. I don't know what she looks like. It's over a year since I saw her. How will I recognize her?"

"What age is she?"

"Nearly four, no, what am I talking about? She'll be six now."

"So she'll be about this high," Anatole holds his hand up to Jan's chest. "And what colour hair does she have?"

"Blonde, curly."

"Well, it might be a little darker now."

"Eyes?"

"Blue," says Jan. "Like cornflowers, my father used to say."

"See, you do remember," Anatole drinks his coffee. "It will be fine, Jan. You'll see."

Jan closes his eyes once more; he hopes Anatole is right.

Marek has arrived. They start to get the vegetables ready. Sacks of potatoes mostly, with some carrots and a few worm-eaten onions. Jan will also be in a sack and will be placed near the front of the cart with the vegetables carefully placed on top of him. Marek reassures him it's only until they're across the border. The border guards are likely to open a sack or two, but from Anatole's observations at the border, it's only ones from the top or round the sides that they pick.

"Once you're safely in Germany, you can get out and ride up in front with Anatole. You'll be hiding for two hours, perhaps three, then Anatole will let you out."

"But is it safe?"

"Nothing's safe these days, Jan, but we'll take the chance."

Jan looks at the sack they've made for him. It stinks of turnips, but he has no choice. He steps inside it and waits for the two men to help him up onto the cart. They place him carefully, making sure he has room to breathe.

"Good luck, Jan," says Marek.

Jan wants to cry, but he mustn't. He manages a squeaky *thank you*, and pulls the sack over his head as they build up his hiding place around him.

* * *

Jan has had many uncomfortable journeys: the truck from his village, the train into Poland, the rubbish lorry from the children's home. None of them were as bad as this. The road is uneven, and he is tossed from side to side as the horse canters along. Potatoes and turnips tumble over him; he's sure he'll be covered in bruises. He'd hoped to sleep, but there's no chance of that. His back and legs ache from lying so still.

The horse slows down, and Anatole shouts, "Ready to go." This is a signal that they are almost at the border, and he has to keep very still. This won't be a problem. He's so stiff and uncomfortable that he thinks he'll be lucky ever to move again. But he gets himself ready anyway. His breath is uneven and loud; his nerves have taken over. He breathes slower to try to control himself. They stop. All around there is the bustle of a border crossing, voices, the sound of cars and trucks, the smell of petrol. Footsteps approach the cart. This is it.

"*Was haben Sie hier?*"

"*Kartoffeln*," says Anatole. Potatoes.

"Show me."

Anatole jumps down from the cart. Jan holds his breath. The weight on his back is lessened as a sack is taken from the pile and opened. He feels exposed. A pause as the contents are checked.

"These are carrots."

"I… Yes. It's mainly potatoes though."

Carrots, potatoes, thinks Jan. What's the difference, they're both vegetables.

"Wait here a moment," the voice says.

It's unbearable not knowing what's going on. Jan strains to hear, but it's so noisy with traffic that he just has to lie still. Is it his imagination or does Anatole say *it's fine, don't worry*?

More footsteps, a different voice. "Are you taking these vegetables to market?"

"Yes."

"*Alles gut*. You can go," says the voice.

As easy as that. Too easy. Jan's still too scared to breathe. But no, they're off, the horse trotting briskly along a road that is better than what they've left behind in Poland. It's not nearly as rough. Jan allows himself to drift off. He hadn't thought he would sleep, but he must have because Anatole is shaking him awake.

"You can come up front with me now," he says.

"Is it safe?"

"How often do I have to tell you? Nothing is safe, but it will be more comfortable."

Jan struggles out of the sack. His limbs are as rigid as those of an old man. He remembers how his grandfather used to complain just before he died about pains in his joints. He's got cramp too. When he jumps down from the cart he flexes his calf muscles to try to ease the pain. Within a few minutes he's all right, but he wants to walk for a while.

"Can I walk beside you, just for the next few minutes?" he says.

Anatole nods and goes into his pocket. He hands Jan an apple. Jan eats it as they go along. The road is empty. Jan studies the countryside.

"It looks just like Poland. Are you sure we're in Germany?"

Anatole laughs. "I'm sure. Did you think the countryside would change at the border?"

Immediately Jan realizes how foolish he's been. He finishes his apple in silence, then asks to join Anatole on the cart. Anatole helps him up.

"What now?"

"It's about an hour to the next village, and there's a market there. I want to try to sell the vegetables there. Once we've done that, I'll take you as far as I can. And then, well, you're on your own."

Not long then. Jan is terrified. His mouth is dry, and he can only think of the problems ahead. He bursts out, "Do you think I'm stupid?"

Anatole considers the question. "No," he says at last, "not stupid."

"But?"

"Perhaps a little foolhardy."

"Why did Marek let me go?" As he says this, Jan wishes Marek were here so he could ask him himself.

"He blames himself for the boy's death. He thinks that he asked the two of you to do too much. You know, other groups chase boys away. They find them a burden, always following them around, eating food that the men need. But Marek took you and Zygmund in, gave you work to do."

Was that a bad thing? Jan isn't sure. He falls silent. Anatole continues.

"Marek thinks he should have sent you away at the beginning."

"But he protected us, gave us shelter."

"I know, but then because of what he asked you to do, Zygmund died."

It's too complicated for Jan to follow. Most likely, Zygmund would have died if Marek hadn't taken him in. He'd been homeless, a Jew, his family dead. Jan doesn't really understand why Marek blames himself. He gives up and concentrates on watching the road.

The village is a bit like his in Czechoslovakia, bigger and noisier, but the people look similar. When he whispers this to Anatole, he laughs and says, "What did you expect? Demons?"

Jan doesn't know what he expected. Not ordinary people like this, though. Old women in shabby dresses, scarves over their heads; old men with faces browned by the sun, wrinkled like apples left at the bottom of the barrel. He stands by Anatole at the cart as Anatole bargains to get the best price for his vegetables. It's a struggle to understand the strange sounds around him. One old woman comes up to him and pinches his cheek while gabbling something at him. He looks at Anatole for help. Anatole shakes his head in warning, then speaks to the woman. She looks down at him and tuts in sorrow. She ruffles his hair before waddling away.

"What did you say to her?"

"Told her you were deaf and dumb." Anatole ducks to avoid Jan's indignant punch.

When the vegetables are gone, they buy some bread and ham for lunch and eat it with some tomatoes they bartered at the market. It is the best meal he has eaten for months. It's so long since Jan has tasted fresh bread he is overwhelmed. Anatole allows him to eat his fill, then gets up from where they are sitting.

"We must be on our way," he says. "I have to get back to the border tonight."

Jan gets up, brushing crumbs from his lap as he does so. A sparrow darts in near his feet and pinches a crumb, flying away as soon as he moves. He's excited to be moving, but terrified too. Listening to the people in the market has reminded him of how poor his German is, far from fluent. He wonders what would happen if he were captured, whether he'd be sent back to a children's home or to a concentration camp like Pawel. He dismisses the thought. It won't do to be so pessimistic. Everything will be fine. It has to be.

The rest of the journey flies past. Anatole is lost in thought, and Jan doesn't want to disturb him with silly chatter. Instead he watches the countryside pass, takes out the map and tries to follow where they are. It's hard to do this, though, when the cart is bouncing around on the uneven road. When they stop to let the horse drink he asks Anatole to show him where they are.

Anatole studies the map. He finds the village where they went to the market and points it out to Jan, then the road, and finally the farmhouse where Lena is. "We're here, I think," he indicates a spot about halfway between the village and the farm.

"How do you know?"

"Look at this green patch with trees on it, that's a forest and we passed by it a little while ago, do you remember?"

"Yes," says Jan, "but there's a green patch there too." He jabs at the map, hoping he's right as it's so much closer to where he wants to be.

"Yes, but look at the road."

Puzzled, Jan looks down at the track beneath him.

"No, not the real road, the one on the map. Look at it, and you'll see that your green patch is on the wrong side of the road. It's on the left, and the one we passed was on our right."

Jan nods. Dammit, Anatole's right. He still has some way to go.

"Put the map away," says Anatole. "It's another two hours before I have to leave you."

Jan wakes with a start. He must have fallen asleep. Amazing, considering the rough ride. They've stopped on the outskirts of a village. Anatole gazes at him.

"Will you be all right?"

Jan nods. He doesn't trust himself to speak. Now that the time has come for him to leave Anatole, he's terrified. Tears prick at the back of his eyes, and he blinks to stop them spilling over.

"Sure?"

Jan manages a strangulated *yes*, and Anatole seems to accept this. He reaches into the cart to get Jan's bundle and hands it to him. They look at the map together one final time, Anatole going over the route until he's sure Jan knows where he's going.

Jan jumps down from the cart and holds his hand out to Anatole. "Thank you," he says. "Thank you for bringing me here." Before Anatole can answer, he's off down the road, as briskly as he can, praying that Anatole didn't spot his tears and can't see how his legs are trembling.

25

Friedrich looks at his watch. The train is due in ten minutes, and on it are the two boys from Berlin. He regrets taking Wilhelm so quickly to his old teacher, and thinks now that he was too rash, for it has taken over a month for the boys to actually come. Gisela sees Wilhelm regularly twice a week; the plan for her to work as Herr Knoller's housekeeper has worked well, but it's harder for Friedrich to see him. He has so much work on the farm to do, and it is so far into town, he has only managed to see him once, the day before yesterday. Friedrich hasn't said so to Gisela, but he was shocked by Wilhelm's appearance. Before he went to Hans's house he was thin, but now, now he's skeletal, his eyes sunken, his jawline sharp-edged. And the look in his eyes: so dark and troubled. It frightened Friedrich. He wanted to ask Hans about him, but was too shy, too in awe of the man who had taught not only Wilhelm but Friedrich too. Instead he muttered his thanks and left, like a thief, furtively, eyes darting everywhere to see if he'd been spotted. He regrets it now, of course. What harm could it have done to ask, *how do you find my son? Do you too see him fading away?* Now it could be another four weeks before he sees him again, and God knows what state he'll be in by then. He closes his eyes in despair.

The screech of the train's brakes brings him round. He moistens his lips. All week he's been dreading this;

it's unbearable to have to put up two Hitler Youth in his home. In vain, Gisela has tried to remind him that it's compulsory for all boys between the ages of twelve and sixteen to be members. He doesn't want to know, walked out of the room when she dared to suggest that Helga, had she been spared, would have had to join the *Jungmädelbund*, the girls' equivalent of the Hitler Youth. In the time since Wilhelm came home, Friedrich has changed from a passive supporter of Hitler to hating the man who has destroyed his family and that of so many others.

Doors open, and Friedrich braces himself. Very few people alight; he counts them, fourteen. He scans them all, looking for the familiar light brown uniform. Nothing. Everyone is too old or too young. He runs along the platform, looking inside each carriage in case they've fallen asleep, missed their stop. God knows what the penalty is for losing two Hitler Youth, but he doesn't want to find out, and he doesn't want the authorities to turn their attention to his family once more. But there aren't any boys of the right age. None. The train starts to move off leaving Friedrich standing alone on the platform, the passengers have all gone on their way.

Friedrich takes the letter out of his pocket and reads it through again. Maybe he's got the date or the time wrong. No, it's there in black and white: *Johann Fischer and Hans Dieter will arrive on the fourteenth of September on the twelve forty-five train from Berlin.* He checks his watch, almost one o'clock, and stops one of the guards. "Please, what date is it?"

"Fourteenth of September, sir." The guard gives him a funny look before continuing to sweep the platform.

Right time, right date. What's going on? Maybe they got an earlier train, but he isn't sure there is one. He chases after the guard. "Excuse me, is there another train from Berlin today?"

"The only other train is the overnight train. It was a bit late; due at seven, but didn't arrive until seven fourteen."

"Did you see any boys on it, any Hitler Youth? I'm meant to meet them here."

The guard shakes his head. "Sorry, sir, I'm not sure." He frowns, thinks a bit. "There might have been one. No, I can't remember, sorry."

Damn. He doesn't know what to do. There might have been one on the early train, on the other hand there might not. And there isn't another train today. Nothing for it, he'll have to go home and hope they're there. If not, he'll have to come back tomorrow.

Gisela is in the kitchen when he gets back. She looks round as he opens the door.

"Well, where are they?"

Friedrich tells her what happened. She puts down her rolling pin. "What are we going to do?"

"I don't know. I suppose I'll have to go back again tomorrow. It's a damn waste of time. I really hoped they'd been on the earlier train and somehow found their way here. There's so much to do just now. I can't spare the time, there's a fence to be mended, hay to be put in the barn. And they're supposed to be a help to us. Bloody hindrance, more like."

"I suppose I could go," says Gisela.

"Mmm. Well, we'll see what tomorrow brings. Is there anything to eat? I'm ravenous."

Gisela serves him with some soup. He eats it quickly, then gets up from the table. "I'm off to try to get some hay into the barn. I'll have to salvage something from this wreck of a day."

Friedrich stands outside the house and wonders what to do first. He rubs his forehead. Barn, he'll go there first. He sets off up the hill.

The sun is blinding. Friedrich squints up at the barn. Is that a figure there? He looks again, yes, there's definitely someone there. Someone slipping inside. Looks like a child. Could it be his missing Hitler Youth? He quickens his step and trips over a stone. When he looks up there is no one there. Perhaps he's imagining things. Wishful thinking, hoping the boys have appeared, for he doesn't know what to do now that he's met the train, and they weren't there. Someone shouts, and he looks round. It's Gisela running hand in hand with Helena. They are hurrying to catch up with him, Helena's golden hair glinting in the sun.

"What is it? Have they arrived?"

"No, not yet. I was just wondering Friedrich, whether I should go and see... you know." She stops there. Neither of them mention Wilhelm by name. Helena has stopped asking for him now, but they can't take any chances.

"Why do you want to see him? You saw him two days ago, and you're due to go the day after tomorrow."

"I know, it's... I don't know, I've got a bad feeling about him."

Friedrich frowns. He hates talk like this. Gisela had a bad feeling the day Helga died, and the day the call-up papers came for Wilhelm. He knows she sets store by it, but he thinks it's superstitious nonsense and won't encourage it.

"You've missed the bus," he says.

"I'll walk. You could watch Helena."

"No," he's decisive. "I won't have it. You're tired enough as it is. Go back home and rest."

"Please." She holds out Helena to him.

He turns away from her and walks on up the hill, leaving her behind. He counts to thirty before looking back. She's set off back towards the farmhouse, her shoulders drooping.

There's a pile of hay beside the barn waiting to be put inside. It's enormous, the sight of it makes him yawn. Damn those boys; in spite of what he said to Gisela about being able to manage, he could do with some help. Friedrich looks inside the barn to try to work out where it should all go. There's a hayloft up above, but he would need help to get the hay up there. He looks up at it, trying to imagine how he could do it alone when he sees movement.

"Who's there?" he shouts.

Not a sound. He listens carefully. It's most likely rats. He stamps his foot, that usually gets them scurrying off. Nothing. That's suspicious. He looks around for a weapon, picks up a pitchfork and starts up the ladder to the hayloft.

There's a small pile of hay left over from last year. He stands in front of it. "I know you're in there. I've got a fork, and I'm going to start prodding if you don't come out." He waits, but nothing happens. Strange, he's sure he saw something. He doesn't want to plunge his fork into the hay, but he's made the threat so he makes a half-hearted stab, then another.

"Ow." The cry of pain makes him step back, he almost misses his footing and falls over the edge of the hayloft. A face appears in the hay. A white, terrified face. The rest of the body appears, a boy of about twelve. One of the Hitler Youth. He knew he'd seen someone when he was coming up the hill. The boy holds his hands up in a gesture of surrender.

"Come out of there you idiot." He grabs the boy by the ear and pulls him out of the hay. "Is your friend there too?"

The boy doesn't answer. Friedrich shouts at him, enraged by his long wait at the station, and the boy's unresponsiveness. He gestures with the pitchfork. "Do I have to use this? Where's your friend?"

A shrug. "Only me."

"Right," says Friedrich, "follow me." He goes down the ladder followed by the boy. At the bottom he waits for him. "What's your name?"

A mumble, it could be anything, but it sounds like Johann. The boy is clearly terrified. Friedrich doesn't think he's ever seen anyone quite so scared. He takes pity on him. "Right, Johann. Let's get you to the farmhouse. Is that all you have with you?" He nods at what Johann is carrying.

The boy nods, holds on to his belongings more tightly.

They walk back to the farmhouse. Friedrich keeps a tight grip on him for he looks like a runner. Now that he's found one of the missing Hitler Youth he's not going to let him go. He's a peculiar specimen, though.

Friedrich thinks of the posters of arrogant young men and women that advertise the *Hitlerjugend* and the *Jungmädelbund*. They show spotlessly clean youth with well-brushed hair, shiny cheeks and gleaming teeth. This is a poor-looking child, filthy with torn clothes and the dirtiest face Friedrich has ever seen. Things must be bad in the city for a mother to send her child away looking like this.

"Gisela, heat water for a bath. I've found one of them."

Gisela comes running to the door. She looks at Johann and shakes her head. "Terrible," she says, "just terrible. Look at the state of him." She looks at the boy and tries to catch his eye, but he is staring behind her. She turns round to see what he is looking at, but there is only Helena, playing with her doll in the corner.

26

Jan can't stop trembling. He's warm now after the bath he's been given, but it's all too much for him: the long walk to find the farm, hiding in the barn only to be caught by a madman waving a pitchfork. He honestly thought he was going to die when it was plunged into where he was hiding, and his shin hurts like hell where it grazed him. The madman seemed to think he is someone else. He didn't understand everything that was said, but the man is obviously a raving Nazi; he kept going on about *Hitlerjugend*. Jan is almost sure that means "young Hitler", and he was terrified at the thought of being in the same house as someone who talks so much about Hitler.

But all that was forgotten when he saw Lena; he didn't know it was her at first; she's grown so much, and her hair is longer, but then he saw it. The dress the doll was wearing, made from cotton with a pattern of tiny pink roses. It was the same pattern as Lena's nightdress, the one she'd been wearing on that awful night. He had stared and stared at her, willing her to turn round, but when she did, there was no recognition in her eyes. She gave him a slight smile, the sort of smile you give to someone you're meeting for the first time.

The woman is less scary than the man, but neither of them are friendly. Their faces are stern. They seem to be angry that he is there, and he doesn't know why.

He doesn't think they're going to hand him over to the police, they mentioned something about "*arbeit*" – he knows this means work. He thinks they're going to make him work. Not that he cares, he's just glad to have found Lena, can't believe his luck.

"*Johann, hast du gegessen?*"

She's speaking to him. She's asked him whether he's eaten. That's easy enough to answer: "*Nein.*"

A bowl of soup is put in front of him. He's ravenous, shovels a spoonful into his mouth and yelps with pain. He waits for it to cool before trying it again.

After he's eaten he's shown to a room, which has one bed and one mattress in it. Both have been made up. He chooses the bed and climbs in. He's planning to try to find where Lena is sleeping and to talk to her. His heart beats faster at the thought of speaking to her, telling her who he is, how happy she'll be. I'll give it half an hour after the old people have gone to bed, then I'll go and find her, he thinks. He closes his eyes to imagine what he will say to her, how he will tell her they'll run away together to find their mother and Maria too, of course. With a smile, he pictures her cuddling into him. His smile fades, he can't keep these images going; there are other, nagging thoughts in his mind: how small she is, how will she manage to walk any distance, how will they get food. He makes a huge effort and pushes them all away. Something will come up; he knows it will. Jan doesn't feel sleep steal up on him; not until he is awoken in the morning by Gisela shaking his shoulder, does he realize he's missed a chance of seeing Lena on her own.

* * *

"Her name is Helena, not Lena," says Gisela for the fifth time. Jan ignores her; he wants to shout *no it's not, you stupid woman*, but of course he can't. He's not managed to speak to Lena alone in the two days he's been here. During the day the man takes him away with him to work on the farm, hard work that tires him out. When he gets back at night, the woman is always hanging around Lena, never more than a few feet away. He despairs of ever being alone with Lena.

Jan's managed to piece together that the couple were expecting two boys from Berlin, sent to help with the harvest. Somehow they think he's one of them. And they think he's stupid. Well that suits him fine. He'll have to make his move on Lena soon, though, because the real boys could turn up at any moment and blow his cover. Amazingly they haven't asked to see any papers, nothing at all. Jan doesn't understand why, but his presence seems to make them very edgy.

Gisela has gone back to making bread. Jan continues to try to engage Lena, to get her to recognize him. "Lena," he whispers, "it's me, Jan." He reverts to speaking Czech. The words lie oddly on his tongue. She doesn't even look at him. He tries again, this time in German. "Helena, *es ist mich*, Jan." This time she does gaze at him and smile, and with a pang he realizes that she no longer speaks or understands Czech. For a moment he wonders if he's made a mistake, perhaps this is not his sister, but no. No one could mistake those huge blue eyes. He smiles back at her.

"Johann, Friedrich will be waiting for you. Run along now." Gisela frowns at him.

He picks himself up from the floor and dusts down his trousers. Moving slowly he goes to the door. Gisela hits him with her rolling pin. "Get a move on, you stupid boy." He looks at her. She seems really to dislike him, and he doesn't know why, for she's clearly very fond of Lena. Lena is always being picked up and cuddled, given extra bits of food, while he is kept hungry. Before closing the door behind him, he turns back to look at them. Gisela is beside Lena, showing her how to knead some dough. The scene reminds him of his home, when his mother used to show Maria how to cook, and he has a wave of longing to feel his mother's arms round him, hear her voice, even if it were only to shout at him. Quietly he shuts the door and sets off up the hill to the barn.

Friedrich is nowhere to be seen when he gets there. Jan wanders round the outside of the barn gazing out across the fields. There is no one in sight. For a moment he wonders about going back to the farmhouse, but the thought of Gisela's rolling pin is not attractive. Anyway this was where he was told to come, so he'd better stay put. It's getting chilly. Summer has turned to autumn, and he is glad of the jumper that Anatole gave him. Even so, it's too cold to stay outside, so he goes into the barn. There's hay all over the floor. It's a right mess. Maybe he could get into favour with Friedrich if he cleared it up a little. Jan looks round to see if there's a broom, but the only piece of equipment to be seen is a pitchfork, the one that gave him the nasty graze on his shin the other day. It's not ideal, but he decides to try it anyway. He picks it up and starts to drag it across the hay on the barn floor, drawing the hay together.

The damn boy has disappeared. Friedrich has been waiting beside the fence that is to be mended for over half an hour. The wind is chill, bites into him, and he shivers. Gisela has been nagging him all day; she went to see Wilhelm yesterday, but, far from easing her mind, it's made her worse. She wants to bring him back, says the Hitler Youth boy is clearly stupid and wouldn't notice anything. She wants him close by to keep an eye on him, and if that's not possible she's going to visit him more often. But he has all this work to do and Wilhelm is safe with Hans. He's thought of a possibility, though. Maybe Johann could look after Helena, to let Gisela go into town. He'll put it to her tonight and with luck that will appease her. Johann seems very fond of Helena, and she likes him. She's friendlier towards him than anyone else apart from him and his wife. But then he's still a child. Maybe all those do-gooders were right; maybe they should send her to kindergarten. He'll talk to Gisela about it, that would give her more free time too. Where is that bloody boy? He can't hang about here all day, he'll need to find him. Friedrich sets off towards the house.

"I sent him to the barn, isn't that what you wanted?"

Friedrich rolls his eyes as he leaves the house. His wife is not her usual self. She's tired-looking, depressed. Even Helena's presence is not enough to liven her up. He plods up the hill; each step is painful, he's so tired. As he reaches the top he sees that Johann is in the barn. What the hell is he doing? He narrows his eyes to try to focus better. Shit, he's dragging the hay across the barn floor; he could discover the hidey-hole at any moment. As a Hitler Youth, he'll be encouraged to spy on everyone, report on anyone behaving in a suspicious manner. Friedrich knew it was bad news to have to have them here. He quickens his step.

"What the hell do you think you're doing?" Friedrich's roar startles himself as well as the boy. Johann drops the pitchfork and stumbles back onto the floor. Friedrich comes into the barn, sees that Johann has fallen on top of the false floor. If he looks down, he'll see the air holes, and that will make him suspicious. What to do, what to do. He'll need to divert him. Friedrich storms into the barn pointing at the hayloft. Johann follows his gaze. He yanks Johann to his feet, shouting, "Did you see that?"

"S… s… see what?"

"That rat! It was enormous." Friedrich is using his foot to sweep some hay across the trapdoor that leads into the hiding place. Even though no one is hiding there, the mere fact that he has an unexplained hiding place would raise suspicions. And after the rumours about Wilhelm's desertion… well, it wouldn't take much to piece it all together.

Johann is still trying to see the rat. Friedrich risks glancing down to see if anything is visible. It's not. He breathes more easily. "Put that thing away," he says. "I want help with the fence."

Johann's face is sulky. "I was just trying to help."

Friedrich relents, no point in being confrontational. "I know, son. Come with me, and I'll show you what to do."

* * *

It's great sleeping in a bed once more. Jan loves it. He's so comfortable he could stay here for ever, but one thing nags at him: he's thirsty. He doesn't really want to get out of bed, and he's a little worried about Friedrich shouting at him – he seems to shout a lot and for very little reason – but he has to have a drink. The ham they had for supper was salty, and it's parched him. Nothing else for it, he gets up and creeps downstairs. He's almost at the bottom when he hears his name. This is too good an opportunity to miss; he has to hear what's being said. Already he's learnt that the third step from the bottom squeaks, so he misses that out and creeps to the door.

"What's happened to the other boy, do you think?"

"I've no idea. I've asked Johann several times, where's your friend, but all he says is *nur mich*. They must have decided just to send the one."

"He's a strange boy, but seems to like Helena, and she likes him," says Friedrich. "You know he gave me a real fright today."

"What happened?"

"He started clearing the hay away from the floor. He'd uncovered the trapdoor, but I managed to divert him and get him out of there."

"Dear God, if he'd found the hiding place..."

"I know. It would have been a disaster. These Hitler Youth, they're deadly little spies the lot of them."

Jan listens, puzzled, what is this young Hitler? Do they think *he's* like a young Hitler? He doesn't like that. Maybe he's misunderstood. He's trying to understand everything, but it's hard.

"I don't think he saw anything, though."

Ah, so that's it; they think he saw something. What could it be? Something in the barn. Friedrich was so angry when he found him there, all that stuff about a rat. Jan thinks hard… Where was he? What have they said? It comes to him, something about a *Tor*; that means door. No, it's too hard; he doesn't get it.

"Mmm, that's good. Friedrich, I must see Wilhelm tomorrow. I know I only saw him yesterday, but I have such a bad feeling about him. Can you look after Helena?"

"No, Gisela, I can't. I must get that fence fixed. I've lost three sheep in the past week." A pause. "Maybe Johann could watch her."

Jan understands this all right. He holds his breath; this is too good to be true. He wills Gisela to say yes. Please, he prays.

"I don't know," she says.

"Please," whispers Jan from behind the door.

"Well, it's that or nothing,"

A sigh. "He's a bit young, don't you think?"

"Old enough to look after her."

"All right, but I want you to check on him every hour."

Yes! Jan wants to scream with joy. This is it; this is his chance. His thirst has vanished; thrilled, he darts back upstairs. This needs some planning.

27

Wilhelm knows he should be grateful he has such a good hiding place. The two girls are pleasant company. They are bright, intelligent girls who are eager to learn and spend most of the day reading. Hans allows them all to come upstairs in the evening. He feels it is safe enough to do that, and they sit round the fire and discuss philosophy and politics. Hans is a good teacher. He lets them have their say, but he doesn't let them get away with anything. Always there are questions: why do you think that, what evidence do you have for believing this? And yet, Wilhelm is not comfortable. In the girls' brown eyes he sees the reflections of other young women; women who pleaded for their lives as he and other soldiers shoved at them with their rifles, pushing them towards the edge of the pits that were to be their graves. He can't bear it.

It's worse when they discuss the war. For some reason they think he's a hero because he deserted. In vain he protests, *I am no hero, I have done terrible things.* The girls smile at him disbelievingly. They think he is a good German, like Hans. And Hans encourages this, says to the girls, *you see, not all Germans are bad. Remember, not everyone believes in Hitler.* Wilhelm can't stand it. He's made up his mind; he'll confess to his crimes and then go. And he knows exactly where he's going.

* * *

Hans has made them a simple supper of bread and cheese. The bread has come from his mother. Wilhelm can't bear to look at her when she visits. Her eyes are so concerned for him, and he doesn't deserve it. He is not worthy of her love. He can't eat the bread. It congeals into doughy lumps in his mouth, which he is unable to swallow. His stomach has cramped into a tight knot, which rejects all food. Sometimes he can take a little soup, if it's not too thick, but everything else is impossible to eat. He knows that Hans worries about him, but he can't help himself; he won't eat.

As he does every evening, he takes a small piece of bread to appease Hans, but leaves the rest for the girls. They need it more than he does. Hans tries to get him to take more, but he pushes it back towards him. Wilhelm sees Hans struggle to take it. He wants it so badly for he is hungry. Until Wilhelm joined them he had to share his rations with the two girls, but now Gisela brings food twice a week, as much as she can, and they are less hungry than before.

"You need to eat, Wilhelm," says Hans. "Your mother thinks I am stealing your food."

"I have told her I give it to you," says Wilhelm.

"But she wants you to eat it."

"I can't."

Hans takes one of Wilhelm's hands. "Why can't you?"

Wilhelm stares back at him. The old man's eyes are cloudy with age. He must be over seventy now. He was an old man when Wilhelm was at school, and he taught his father too. "Hans," he says, "why do you think I deserted?"

"Because you are a good man," the words come easily to him.

Wilhelm shakes his head. "It's not true."

"You refused to carry out the evil tasks that they asked of you."

"But don't you understand? I didn't immediately refuse. I was in the army for months before I got the chance to escape. I did terrible things. Terrible things."

Hans sighs. "I know. But who am I to judge you? What might I have done, if I had been in your place?"

"I killed children, in a village in Poland; Jewish children, in their mothers' arms. I may have killed their mother for all you know," he nods over at the two girls.

Over in the corner the two girls are listening, their faces pale and pinched. They've never considered this possibility, never for all their philosophical reasoning given any thought to the possibility that Wilhelm might be a murderer. They know he was a soldier, but have believed all that Hans said about him being a good German. Hannah, the younger one, begins to cry. It almost kills Wilhelm to hear her sobs. She's so young, and he knows she looked up to him as a hero. He can't stand having to disillusion her, but neither can he continue to live this lie.

"Tell me about it," says Hans.

"I can't tell you everything. You'd hate me."

"Wilhelm, that's not true."

"I had been in the army for six months when it started. We were sent from village to village. In the first village we killed only men, but in others…"

Hans is kneading his forehead with his knuckles as if he's trying to get rid of images of death. "What happened?"

"The east of Poland was the worst. In every village we were told to look for Jews. When we found them, we killed them, and then buried them in mass graves." He stops speaking; tears are running down his face. "I can't bear to think about it."

The room is silent. Wilhelm senses the revulsion of the others. He cannot look at them. Slowly he rises to his feet. "You see now why I won't eat. How can I, when so many deaths lie on my conscience?" He walks out to the hallway and goes into the cupboard under the stairs. "I'm going to bed," he says to Hans, who has followed him.

"Will you be all right?"

Wilhelm doesn't answer him. He lifts the trapdoor and disappears down into the cellar.

"What do you mean, he's gone?" Gisela shouts at Hans.

"Ssh, someone might hear you."

She sits down at the kitchen table. "Where is he?"

"I don't know. I couldn't stop him."

It is what Gisela has dreaded. She knew something was wrong, felt it in her bones. Friedrich was scornful of her feelings, but she knew that morning, when Helga was knocked down, that all was not well, and she has the same feeling now. "When did he leave?"

"This morning, I think. I'm not sure. Or it could have been last night," admits Hans.

"Last night!"

"Well I don't know for sure when it was. He told us about the terrible things he did, and then went to bed. He was sleeping when the others went down to the cellar. Gone when they awoke. So it could have been any time between midnight and seven this morning." His voice quavers. "I'm so sorry, Gisela. If I thought he was going to disappear…"

She can't stay angry with him; it's not fair. Gisela lets her hand rest on her arm. She's wretched with worry, but it's not his fault. She has to get back to the farm to tell Friedrich, though what he can do is beyond her.

The bus has never seemed so slow. It stops several times to let passengers on and off. Gisela sits near the back, praying that no one she knows will come on for she doesn't want to speak to anyone. The lump in her throat is too huge to let her speak.

"Gisela." Her heart sinks at the sound of her name. She looks up. It is the parish priest. She nods, not trusting herself to speak. He sits down beside her.

"Have you heard the news?"

"No" – a whisper.

"I'm afraid it's not good. Herman, you know, Marguerite Durr's son, he died at the Eastern Front last week."

Gisela turns her face away so he can't see the tears fall down her face. Poor Marguerite, all her efforts to protect her son were in vain. She can't feel angry with her any longer in spite of all the pain she caused her. Beside her the priest prattles on, but his words wash over her, until, at last, it is her stop. She gets up and squeezes past him.

"I'll give her your condolences," says the priest.

It would be better to say nothing, but of course she can't admit that, so she nods instead and hurries off the bus.

She's glad to see the house. The rain that started five minutes ago is getting heavier, and she's soaked through in seconds. She puts the post she picked up from the postbox at the bottom of the track into her bag and starts to run. When she reaches the house, she pushes open the door and shouts out for Friedrich, then Helena. But there is no one there. Friedrich must have gone to mend the fence and taken the boy and Helena with him. She'll have to find him and tell him what has happened. He'll know what to do. First though she must eat, for she's weak with hunger. She puts down her bag on the table, remembering the post as she does so. She takes it out and examines it: three letters for Friedrich, two bills and something official looking. This catches her eye. He won't mind if she opens it. She shouldn't, but she's so anxious, and it could be about the other boy from the Hitler Youth, there's been no word about him. She rips open the envelope and starts to read. It's impossible, they must have got it wrong or she hasn't understood properly. She reads it again, but it's clear – *thank you for your cooperation… have to inform you… boys' parents have decided to keep them in Berlin.*

Gisela can't breathe. She drops the letter, tugs open the top button of her blouse. It can't be true, it can't. All that effort to try to keep Wilhelm safe: entrusting him to someone who only a few weeks ago was almost a stranger; the risky journey that he and Friedrich had to make; the pretence that she was Hans's housekeeper; having to go hungry so that she could give extra rations to Hans's household. All that damned effort, and for what? She'd wanted Wilhelm near her so she could look after him and now he's disappeared to God knows where. Dear God, he could have been safe with her all along. They needn't have gone through any of this. If only the letter had come sooner. But now… now there's a stranger in their midst, calling himself Johann. Who is he, and where is he now? And Helena, where is she? Could he have stolen her away? No, it's not possible; what would a boy like him want with a child so young. Gisela's breath is coming in gasps, her chest is taut. She sits down and tries to calm herself. She'll be no good to anyone in this state, and she has to be strong. Her two children are out there somewhere, and she has to find them. Once she's found them, then she can worry about what to do about the boy.

28

Wilhelm stumbles over the fields towards the farm, but he's not going home. Although he longs to be with his parents he knows that seeing them will weaken his resolve. And he must do what he has to do. It is only right. He's sorry for the pain he will cause his parents, but it's better this way. His legs can barely hold up his body; he's weak from hunger. He's been walking since early this morning, not caring whether he was seen or not, though in fact he has not met anyone.

It starts to rain, gently at first, then harder. It soaks into his thin clothes, chilling him. He thinks of the fire in his mother's kitchen, the smell of bread baking in the oven, the tang of wood smoke in the air. How he yearns to be with his family, but he mustn't give in to this feeling. On and on he staggers, feet sinking into the mud in the fields. Most of the crops have been harvested, leaving the fields bare and empty.

The rain is coming down in torrents now, bouncing off the ground. He can hardly see two metres in front of him, but he carries on with one aim in mind. It can't be far now.

At last, Jan is on his own with Lena. He rushes into her room and grabs some clothes from a drawer, making sure he has some jumpers and a coat. The sky is overcast, and they have a long way to go. He's going to make his way back to the border and try to reach Anatole's house. From there perhaps he'll be able to find Marek. It's not too far, he tells himself, and Marek will help them, he knows he will. Once he has bundled her clothes together he searches for food. Bread and ham, that will be good, and there's cheese too. Lena ignores him as he dashes round the farmhouse. She's playing with her doll, dressing her up in a blue cotton dress that Gisela made.

Jan has gathered everything together; he's ready to go and rushes over to pull her up from the floor. "Come on, Lena, we have to go."

She bursts into tears, frightened by the sudden movement. Jan closes his eyes, wishes for patience. He drops down to her level. "Do you want to play a game?" he says.

Her lip is pouted, and she doesn't answer.

Jan wants to shake her. Friedrich said he'd be back in an hour, and it's already fifteen minutes since he left. Every second is vital. Deep breath and a casual "We could hunt for treasure".

A flicker of interest. "Where?" she says.

"Out in the field, come on, let's put on your shoes."

Lena sits passively while he puts on her shoes. When she's ready, he holds out a hand to her. He mustn't rush her. "Ready to go?"

She takes his hand, and he wants to cry with relief. "Let's go," he says.

It's much colder outside today than it has been for some time. Jan pulls Lena up the hill. He's going past the barn towards the woods, where there's a track that will take them on their way. The main road is in the other direction, and he trusts that when Friedrich discovers they're missing, he'll think they've gone that way. Jan has dropped the cardigan Lena was wearing earlier, on that path, hoping that this will divert them long enough to give him and Lena a good start. They've been walking for five minutes when it starts to rain, very quickly changing from a soft drizzle to a thunderous torrent. He curses. This is disastrous; they'll have to shelter. Still pretending it's a game, he runs with Lena to the barn, praying that it will go off soon.

"We'll sit here for a minute," he says to Lena.

"Is the treasure here?" she asks, shaking the rain from her hair.

"Not here, no. We'll wait until the rain stops, then we'll go on." Jan catches his breath as someone dashes into the barn. Damn! Is it Friedrich? He pulls back into the shadows, taking Lena with him. But it isn't Friedrich, it's someone much younger. The young man scans the barn, and Jan holds his breath; what if he spots him and Lena? But it's so dark he doesn't see them, and fortunately Lena doesn't notice what's going on. What's he doing? He's sweeping the hay aside, and now he's kneeling on the floor, pulling at something. A trapdoor rises, and the man disappears beneath it, closing it behind him. Jan is baffled, then remembers the conversation that Gisela and Friedrich had. This must be what they were talking about.

Wilhelm climbs down into the hidey-hole. He'd forgotten how small it is. Doesn't matter, he won't be here much longer. The blankets, lamp and matches are still there. Good, he wants some light to comfort him. Everything's worse in the dark, more frightening. Wilhelm lights the lamp and shakes out the blankets. He wraps one round him, settles into the corner and gets out his razor from his jacket pocket.

Jan can't help himself. He wants to know what's going on. It's still raining hard, so he might as well take a look and see what's happening. Lena's almost asleep; he'll leave her for a second to check it out. He creeps across to where the young man vanished and examines the ground. There is a trapdoor, and it has holes in it. Jan's heart beats faster. There's light coming through the holes. He kneels down and puts his eye to one of them and squints to see what's going on. It takes him a second to adjust to the change in light. It's a deep hole, a hiding place. The man is down there; he takes up most of the space. He's wrapping a blanket round himself. Jan wishes he had a blanket; it's so cold today. The man settles down, leans against the wall. It looks cosy in there, Jan thinks. He wonders why the man is hiding and hopes he is not an enemy of Gisela and Friedrich, for although they're not very nice to him, they dote on his sister, and he wouldn't want to see any harm to come to them. But it's not his concern, and he really should be on his way; the rain is tailing off. One last look… Jesus! The man has a razor and is holding it to his wrist. Jan looks down at him in horror.

Gisela runs out of the house, but the rain forces her back inside. As she goes to close the door, she sees Friedrich appear. He's drenched through. She pulls him inside.

"Some day, eh?"

"Never mind that. Where's Helena?"

"With the boy."

"There's no one here. And look," she says, thrusting the letter at him, "he's not who he said he was." Her voice rises. "Who is he, Friedrich?"

Friedrich scans the letter, a deep frown on his forehead. "I don't understand."

"Neither do I, and there's more. Wilhelm has disappeared from Hans's house. He walked out earlier today. Hans said he was behaving oddly and was very depressed." Gisela sinks onto a chair and bursts into tears. "We have to get out there and find them. But where do we start?"

"Wilhelm could be anywhere, but the children can't have gone far. You go down towards the main road, and I'll go to the upper fields."

"No, they can't have gone down to the main road. I would have passed them on the way back," says Gisela. "We'll concentrate on the upper fields." She puts on her coat. Rain or no rain she's going out to find them.

Outside the farmhouse, Friedrich spots the red cardigan that Helena was wearing. It is by the side of the path, which leads to the main road. "Are you sure you didn't miss them?"

"Yes, I told you. There's no way I could have missed them. I'll go up to the barn, and you go into the woods. They can't have got far in this rain." Gisela starts to run up to the barn closely followed by her husband.

The mud is treacherous, slowing her down. It's too hard to keep going at speed; she has to stop to catch her breath. I'll get there, she tells herself. Two minutes, and I'll be there. The rain is hammering down, sheets of it.

* * *

Jan scrambles down the steps to the man and crouches beside him. The man is unconscious, his shirt covered in blood. Jan's head is swimming; he can't stand the sight of blood, and there's so much of it here. He's never seen so much since the morning his father died, all those men, lying in front of Horak's barn, drenched in scarlet. Mustn't think of it, concentrate on what's happening now, get the razor off the man. He swallows hard to try to control his nausea and reaches across to move the razor away. As he does so the man stirs; his eyes open and lock onto Jan's. They are pale blue, lifeless. Jan starts to speak, to say something comforting, but the words won't come. Scenes from the past are crowding in on him. He's back at Horak's farm, in the cherry tree, watching men like this one slaughter his father and friends; he's in a forest in Poland listening to a man plead for his life, begging to see his wife and children once more. He can hear Marek chiding him: *They're the enemy. Do you think they'd show any mercy to you?*

Jan hesitates. He can't save this man, how can he? He's a German, a Nazi, a murderer, and he deserves to die. He'll leave him here; it's what Marek would want. He'll climb back up, grab Lena and run, get far away from this hellish place.

But Marek wants more than that; his voice is insistent: *Come on Jan, don't let this opportunity slip by you. You could kill him; see how easy it would be. Grab the razor, slit his throat, there's no fight left in him. Finish him off. Avenge your father's death; it's your duty.* The voice is so clear he looks up expecting to see Marek, but there's no one there.

Jan seizes the razor and looks at the man. He tries to read the expression in the man's eyes. It should be terror, but there's no fear there. Resignation, that's what it is. He wants Jan to kill him. Jan drops the razor. He can't do it. He can't kill a man in cold blood. He closes his eyes in despair. He can't even leave him to bleed to death; he'll have to try to stop it.

"No," the man yells. His eyes are full of the terror Jan expected to see when he grabbed the razor from him, but he's looking past him up to the opening of the hiding place. Jan turns round to see a pitchfork coming towards him. Just in time he moves out of the way. It crashes into the hiding place, grazing his thigh. Jan squints up to see who threw it. It's Gisela, her face red with fury. Behind her is Lena, crying, looking terrified. At first Jan thinks she is weeping for him; his heart leaps that she cares, but no, she is calling another name, *Willi*, and pointing past him at the man. She doesn't seem to care that Gisela has just tried to kill him. The thought hurts him more than anything. "Help me," he cries, "he's bleeding to death." He climbs up the ladder, his legs trembling so much he thinks he'll fall.

Gisela grabs him and shakes him until he can hardly breathe. "What did you do to him, you little bastard?"

Somehow he finds the strength to free himself from her grasp. "I didn't do anything. He's cut his wrists with a razor."

Gisela pushes past him and climbs down the steps to the man. She rips her skirt to make bandages. The man speaks to her. "I did it, Mother. The boy was trying to save me." A moment later he slides back into unconsciousness. It doesn't look too good to Jan. Gisela wraps the material round each wrist, and pulls as tight as she can. "Go and find my husband, he's in the fields," she shouts up to Jan. "Tell him I've found Wilhelm. Tell him to hurry. Please!"

Jan doesn't know what to do. He wants to grab Lena and run – but if he does, the man could die, and he owes him. If it weren't for him, Jan would be dead.

Lena is terrified by all the shouting. Before he can stop her she starts to climb down into the hidey-hole. "Willi," she cries. "Mutti!" Jan pulls her back up, but she resists and keeps trying to get down beside them.

"Come with me," says Jan, but she screams and pulls away from him. In despair he shakes her. "Please Lena, come with me," he says. But again she screams out, "No." He tries speaking to her in Czech, but she ignores him. From the hidey-hole, Gisela is still yelling at him to get help. He wants to run away, but he can't, he has to help. "Forgive me, Tati," he whispers as he goes out into the rain to find Friedrich.

Gisela holds her son as if he were a baby. "Hold on, hold on," she says over and over. "Vatti's coming." It kills her to see her son like this. Wilhelm opens his eyes, but she can see he isn't focusing. Her heart is torn in two. Where is her husband?

"Gisela, you come up here so's I can get down there and bring him up." Friedrich's voice is just above her. "We need to get him back to the farm." She's reluctant to leave Wilhelm, but Friedrich should be able to carry him, she certainly can't. She climbs up and lets Friedrich into the hole, watching as he struggles in the tiny space to hoist Wilhelm over his shoulder.

The rain has stopped, thank God. Friedrich carries Wilhelm back to the farmhouse. Gisela has run on ahead to start heating some water to warm him up. If he doesn't die from loss of blood she fears he will die from the cold. The two children trot along behind her, Helena's finding it hard to keep up. Gisela's yet to find out who the boy is and why he has come to their farm, but already she's thanking him in her heart for saving her son.

I had no choice, thinks Jan. I couldn't leave him to die. And Lena knew him; he must have been a friend to her when she arrived here all alone. He saved my life; I couldn't leave him to die. The arguments sound shallow to him. What would the partisans have done? They would have slit his throat without a second thought or at the very least left him to die – a German man, the age to fight. He was the enemy after all.

But if he is the enemy, why is he hiding in a farm in Germany and not fighting in the army? Jan can't understand what's going on. And why did he try to kill himself? It doesn't make sense.

29

Despite his mother's care and his father's entreaties, Wilhelm is fading away. He resists eating and turns his head to one side whenever Gisela tries to feed him some soup. She's frantic with worry. He lost a great deal of blood, and if he doesn't eat he has no chance. For two days she leaves his side only to go to try to make something to tempt him to eat, but nothing works.

Friedrich is very quiet. He knows that Wilhelm has lost the will to live, and he can't bear it. He hasn't left the house since he carried Wilhelm home; he couldn't care less about the farm and all the work that has to be done. What's the point when his only son is dying?

Jan sees their preoccupation and thinks this would be a good time to flee, but he can't get Lena to budge. She's stuck to Gisela's side all the time and is wary of Jan. I'm her brother, he tells himself, and I can't get her to come with me. He doesn't want to admit it, but Lena has grown away from him, changed beyond recognition.

He listens to every conversation he can, makes himself useful round the house. He picks up that Wilhelm has been in hiding; that he has run away from being in the army. This confuses Jan. Does this make him a good man, does this mean he doesn't agree with what the Nazis are doing? It must do, otherwise why would he run away? Perhaps he's like the soldier who saved him over two years ago, the young man who leant against the tree, vomiting, his eyes so full of fear when he looked up into the tree and saw Jan hiding there. He didn't want to kill. But he didn't have to follow orders, thinks Jan. He could have shot the man who told him to do it. A little voice argues back, *But then he would have been killed too, and the men in our village would still have been shot because some of the soldiers were enjoying it, laughing as they stood around in their break from the shooting, they would never have joined in a rebellion*. It's all too confusing for Jan. He had thought all Germans were bad, and now he can't make up his mind about Wilhelm and his parents.

At night he can hear Gisela sobbing. It's hard listening to a grown-up cry. Jan used to think that adults didn't cry for he never saw his mother or father weep. Now he realizes how lucky he was. In this family there is much sadness.

Jan stays quietly in the background watching the drama all around him. He makes himself useful, terrified that Gisela and Friedrich will throw him out, but they don't even seem aware of him, they're so desperately worried about their son. Once, when Gisela was washing herself, he crept into the room to look at Wilhelm. There's little left of him. Jan has seen death many times, and death is in this room. He jumps back, startled, as Wilhelm opens his eyes. "You were going to kill me, weren't you?" he says.

Jan nods, miserable.

"I don't blame you. I have done terrible things." Wilhelm turns his face to one side.

"Men like you killed my father, killed all the men in my village," says Jan. "I wanted to avenge them." He tells Wilhelm about the massacre, watches while Wilhelm weeps for the deeds of his country. He's about to tell him about Lena when Gisela returns, shoos him out of the room.

"Mother," whispers Wilhelm, "Mother, I have something to tell you. Can you get father?"

Gisela, who is half asleep, stirs. She's terrified at what is happening to her son. She runs to the bedroom where Friedrich is blessedly asleep and shakes him awake. "Come quickly, Wilhelm wants to speak to us." Friedrich jumps out of bed and comes through to the bedroom.

Wilhelm's voice is weak. "The boy, Johann. He's not German."

"How do you know?"

"He told me. He's from Czechoslovakia. All the men in his village were murdered by our soldiers." Wilhelm has tears in his eyes.

"Hush, Wilhelm, you don't need to speak. You must rest, get back your strength. Shall I get you some chicken soup?"

He shakes his head. "Please, just listen to me."

Gisela falls silent as he tells them about the massacre in the village and how the boy saw it all.

"His face haunts me," says Wilhelm. "Because of us, he is alone in the world. He must have seen everything. His father was been killed, perhaps uncles, brothers. I don't know. But he saw it all, a slaughter just like the ones I took part in. And yet, he doesn't hate me."

Gisela makes a comforting sound, but there's nothing she can say really. Her son is tortured by what he did, and nothing she or Friedrich does or says will change that. She and Friedrich are as close to Wilhelm as they can be, for his voice is weakening terribly. Gisela urges him to stop, save his strength, but he insists on going on.

"It will be all right, don't you see? I'm dying—"

"No!" wails Gisela.

"Don't be afraid. My faith has returned. If a child like the boy can forgive me, then God in Heaven will show mercy. I am so sorry for what I've done. And the boy, he will be a comfort to you. You must look after him." He closes his eyes.

"Wilhelm! Look at me. You're not going to die. You're not." Gisela is almost hysterical. Friedrich takes her into his arms to try to comfort her.

Downstairs, as he's cutting bread and cheese for his supper Jan hears the wail from the room above and bows his head. In spite of everything he feels sorry for Gisela and Friedrich. Even at his young age he can see how terrible it is to lose a son.

They bury Wilhelm in the hidey-hole. Jan has to help Friedrich carry the body up to the barn. Friedrich wants to do it himself, but he has eaten nothing since Wilhelm's suicide attempt, and when he starts off he stumbles. He carries Wilhelm's body back into the kitchen and indicates to Jan to help.

It's dark and cold outside. Winter isn't far off. There's a smell of snow in the air although it's not yet November.

Jan can hardly hold on to Wilhelm's legs he's shivering so much, but he grits his teeth and concentrates, and somehow they reach the barn without dropping him. Jan stands aside as Friedrich carries his son into what was a hiding place and will now be a tomb. Friedrich spends some time arranging Wilhelm's body, and Jan begins to worry that he will never resurface. But a moment later he does.

"Tomorrow, we'll bring earth from the field and fill this in," he says to Jan. They're the first words either of the parents have spoken to Jan since the incident. Jan says nothing in return, but follows Friedrich down to the farmhouse.

It takes most of the following day to fill in the hidey-hole. Friedrich is crying and never speaks. Gisela is back in the farmhouse, sitting at the table, staring into space. Not even Lena can make her smile. Jan feels the burden of their sorrow, feels that somehow he is to blame. If he only had to consider himself he'd leave this instant, but he has Lena to worry about.

She's unhappy; he can see that. She's picked up on the adults' mood and is very quiet. Once or twice he tries to play with her, once she manages a smile, and he is delighted. But the next minute she runs and buries her head in Gisela's lap.

In this way, they exist beside each other for several weeks. The adults ignore Jan save to give him food and occasionally ask him to do some work. Jan in turn stays out of their way as much as possible, does as he's told and tries to be helpful. The weather has fully turned now, and he dreads being thrown out. He'd be lucky to last a day out there. It's a tense existence, though, and he's constantly wary.

One night at supper, Jan is taken by surprise when Friedrich addresses him. He's so used to being ignored most of the time, that at first he doesn't realize that Friedrich is speaking to him. When Jan takes too long to answer, Friedrich loses his temper and shouts at him, "Who the hell are you?"

"Johann," stutters Jan.

"No, you're not." Friedrich gets up from the table, goes to the cupboard, and takes out a piece of paper. He waves it in front of Jan. "You're pretending to be a Hitler Youth, yet this letter says they're in Berlin with their parents. It's time you told us who you really are."

Jan finds this hard to follow. He says nothing.

"You're not German, are you?"

Nothing, safest to say nothing.

"Wilhelm told us. The day before he died, he told us what happened in that village in Czechoslovakia. He said you saw your father die. Is that right?"

Dear God, what can he say? His cover is blown, and these people are mad with grief. Why did he tell Wilhelm who he really was? "*Meine Name ist Johann*," he says, trying to sound convincing.

"No it isn't," roars Friedrich. "Your German is poor. You have a funny accent. You don't understand all we say. You're meant to be a Catholic. Say the *Our Father*. Go on, say it!"

"I am a Catholic."

"Say it then, the Our Father. You're old enough to know it by heart."

"*Unsere Vater, wie...*" Jan falters. He has no idea how to continue.

"Tell us the truth," Gisela's voice is deadly quiet. In a way, Jan prefers Friedrich's shouting. He hangs his head.

Still quiet – "We know where you're from, but we don't know why you're here."

Jan gives in. They know too much. "You're right," he says, "I'm not German; I'm from Czechoslovakia. My father was killed by German soldiers. My mother was taken away to a camp, and my older sister disappeared. But my little sister is here in this room. I have been searching for her for over a year."

He's shocked them with this. They thought they knew his story, but they were wrong. Gisela's face is white with fury. "Prove it," she spits.

Jan speaks to Lena in Czech. "Lena, don't you remember me? I am your brother. You remember Mama and Tati, don't you?" Her eyes are wide as he says this, but she doesn't respond.

Gisela smiles. "Helena, *wo is dein Papa*?" Lena points to Friedrich. "*Und deine Mutti*?" Lena blows Gisela a kiss. Gisela turns to Jan. "You're lying."

Jan jumps up from the table. "I'm not lying. It's the truth," he shouts. Lena is watching all of this, her face pale. She has stopped eating. The baked potato is on her plate untouched. In an instant, it comes to Jan. He doesn't know whether it will work, but it has to be worth a try. He crouches down beside Lena and starts to sing:

"*Jedna dvě tři čtyři pět, cos to, Lenko, cos to snědl? Brambory pečený, byly málo maštěný.*" He's getting through to her; he can see it in her eyes, there's a dawning light there. He sings the old nursery rhyme once more, pointing to her potato. "One, two, three, four, five. What have you eaten, Lena?" He pauses and she joins in, laughing. "Baked potatoes, too little grease on them."

"What is this? What are you doing to her?" yells Friedrich.

Jan ignores him, tries another old song. This is one she loved when she was tiny; she used to play it with him a lot, she must remember it. He takes Lena's thumb between his thumb and forefinger and shakes it. "*To je táta*, this is dad" – he goes to her next finger – "*to je máma*, this is mum." He waits for a second as he always used to. She grabs his finger and finishes the rhyme: "*To je dědek*, *to je bába*, *to je vnouček*, *malý klouček*." This is grandpa, this is grandma, and this little boy is the grandson. And as she always did when she was little, she tickled him as she said the last line. Jan laughs with joy. He tries some more Czech. "What is your name?" and this time she answers, "Lena." A breakthrough. "Tell them who I am," he whispers. "*To je Jan*," she says to Gisela and Friedrich, adding to his delight, "my brother." He couldn't have asked for more.

Jan feels sorry for the couple. They are devastated, Gisela waxen, Friedrich looking as if he's aged ten years overnight. And after Wilhelm's death they have no fight left in them. Friedrich sits down heavily in his armchair, which creaks in protest. Gisela flees the room. Jan looks at Friedrich unsure what to say, his feeling of triumph fading in the face of so much distress. "She's my sister," he says again. "I've been looking for her for over a year."

Friedrich stares at him with bloodshot eyes. "How did you find us? I don't understand how you managed to find us."

"It's a long story," says Jan. "Maybe we should wait until your wife..."

Friedrich's shoulders slump. "She'll never recover from this, never." He gets up and rummages in a cupboard for a few seconds, bringing out a bottle of schnapps. He pulls out the cork with his teeth and gulps down a mouthful, grimacing at its strength. The colour returns to his cheeks. "God knows what she'll do now."

Jan doesn't say anything. He's more afraid of what Friedrich might do. He feels years older than twelve, decides he has to take a lead. "We're all tired, perhaps we should talk about it in the morning." When Friedrich nods, he holds out his hand to Lena and leads her up to her bed. As they pass Gisela's bedroom, he quails at the strength of the sobs coming from them, glances at Lena to see whether she's noticed and is relieved to see that she's so tired she seems oblivious. He puts her to bed, then goes to his room where he places a chair under the door handle to stop anyone getting in. He doesn't really think they'd harm him, but they are desperate in their bereavement, and he's taking no chances.

Jan lies in bed worrying about what to do. He feels they have an advantage over him; they could take him to the authorities and hand him over. No one would do anything about Lena. As far as the authorities are concerned she's legitimately adopted. He hates himself for even thinking it, but resolves that if they try to betray him to the authorities he'll tell them about Wilhelm.

In the morning Friedrich admits they've had doubts about Lena from the beginning. "It didn't add up," he says, "the details about her past were so sketchy. We didn't understand how she could have been in a fire where her mother died yet had no burns and showed no fear of fire. And her accent was so strange."

"What are you going to do?" asks Gisela. Her voice is thick with tears.

"Take Lena, find our mother and go home," he says with more confidence than he feels.

Gisela shakes her head. "I won't let her go."

He takes a deep breath. "Then I'll tell people about Wilhelm. About how you hid him."

"Do you think I care? What good will that do?" she says. "Anyway, you do that, and I'll tell them that you pretended to be someone else. It's probably a crime to impersonate a member of the Hitler Youth."

She's right. It will do no good. They're trapped with each other. He can't tell anyone about Wilhelm without questions being asked about him. He has no identity card, nothing. At the same time, they can't betray him for fear of what he might say about Wilhelm. Dismayed, they glower at each other.

"How far do you think you would get with Lena in tow? She's a small child; she tires easily. You'd never get anywhere."

Jan scowls; this is what every adult has told him, all the partisans used to laugh at him when he told them his plans. Now this woman is telling him the same thing. "I found my way from Poland to Germany," he says. "I can find our mother."

Friedrich is more patient than Gisela. "How did you get here?"

Jan doesn't want to say, because he knows he couldn't have done it without the help of the partisans, not easily anyway. Reluctantly he tells his story. To his surprise, they don't point out how much help he had.

They say nothing at first when he finishes, then Friedrich speaks. "It's an amazing story," he says. "You must have wanted to see your little sister very much indeed." He sounds sympathetic.

Jan doesn't want to trust the couple. They stole his sister after all. But he has to admit that they really seem to care for Lena. Perhaps not all Germans are bad, perhaps some of them don't hate everyone who is not German.

"Please, don't do anything today. Don't do anything hasty," says Gisela. "Perhaps we can work something out."

Jan doubts it, but their haggard faces convince him that he shouldn't do anything too quickly, so he agrees.

They've sat up all night arguing about what to do. Gisela is terrified of losing Helena, yet she can't help wondering about the mother, about what she must be feeling. If she's alive that is. And there's the rub. No one knows for sure where she is; no one knows she is still alive.

"I think we should encourage him to go," says Friedrich. "We'll be able to persuade him to leave Helena. He knows she'd never survive out there. But we could say that if he comes back with his mother, Helena can go with them. He'll not get far without someone capturing him. Then he'll be out of our way for ever. We won't have to worry about anyone claiming Helena."

"We don't know that," says Gisela. "He's a bright boy, he found us. He never gave up hope of finding his little sister. What if we do let him go, and he finds his mother and then they come back?"

Friedrich pours another glass of beer. If he were a ruthless man, he'd kill the boy. But he's not. He could no more harm Jan than he could his own son. He winces at the thought of his loss. "Maybe there's another way. I think there's little chance of that woman still being alive."

"What are you saying?"

"We could try to persuade him to stay. Everyone thinks we've got a Hitler Youth staying with us. I'm sure we could get an identity card for him; we could say he lost his. All his details are in that first letter that was sent to us." He pauses. "It's worth a try." He doesn't want to bring Wilhelm into the argument, but decides he has to. "And Wilhelm asked us to look after him."

"No, he could never replace Wilhelm. Never."

"I think Wilhelm was trying to tell us something important that night." Friedrich isn't a philosophical man, so he struggles with the ideas that are coming to him. "I think he saw it as fate that Jan turned up here, a boy without a father. He knew he was dying…"

"You think he wanted you to become his father, for the boy to take his place as your son? Where does that leave me? His mother could still be alive for all we know."

"I'm not explaining myself well. But you must admit, it does seem like fate, Helena comes to us, then Jan. We can keep them safe for the time being."

Gisela shakes her head. It's well after midnight, and she's tired. But she can't think of any other solution. "All right," she says, "we'll ask him to stay, but I will never see him as my son. Never."

In the morning they put their proposal to Jan. They tell him he can stay with them until the war is over, then he can try to find his mother. They don't mention Helena; they won't make any promises about what will happen to her.

Jan has agreed to the plan. He's not sure why, except Lena is happy here, and it seems safe. After all his hardship of the past two years he wants some comfort, and Friedrich has assured him that the war will soon be over. Once Germany is liberated he can find his mother. He hopes he can find his mother. At times like this he fears he will never see her again, and even if he does he won't know her or she won't know him.

Soon he settles into a routine. During the day he helps Friedrich with the farm. In the evening he plays with Lena, talking to her about her real family. Gisela and Friedrich don't like this, but they are too desolate about Wilhelm to stop him. Sometimes Gisela allows him to help in the kitchen, and he loves that. It reminds him of home. Slowly he becomes, if not attached to these people, then at least more trusting, and he stops blocking his door at night. It's almost like home he thinks, almost, but not quite.

In this way November and December pass. They don't celebrate Christmas. For one thing, Gisela and Friedrich are still in mourning. For another, they are aware that all the Hitler Youth who were billeted in local farms have now gone home, and they are wary of people asking questions about Jan. So when people call at the farm to offer their season's greetings, they are not invited in. Word gets round, and soon the visitors stop calling.

In the New Year, Hans comes to see them. Gisela is shocked by his appearance: he is old and frail, and it has exhausted him to trail all the way out to the farm. He's distraught when he hears about Wilhelm, blames himself, but Friedrich won't have it.

"He couldn't live with what he did," he says. "It's as simple as that. If anything's to blame, it's this evil regime. You did your best. So did we."

"Such a terrible loss," says Hans.

Gisela interrupts him; she doesn't want to talk about Wilhelm. It's too upsetting. "Why are you here?"

"We need food. The girls and I, we're starving to death. I was hoping… anything you can spare. We'd be so grateful."

"Of course," murmurs Gisela.

They send Jan down to Hans twice a week with food parcels, as much as they can spare. He has to go at night for he mustn't be spotted. This doesn't bother him; it's like being back with the partisans once more except he goes back to a warm bed instead of shivering in a hole in the ground. He enjoys these visits; Hans is welcoming, and often he stays for an hour or more, chatting to Hans and the girls.

Some weeks later the war ends. Jan's immediate feeling of relief is quickly followed by dread. There are terrible stories coming from the east about acts of revenge on German civilians with many men being shot. Friedrich and Gisela are terrified about what will happen. So instead of setting off to find his mother immediately, he agrees to stay. When the liberators come he will be able to tell them how the Germans gave him and his sister shelter during the war.

The Russians have demanded to see the family in the town hall. Gisela and Friedrich get themselves and the children ready with fear in their hearts. The journey into town is agonizing. What if they have not done enough to be spared? What if Jan turns against them? They know in their hearts that he won't, but they worry nonetheless. These are such confusing times.

The town is unrecognizable. Just before the end of the war, it was bombarded two nights running, a time of terror for them as they listened to the falling bombs only a few kilometres away and wondered if one would strike them instead. Now, seeing the damage that has been done, they realize they were not frightened enough. They pick their way through the rubble, at times having to clamber over great chunks of stone to get to the Town Hall. It is undamaged, but filthy with the dust from the ruins of other buildings. Gisela looks around at the children. She wasted her time getting them all spruced up for this interview. They are covered in grime, Jan has somehow torn his trousers. What does it matter? The Russians won't be interested in how they look.

Inside the Town Hall, there's a queue of civilians. A soldier takes the letter from them and shows them into a room. They are left standing in front of a desk. Gisela's mouth is parched with nerves. She jumps as a soldier comes into the room. He sits down behind the desk and indicates to them that they should sit.

"I have asked you to come here because I have information that you helped two Jewish girls hide during the war." His voice is stern, and Gisela quails. She had thought it would work in their favour, could she have been wrong about that? She nods and says, "Yes, we gave them some food."

He looks down at the paper on his desk. "Mmm. That is what it says here. When the Jewish girls were freed from their hiding place, they testified to the help given to them not only by Hans Knoller, whose cellar they were hiding in, but also by the couple who live in Grunfeld farm. That is you, I assume?"

"Yes," says Friedrich. "That is us."

"Good, good. They said that without your help they would surely have starved to death."

Gisela thought she might faint when he nodded his approval. For a few seconds she had thought that perhaps in the Soviet Union as well as Germany, it was a crime to help Jews.

The soldier questions them about the children. Determined to hide nothing, Friedrich tells them everything about how Lena and Jan came to be with them. The soldier writes it all down in a notebook and smiles at

Jan on hearing about his time with the partisans. When they have finished, he gives them new ration books.

"You're free to go," he says. "I will pass on the information about the children's backgrounds to the Red Cross. They are trying to reunite families. You will hear from them in due course. Good afternoon to you."

They are dismissed. The little group leave the Town Hall with a mixture of emotions. Jan is jubilant at the thought he might see his mother again soon, Friedrich and Gisela relieved that they are not going to be imprisoned or worse, but devastated at the thought of the Red Cross seeking out the children's mother. Only Lena is oblivious. She holds Gisela's hand as she skips down the street. "Can I have a new ribbon?" she asks as they pass the haberdasher's shop. She doesn't seem to have noticed it's in ruins.

30

The long awaited day is here. When the letter from the Red Cross came last week, Gisela wanted to burn it without reading it; she knew what it would say. Friedrich wouldn't let her. He was gentle with her, took her face in his hands and said, "We cannot keep what is not ours." She didn't argue with him, but inwardly she disagreed.

Jan has hardly been able to sleep he's so excited. It's four years since he saw his mother; he imagines the look on her face when she sees him and Lena. Perhaps – though this is too much to hope for – she'll have found Maria, and they'll all be together again. He's so excited he doesn't notice how quiet Lena is whenever he talks to her about their mother. When he mentions "mama" she looks confused and glances furtively at Gisela. Gisela sees this and feels quietly triumphant, but she knows it will mean nothing when the time comes.

The house has been scrubbed from top to bottom. The children are dressed in their finest clothes; their hair is brushed until it shines, and they have each had two baths this week. Gisela has not stinted on spending money on the children. She buys only the best for them and vows that whatever happens, this woman will not be able to say that she did not look after them properly. She is dreading today. They have been almost happy this past year. Lena is a darling, and the boy, once they got used to him and he began to trust them, well he's a spirited little thing and a damn good worker. She can't bear to think about the future. They've never discussed it, Friedrich and her, and she fears they never will. The day will end, the children will be gone, and they will say nothing about it. She wonders if perhaps they'll live in silence punctuated only by *what's for supper?* and *it's cold today isn't it?* It's unbearable.

"They're here, they're here." Jan's shouts pierce her thoughts. Two slight figures are trudging up the track, the Red Cross worker and the mother. Gisela tries to smile. "Well, on you go, go out and greet her."

Jan doesn't move.

"What's wrong?"

"That's not my mother. That's an old woman."

The women coming up to the door do indeed look too old to be Lena's mother. Jan had told her his mother was thirty-eight, and neither of the women look as young as that. But the war has aged everyone; she should know that. Knows it only too well when she looks into a mirror and sees the haggard wrinkled face and the dark hair liberally striped with grey.

"Jan," she says, "remember it's been nearly four years, and your mother has been through a great ordeal."

He nods, but still looks uncertain. The women are at the door now, and Friedrich has gone to let them in. Gisela digs her fingernails into the palms of her hands to try to stop the pain in her heart. It doesn't work. She forces herself to smile at the two women. She knows which one is the mother immediately. One of them is drinking in Jan with her eyes at the same time looking round for Lena. There is an air of desperation surrounding her. She steps towards Jan, who steps back.

This is not how it was meant to be. He was going to run down the path and into his mother's arms. She'd swing him round the way she used to when he was a little boy. She'd be laughing and crying all at the same time, and Lena would be right there too, and she'd gather them both in her arms and everything would be all right again. And then she'd say "Guess who I found outside", and Maria would appear looking beautiful. This was how it was meant to be.

Jan keeps staring at the woman. She looks a bit like mama, but thinner and older and oh so tired. She's not laughing, there's a little smile on her face, so little, Jan isn't sure that it is a smile. This can't be his mother; his mother would scream with delight at seeing her children once more. This woman looks scared as she comes towards him.

"*Ahoj*, Jan," she says in a quiet voice.

It sounds a bit like her. He holds out his hand and says hello back. Her face falls, and he realizes he's done the wrong thing, that she's waiting for an embrace, but he can't do it. He drops his eyes. His mother looks round at the other woman for help. She steps forwards.

"Well, well, so this is Jan. I've heard so much about you. You're quite a hero, the way you found your little sister. Your mother hasn't stopped talking about you all the way here. Why don't we all sit down, and perhaps Frau Scheffler can get us something to drink."

Gisela's face flushes at this, and Jan realizes she feels rebuked for not offering them something straight away. He wants to help her, so gets up and says, "I'll get the drinks." But the Red Cross woman tells him to stay and talk to his mother. Trouble is, he can't think of anything to say.

"Where's Lena?" asks his mother.

Friedrich pushes Lena forwards, but she starts to cry when she sees the two women. With a shock, Jan understands that his mother and Lena are total strangers to each other, that they haven't seen each other for three and a half years, half of Lena's age. Mother tries to cuddle her, but Lena clings to Friedrich's leg and won't budge. The Red Cross woman looks irritated, an angry flush sweeps over her chest. A cross, red woman, thinks Jan. "Come on, give mama a kiss," she says. Lena runs over to Gisela and hides behind her skirts. Jan's mother starts to cry.

This is unbearable, not how it should be. Jan wants to reassure her, but she's a stranger, how can he approach a stranger and comfort her?

They've been here an hour. The Red Cross woman is looking at her watch, and Jan predicts that any moment now she'll say the fateful words. Now the time is here, he's not sure he wants to go.

"Right," she says, "time to go."

Gisela has packed suitcases for them the night before. They're by the door. The Red Cross woman picks up one and gestures to Jan to pick up the other. "My car is not far," she says. Jan can hardly stand, his legs are trembling so much. He holds out a hand to Friedrich, who grabs it and pumps it up and down. Jan thinks he'll never let go. Lena is still clinging to Gisela; she hasn't looked at her mother. He goes over to Gisela and hugs her. Then he holds out his hand to Lena. Lena ignores it, holds out her arms to be lifted up by Gisela. She's reverted to being a baby.

Gisela pushes Lena away. It breaks her heart when she wants to comfort the child. Lena screams when she does this, her face contorted with terror. "Hush, *Liebchen*. This is your mother. You must go with her. Jan will be there."

"No," screams Lena. "I won't go. She's not my mother. You're my mother. Why are you doing this? I don't want to go."

Gisela turns away. She can't bear this. Lena grabs her arm. Gisela has to unpick her fingers to loosen the grasp; she can't look Lena in the eye. Lena kicks out at her, and she winces, but who can blame her? "Friedrich," she pleads, "help me."

The woman from the Red Cross strides across the room and pulls Lena away from Gisela. "I haven't got time for this. You're coming with your mother now."

Lena is hysterical. Gisela runs over and grabs her back. She can't let her go in this state. It's inhuman. Lena is shaking with fright.

Lena's mother stands by, looking on with helplessness. Tears stream down her face. Jan wants to scream at her, *do something, you're her mother*.

Gisela is speaking softly to Lena, whispering in her ear. Jan can't hear what she's saying. Lena's sobs grow quieter.

"What did you say to her?" asks the Red Cross woman.

"I told her she has to go away, but that she can come back and visit us."

"I don't think—"

"I don't care what you think," interrupts Friedrich. "Look at the state of the child."

The woman's face gets even redder. There's sweat on her forehead. "We have to go."

Lena's mother turns to Jan and speaks to him. He says to Gisela, "My mother says you're right, and we will come back to visit. She asks if there's something you can give to Lena, something that she'll have to return to you. To prove to her that we'll be back."

Gisela looks round the room. They have so few possessions, little that is valuable. What is there that would convince Lena that she will be back? Her glance settles on a photograph of Wilhelm. She goes over to the dresser and picks it up.

"Lena," she says, "take Willi with you. But just for a few weeks, and then you must come and see us and bring him back. Will you do that?"

Lena is calmer now, still crying, but no longer hysterical. She nods and takes the photograph. Jan leads her out to the car.

As the door closes behind them, Gisela stuffs her fist into her mouth to muffle the roar of grief that is welling up inside her. She knows they'll never be back; the mother did what she had to do to comfort Lena. Friedrich goes to her and hugs her. They stand in a close embrace, sobbing as their reason for living leaves.

* * *

Outside, Jan, his mother and Lena reach the car that is waiting for them. As he waits for the Red Cross woman to open it up, Jan looks up at his white-faced mother. She gazes back at him as if she's trying to remember who he is.

"Will we come back to see them?"

She brushes the hair back from his forehead. "I don't know, Jan. I just don't know. It's so far away..." Her voice tails off.

He slides into the back seat, Lena is already there, still crying. The engine starts, and they're off, the car bumping down the rough track to the main road. Jan twists round in his seat to gaze at the farmhouse for one last time. It looks like home.